THE
GARDEN
OF
SECOND
CHANCES

T0282034

THE GARDEN OF SECOND CHANCES

A NOVEL

BY MONICA FRAZIER, WRITING AS
MONA ALVARADO FRAZIER

Published by SparkPress, a BookSparks imprint,
A division of SparkPoint Studio, LLC
Phoenix, Arizona, USA, 85007
www.gosparkpress.com

Published 2023
Printed in the United States of America
Print ISBN: 978-1-68463-204-6
E-ISBN: 978-1-68463-205-3
Library of Congress Control Number: 2022919515

Book Design by Stacey Aaronson

She Writes Press is a division of SparkPoint Studio, LLC.

To my mom, who showed me resilience in the face of adversity and has always been my supporter.

"But when we leave the garden /
always we carry something with us /
A fragment of our innocent selves . . ."

—BENJAMIN ALIRE SÁENZ

AUTHOR'S NOTE

This novel references drug use, intimate partner violence, emotional and sexual abuse, racism, and violence within a juvenile correctional facility. These realistic plot elements may be uncomfortable to read.

GLOSSARY

Abuela — grandmother

Al rato — bye, later

Asco — nausea

Ay, cabrón — oh, shit

Bofo — idiot

Cabrón — bastard

Chanates — African Americans (derogatory)

Chisme — gossip

Compa — prison living unit (slang)

Consejo — advice

Cumbias — type of Mexican music (fast)

Curandera — healer in the Mexican tradition

Dichos — proverbs, sayings

Escándalo — scandal, ruckus

Eses — guys, girls

Firme — alright, cool

Gacho — not cool

Gavacha — Anglo girl

Gracias a Dios — thanks to God

Grillo — cricket

Güero — light skinned, pale

Hyna — girlfriend

Jefa — female boss, mother

Jefita — mother

Jura — police

Lechuza — owl

Leva — ostracize

Mal Ojo — evil eye

Malfloras — lesbians (derogatory)

Malillas — malaise, ill

Mayata — African American (derogatory)

Mercado — market

Mi vida loca — my crazy life

Milagro — miracle

Mosca — fly, pesky person

Norteña — person from the north

Órale — hey

Paisa — short for paisana or girl from the same country

Palatero — ice cream vendor

Palomas — doves

Pesay — protective custody

Pinche — fucker

Pinta — prison

Pobrecita — poor thing, poor girl

Por vida — for life, always

Pruno — prison-made alcohol

Qué bonita nombre — what a pretty name

Qué lastima — what a shame

Qué pues — what's happening?

Rata — rat, informant

Sabes — you know

Sancho — boyfriend, sugar daddy

Secundaria — junior high school, middle school

Serio — seriously

Siempre — always

Sinceremente — sincerely

Skonka — scandalous female

Te lo juro — I swear to you

Telenovelas — soap operas from Latin/South America

Tio — uncle

Trucha — be aware, be on your toes

Yerba Buena — mint

Wachala — look at her

ONE

I didn't run because I killed him. I ran because I didn't. The handcuff on my wrist clacked against the window with every jolt of the transportation van. I twisted a hole in the knee of my orange jumpsuit with my free right hand and made it larger, exposing my skin, now a lighter shade of brown from lack of sun. If only I could pour myself out of the hole and escape this situation. If only someone would listen.

The girl we picked up at the last juvenile hall sat a couple of feet away from me, her eyes closed. *How could she sleep through this trip while my mind sped through my past?* The van shook, the heel of my foot bounced off the floorboard.

The girl's eyes blinked open. "What're you looking at, bitch?"

Like the hiss of a snake ready to strike, her voice made me shudder. The tattooed number thirteen rose over her dark eyebrow. A scary clown inked on her neck stretched behind her ear and disappeared into her short black hair.

We had chains around our ankles, so I knew she couldn't kick me. I turned away and leaned my cheek against the cold window.

Places I'd never visited before flashed by on the freeway signs: BELL GARDENS, COMMERCE, 5 NORTH. I read them until the road disappeared into a foggy area and came out again onto city streets. People went about their mornings like a normal day. I stared out of the window. I wanted to remember what the world looked like before I got to prison. Remember the trees, houses, and cars. Watch people catching buses and kids walking to school. I needed to remember the life I had, the one slipping away as fast as the wheels turned. I would never forget who I left behind.

The crackling of the officers' radio in the front seat broke the silence. I glanced up. The red lights of the truck ahead of us grew larger. Fast. We lurched to a stop. I slid forward, braced myself against the mesh screen. My stomach bounced back and forth. I gagged. My hand flew against my mouth.

The girl next to me banged on the divider separating us from the officers. "Give me napkins. She's gonna fucken hurl on me."

The lady officer pushed a paper towel through the opening. I grabbed it. The tattooed girl's upper lip curled, baring her chipped front tooth. The piercing black of her eyes warned me to hold everything inside. I slid a trembling hand under my thigh, tried to make myself smaller.

"Give *me* the damn towel. No, give me two." She hit the screen again.

"Knock it off," the male driver shouted.

My shoulders pinched together with each clanging blow of her fist against the screen. My eyes squeezed shut. My body remembered. Alek's face loomed in front of me, his loud voice shrinking me into a corner. I gasped for breath, opened my eyes, and dropped my gaze to the lumpy seat.

The van exited the freeway onto a one-lane road, twisting up bare hills. The sound of our handcuffs clicked against the window like tapping fingers waiting. Farther away from home. Further from who I left behind.

A sign on a chain-link fence read INMATE PROCESSING. We turned onto a side dirt road. Closer now. The tires dipped and bumped, stirring up clouds of the earth as if I entered a whirlwind. I smelled my sweat and panic.

The van jolted to a stop in front of a soaring gate with crisscrossed steel patterns. Silver coils like the thin ropes of a lariat curled across the top of the fence. Razor-sharp edges flashed. The gate rolled open. My chest clenched.

The driver's yellow-brown eyes stared at me in the rear-view mirror like the iguanas my brothers caught in my hometown of Santa Isabel. "Welcome to Disneyland. Time to do your time."

He jumped out of the driver's seat, slid open the door, and unlocked the tattooed girl's wrist. She jumped to the ground. Still in her leg irons, she shuffled to the white line on the asphalt and leaned back with her chin raised like she didn't have a care in the world.

Officer Iguana helped me off the van and led me by the inner elbow next to the tattooed girl. The chain clinked with each small step. The closer I came, the more the girl scowled. She was much taller than me, broad and powerful looking. With one punch, she could knock me down. I prayed the officer wouldn't loosen his grip or my legs would crumple.

Concrete, barred windows, and tall fences surrounded me.

Off in the distance, a brick tower stood with barbed wire twisted beneath its huge windows. I'd be here for years. More girls like the one next to me. Every. Day. My legs trembled, thinking of the thousands of days and nights. Nerves shot through my belly like lightning. Everything in my sight spun. My stomach bubbled. Milk and oatmeal rushed into my throat, splattered to the ground, and sprayed the bottom of the girl's jumpsuit.

"You stupid ass!" She growled and jumped back.

"Shut up, or you'll clean it." The lady officer pulled me away and gave me more paper towels.

The sour odor rising from the asphalt gave me asco but I clenched my teeth against my nausea and dropped the paper on the mess. Then I carried what was left of my panic to the trash can.

The door opened at the end of the building, and another lady appeared. She didn't wear a uniform like the officers, but tight jeans and a long loose blouse. Several keys and other items hung from a thick black belt cinched at her waist. She strode over to us in her white tennis shoes. Officer Iguana handed her thin files. "They're your problem now, Montes."

"Yeah." She glanced at the papers, flicked her eyes at the other girl and me. Her chewing gum popped, releasing a minty scent. "Ivanov, Juana and Gonzales, Dolores."

Dolores. The girl's first name meant pains. A name I knew she'd live up to.

"Don't call me that, Montes," Dolores spit on the sidewalk. "You know my name's Jester."

"Whatever. Another *vacation,* huh?" Montes snickered. "Follow me."

Her voice was as tight as the ponytail that stretched the sides of her eyes up towards her poofy bangs. With one hand, she pulled open the door and motioned for Jester to step inside first. The sharp odor of pine cleaner filled the damp air and stuck in my throat. My belly rolled again.

The jingle of Montes' keys followed behind us. We disappeared into a dark hall that looked like the caves back home where I'd follow my older brothers, stepping inch by inch, hesitant to move for fear bats would fly out.

"Hold up." Montes went around me and yanked open the next door.

Bright lights glared on shiny linoleum floors. I blinked and tried to adjust my eyes. Orange doors lined both sides of the hallway from the top to the end.

"You remember the layout, Gonzales. The rooms." Montes swung her arm left and right. "Same set up on the other wing." Her voice was flat and distant like she had shown the place to hundreds of girls before me and was tired of talking.

At Centre Juvenile Hall, where I was before, we didn't have locked doors. We slept in a big room all together. Each of these doors had a narrow window in the middle and a slot at the bottom like where a mail carrier puts letters. I wondered if I'd get my own key to my room.

"Walk to the top of the hallway and stop at the staff desk," Montes said.

We moved up to the wood counter, where a man in a tan and green uniform stood on the other side. A calendar taped to the wall next to him said 2002, although we were in January of the new year. On the other side of his desk was the empty dayroom where windows filled one side. The other walls were brick but painted a dingy beige.

Montes waved us to her left. Black letters over the hall said Alpha. "The second one is your room, Gonzales."

Jester tapped her white slide on the floor, crossed her arms over her chest while Montes unlocked the door. "Who lived here before me? Better have been another Latina."

"This isn't a hotel. Get in." Montes shut the door behind Dolores and opened the next one. "Inside, Ivanov. You start your twenty-four."

"Twenty-four what?" I asked.

"Everyone gets locked in for twenty-four hours while we check out your files."

The door lock clanked shut. There would be no key. Dusty brown brick walls and grey paint peeling off the ceiling surrounded me. The strong bleach scent made me wince and hold my breath as I moved to the skinny bed and locker on the right side. A metal sink and toilet were on my left. Goosebumps rose on my arms.

I climbed on the thin mattress, curled up on my side. If I were lucky, I'd sleep away the next hours. If I couldn't sleep, I'd think of how to tell these people what a mistake they made.

"Hey, Mouse," Jester shouted from the next room. "You owe me for barfing on my leg. You one of them Mexican Indians, huh? You hella short."

The teasing began sooner than at Centre. I ignored the question and tried to make conversation. "My name is Juana Maria."

"So fucken Mexican. *Juana Maria*. And you got a weird last name too. From now on, you're Mouse. Got it?"

6

Mouse? Mamá gave me my name, and a stranger thinks she can give me another? But it was better than what Papá called me. Pulga. A flea. "You're always after your mamá, hermanos, and hermana." He said I was a nuisance, but I was the youngest and wanted to be with my brothers and sister.

"Hey, Mouse, heard you killed someone."

"I kill no one."

"Lied, huh? Took the rap for somebody?"

Too many questions. I remained silent and reminded myself to breathe, stay calm like one of the nicer counselors at Centre had told me, but each time a lock bolted or a tennis shoe squeaked on the floor, my chest tightened.

Muttering voices streamed into the hallway. I sat up.

"Órale, Jester, you here again?" a girl yelled. "Who came in wit' you? Anybody I know?"

"Some mousy chúntara."

Chúntara. Wetback. A word spoken at Centre every day from the Mexican girls born in the US. There was a divide between us and them, us and staff, us and everyone.

"Oh, one of them mules, huh? Popped coming across the border?"

"Nah, heard she knocked somebody off," Jester said.

"Quiet. It's count time," Ms. Montes shouted. Brown eyes and bangs peered through the skinny window in my door. "Ivanov, stand against the far wall. Here's your issue. Change and fold up your jumpsuit."

I leaped off the bed and against the wall. She threw a paper sack, a pile of worn-looking sheets, and clothes on my mattress. The door shut with a thud. I found an apple juice box, a white bread bologna sandwich with a yellow plastic square of cheese, and a brown cookie inside the wrinkled lunch bag. We had hot food at Centre.

Hunger made my stomach growl, but I couldn't eat. I stared at the pile of clothes. The faded blue jeans and tee shirt were too big, but I put them on, rolled up the cuffs, and moved to the window.

Scratches on the glass and metal frame around the opening had the names of girls before me. Flaca '72, Misty '81, Jada '99. Too many names. Three metal bars stood behind the screen and blocked part of my backyard view. One lonely tree stood in the center, naked. Someone pruned back too many branches.

"Qué lástima" Mamá would say if she were still alive. What a shame. So much earth, and no vegetables, no flowers, nothing but yellowed grass and concrete.

I sat back on the bed. A wave of loneliness and dread covered me like on my first night at Centre. I reminded myself that my baby was safe.

At Centre, we had dozens of bunk beds in an area staff called a dorm. The girl in the bunk next to me sobbed until she hiccupped. A girl yelled at her to shut up, or she'd shut her up. I lay in my bed too scared to sleep and stayed quiet that night. Like now. I'd already learned to force myself to remain silent and cry inside until I ached.

A thump at my door made me jump. In the shadowy dark, I couldn't see anything. The room light flicked on. A voice in the hallway announced, "Ivanov, mail."

Gracias a Dios. Finally, a letter. My sister, Lupe, used to write me every month, keeping me up with the news about my baby, her engagement to José Luis, their marriage. But, during the last couple of months, she hadn't written. Maybe she sent another photo of my baby, Katrina, who was seven months now. I wondered if she sat up by herself or crawled yet.

The opened envelope slid through the doorframe and dropped on the floor. I scooped it up and read the postmark: December 21 from Phoenix, Arizona. Three weeks ago. Someone wrote "Forward" and "Translated," on the front under the original address to Centre Juvenile Hall. I didn't know anyone in Arizona. I slid out the piece of lined paper.

Dear Juana,

Your sister is going to have a baby, due in July. There is no work in Santa Isabel or in the city. I had to leave again. I want Lupe to come to Arizona to be with me. She didn't want to tell you, but you must find someone to care for your baby. Please ask your brother and his wife.

With respect, your brother-in-law, José Luis

Lupe's pregnant? I paced back and forth from my door to the window, chewing on my knuckle, sitting then standing. Katrina couldn't stay with my older brother and his wife. They had kids of their own. I hadn't seen them since I left Mexico three years ago. My father's disabled. How could he care for an infant? He wouldn't agree anyway.

Lupe couldn't leave. I had to get ahold of her and beg her to keep Katrina in Mexico until I got out. She promised me. I rubbed at the knot in my chest.

"Ivanov, don't you hear me calling you? Dinner."

I glimpsed Ms. Montes through the window in the door. Next to her, a girl in a black hairnet slouched against a cart filled with food trays. She picked at her teeth with her pinkie finger.

"Miss, can I call my sister? It's an emergency."

"Everything's an emergency, Ivanov. No phone privileges until your twenty-four is over tomorrow. Write a letter."

"Can I have paper then?"

"This isn't the time."

"But my sister, she's—"

"Ivanov, back up from the wicket. Take this now, or don't eat." Montes's eyebrows scrunched together.

"Can I get paper later?" My voice cracked. "I need to write a letter."

"Jones, give her the tray."

The slot at the bottom of the door flipped open. A yellow container skated across the floor, leaving a pile of gray noodles behind. A red apple rolled to my feet. Fishy stink filled the room.

"The food fell on the floor," I shouted between the door-frame.

"Oops, my bad," Jones said. "And the tuna noodle casserole's one of our best." Her laughter echoed down the hall.

What's the use of asking them for anything? I punched the hot and cold buttons on the sink, tried to get water out of the faucet, and wet the thin washcloth. Cleaning the mess on the floor reminded me of how I started my morning, wiping my vomit up.

Creaky wheels of the food cart stopped at my door. I glanced up. Jones curled her finger at me and blinked her big blue eyes. She must have another tray for me. I moved closer to the door window.

"Don't *ever* front me off again, Mouse. You're here for a long time. So am I."

TWO

The lock turned with a loud click. Montes swung open my door and told me to stand "on quiet." Which I guessed meant no talking. I waited in the hall while she unlocked the next door. Gonzales stepped out, tilted her chin up at me.

"You owe me," she mouthed.

I gulped and jammed my hands in my jean pockets, trying to keep my legs from wobbling.

Montes stopped at the top of the hallway, pointed to a yellow stripe on the floor, and motioned for us to move up. Like at Centre, the staff had their hand signals. The mean ones shouted out directions like people who trained attack dogs.

"To the line. Hands behind your back. Move to the dayroom," she yelled.

No mistaking what kind of staff Montes was. An older lady sat at the desk. The twisted bun on her head was silvery white. Her little round eyeglasses reminded me of an abuelita.

The sound of washers and dryers rumbled through the room. I glanced to the two back offices. One sign said LAUNDRY and the other said STAFF. Powdered detergent and the odor of musty clothes hit my nose making me scrunch up my face.

"Take a seat, Ivanov," Montes said.

She waved me to the green chairs in the middle of the room, where three other girls sat in the crooked circle. Jones, the kitchen girl, was one of them. Her eyes followed me when I inched past her chair and around her outstretched legs. I took a seat between two girls. One wore black-rimmed glasses, and the other stared at her lap. Jester dropped into the chair next to Jones. Both of them frowned at me.

I wiped my sweaty forehead, brushed my hair away from my face. I couldn't show them I was afraid. The girl with the eyeglasses glanced at me, lifted her chin, and gave me a smile which I returned.

A tiny pale girl entered the dayroom with her arms wrapped around her chest. Her face, flushed and damp, looked like she had the flu. Jester winked at her as she tilted her chin up. The corners of the girl's lips rose in a smile before she slumped into the last empty seat.

"Welcome to the Mariposa living unit, *ladies*."

Montes said the word like it was bitter fruit. Her nose even wrinkled. I could tell she'd be like the worst staff at Centre, the ones the girls called "tight ass bitches." My parents always told me to respect authorities, so I never called them names.

"I'm your correctional counselor. For the benefit of the new girls, I'll run through an orientation. But before we begin, meet our unit supervisor. Any words, Mrs. Shaffer?"

The older woman at the desk stood, crossed her dark arms against a yellow floral blouse. "Ladies, you're not here for singing too loud in the choir. You made serious mistakes. Follow the rules, take the program seriously, and we'll all get along. Understand?"

The other girls sat up, even Jester. The woman's deep voice did not sound like a grandmother's.

"Thank you, Mrs. Shaffer. Now, listen up." Montes pointed to the pale girl and me. "The administration building and the communications tower are over there. Across the roadway, that brick building is another living unit like Mariposa. There are seven other units like this one. Don't get lost cause I'm not buying it."

Jester leaned into Jones, pointed to me. "Check her out. She's floating in her blues."

They laughed, reminding me of the cackling hens in our backyard at home. As soon as I could find a sewing needle, I'd fix this uniform.

"Any questions?" Ms. Montes asked.

"Miss, can I have a paper to write a letter now?"

"Ivanov, this is group time. So no." She turned away from me. "Gonzales, you know the rules already. Just follow them this time around."

"Why you keep calling me by my last name? The name's Jester, Montes."

"It's *Ms.* Montes, *ward* Gonzales. Address staff as Ms., Mr., or Mrs. I'm not your friend." She ran long red fingernails through the bangs on her forehead. "You're all wards of the State of California. You're here to attend group counseling and school. No fighting, no profanity, no drugs. And mind your own business." She turned to me and shoved a plastic badge in my face. "Memorize your number. Keep the ID on you at all times, left side of the chest."

The ID showed five numbers beneath my photo with my

name on the right side, IVANOV, Juana M. Seeing my last name in print made me think of Alek again.

She flapped a pamphlet in front of my face. "Read this," she ordered then disappeared into the back office.

The papers had a few English words I didn't understand. I pointed to one. "Jester, what does this mean?"

"Can't you see I'm busy?" She flicked her hand at the tiny girl. "My homie, here's malillas. She's kicking, sabes?"

The word malillas sounded like Spanish but mashed together with another language.

"Pobrecita. You tell staff about her?"

"Her name's Babydoll, and don't tell me what to do, paisa. Remember, you owe me."

Babydoll's eyes fluttered open. Their color startled me. They resembled huge green olives and were almond-shaped like those of the beautiful women in the old Mexican movies my mother used to watch.

Jester leaned forward in her chair, tapped Jones's knee. "Check this out, Gina. When the van pulled up to the gate, this hyna shook like a scared mouse. Puked right on my jumpsuit."

Gina curled her lip, scrunched up her nose. "Oh my gawd, so nasty."

"Gacho," Babydoll said. She rubbed the blue teardrop on the corner of her right eye. "You owe Jester big time now."

Ms. Montes walked back into the circle with her hands full of green file folders. "Now, for the rules during group counseling. No nicknames, profanity, or jumping out of your chair. We'll talk about your commitment offense, your crime. Mariana Johnson, you speak Spanish. Translate for Ivanov if she needs help."

The woman next to me lifted her head. Her round cheeks rose in a shy smile. I noticed the warm brown color of her skin, like piloncillo, the raw sugar cones my mother used to make champurrado.

"Me llamo Mariana," she said.

Her voice was so low I had a hard time hearing.

Ms. Montes clapped her hands together. "Okay. You, new girls, need to understand what the Corrections Board expects at your initial hearings next month. Gonzales, since this is your third go-round, tell the group your original crime and what brought you back here."

"Check this out." Jester grinned. "Me and the homies were kicking it at our park when these hynas from another set come over. We start fighting." She jabbed the air. "Stabbed two of them."

I sucked in my abdomen, imagining Jester plunging a knife into someone's body.

"They didn't belong in our territory. Lucky, they lived. Did three years, got out when I was seventeen."

Jester was only fourteen when she stabbed people? This frightened me more than her earlier words. I leaned back into my seat, curled my legs into the chair.

"And your latest violation?" Ms. Montes said.

"Stayed free almost five months 'til my punk-ass parole agent hooked me up for hanging around gangbangers. My own friends. Psst. And I had a knife. Big deal."

"I should have asked ward Anaya." Ms. Montes pointed to the girl wearing glasses. "Ivanov, your crime?"

A swooshing sound filled my ears before I realized it was my heartbeat. My cheeks grew hot. Whenever I think of what happened that night, my throat tightens until I can barely breathe. My mind flashes to the sound of Alek's body falling down the stairs. Heavy thumps, curse words, moans.

"Ivanov," Ms. Montes snapped her fingers. "Tell us your crime."

"The court, they say I, um, my husband died because—"

"This chick's married?" Gina leaned forward, her chair scooting back.

"Tole you she knocked someone off," Jester said.

I rubbed my hands together, took a breath. "No. Uh, yes, I had a husband, and I have a baby—"

"She in foster care?" asked Babydoll. "Who gots her?"

Mariana translated everything.

"It's okay, I understand," I waved my hand at Mariana.

"Everyone be quiet," Ms. Montes said. "Ivanov, what are you sentenced for?"

"Uh, the um, voluntary thing?"

"Your commitment offense is voluntary manslaughter."

"Yes, Miss, *Ms.*, but I—"

"Órale, this mouse of a girl gots balls." Jester's laugh echoed in the dayroom.

The girls' voices swirled through the air. Who did she kill? How? She use a gun or what?

This is the reason why I never wanted to talk about what happened. Everything sounded horrible. People thought I was a terrible person.

"Speak up, Ivanov." Ms. Montes's eyes focused on me. "Surely you had to recount your crime in juvenile court."

"I didn't hurt my husband."

"The judge found you guilty. That's all that matters." Ms. Montes glanced at her red wristwatch. "Group time's up. Mariana Johnson, you'll have to present your crime next week."

"Yes, ma'am," Mariana's soft voice said.

"You're in here?" I asked her in Spanish. "I thought you were one of the staff."

Mariana shook her head. Her thick curls vibrated against her shoulders.

"And you, Ivanov." Ms. Montes scribbled something on her clipboard. "Be better prepared next time."

What happened was not something I could talk about in front of everyone. Even though I retold the account to the police, the detention staff, and the judge, none of them believed me. When the time comes to tell my daughter about her father, what do I say? How do I explain his death? Will she believe me?

THREE

Unable to sleep, I reached into my locker and took out the photograph of my baby. While I was in Centre, Lupe sent me a photo of Katrina, at five months old. I held it inches from my nose so I could see every detail. She wore a bright pink dress and a tiny ribbon in her dark hair. Her eyes reminded me of Papá's, the color of honey, and her shy smile like the one Alek first showed me. The smooth softness of her cheeks made my eyes water because I wanted to feel her warmth in my arms.

Kissing her little face, I hugged her picture against my heart. It was the only photo of her I had. The others I left in our apartment when I fled into the night.

The chill in the cell reminded me of that evening. The bus ride through San Bernardino to Indio and the desert took six hours. Frightened, I stay huddled in my seat, rocking my baby and thinking of what I'd do once I arrived in Calexico.

I thought Papá might accept a collect call from me, maybe he'd forgiven me and tell me to come home, but when I picked up the telephone handle, I remembered his anger and letter. After I arrived in Los Angeles, I wrote Lupe. Papá wrote back instead:

How dare you disobey me and leave your family for a stranger, an Americano, after my brother and your tia gave you a home. Now you say you'll make lots of money, in the Estados Unidos, send some to us? We don't want your money. You're an embarrassment.

At the bus station, I couldn't bring myself to call Papá or tell him that I had run away from Alek and needed help. Instead, I phoned my cousin Maribel in Mexicali, across the border from Calexico, and asked her to meet me. A short time later, she burst through the bus station entrance, threw her arms around me, and hugged me tightly. We hadn't seen each other for nine months.

Maribel examined my face, put her hands on her full hips. "You have marks on your neck. What did he do?"

"Nothing. We argued, an accident." I rested my hand on the side of my neck. "He's been drinking. He lost his job. I just had to get away for a little while."

Her long straight hair fanned out when she shook her head. "No, Juana. Stay with us. We'll make up a reason why you're here."

"How do I face your parents? They don't know I had a baby."

She took the blanket off Katrina's sleeping face. "She's so little. Tell them and your papá the truth."

"No. I can't, Mari. I'm going back and try to work things out with Alek. Please, take care of Katrina."

"You can't just leave her with me. Come to the house, and we'll tell my parents together."

I kissed Katrina's cheek and breathed in her baby scent. For a second, I hesitated and kept her snug against my chest. My hands trembled. Was I doing the right thing? Should we both go back? Alek's shouts crowded into my mind, and my body remembered the fear.

And then I remembered the times he cuddled Katrina and me, calling us his family and telling me how happy he was with us. There were good days too. I could convince him to return with me to Calexico, where he could find another job. If only he'd stop drinking.

I pushed Katrina into Maribel's arms. "Please, take her. Alek will be all right today, and he'll listen now. We'll be back in a couple of days, together, and then I'll tell Papá about Katrina. I promise."

But I didn't return. I couldn't.

Maribel called Papá and told him I had left my baby with her and her parents. I wrote and told him I didn't know I'd be arrested. He wrote back while I waited for court in Centre Juvenile Hall.

Now, you're in prison? Did you do what they accused you of? Lupe can't work because she cares for the baby. We struggle to buy my medications and all the things a baby needs. What kind of mother are you to leave a child? You should never have gone back to Los Angeles. You've dishonored me. You're not my daughter anymore.

My plan to help the family was a failure. Not only was I a bad daughter, but I shamed him and left him and Lupe worse off.

The humiliation of all I lost kept me from writing back to explain why I left Santa Isabel for Mexicali. I wanted to make money to contribute to buying the prosthetic arm Papá needed. He'd be able to work again, not spend his days depressed and angry. Life would become better for him, me, and Lupe if he had a job.

But all that was over now. I crumpled Papá's letter in my hands and twisted the paper back and forth before throwing it into my locker. I dropped onto the bed and hit my fist against the thin mattress. Hot tears streamed over my face onto the flat pillow. How stupid I was. If I could only talk to Papá, if he knew why I ran from Alek, why I left Katrina with Maribel, maybe he'd forgive me.

Speakers crackled throughout the evening. Girls yelled out their doors, and the staff hit the bars of the windows outside with their flashlights. Despite the noise, the emptiness inside me made me yearn to talk to someone. I knocked on the wall of my room.

"Mariana? Awake?"

"Huh? Um, yes."

Her wobbly voice was the kind I had after crying for hours. Tired, defeated.

"When did you come here?"

"Two weeks ago."

"How do I get paper and stamps for a letter?"

"Canteen. Ask Ms. Montes."

"She's mean, tells me 'Not now, Ivanov' when all I want is paper to write a letter to my sister and father. I don't have money for the canteen."

Mariana didn't answer, so I kept on talking. "How do you know Spanish so good? Jester's Mexican, and she doesn't speak—"

"I . . . I don't want to talk. Um, not tonight."

"You no feel okay?" I thought she'd be friendly since she translated words for me. But I understood when people wanted to be alone in their thoughts. "We talk later."

I pulled open my screened window for some air. The street-lights on the road glowed yellow, illuminating the top of the chain-link fence that surrounded the living unit. I couldn't see the tree in the backyard.

Jester's voice yelled across the wings of our building. "The chick's a norteña. You can't talk to her anymore."

"But you told me Anaya's not a gangbanger," Babydoll said.

"So what? We got word from the big pinta we don't talk to norteñas."

"Gina comes from Los Gatos, up north. Can we talk to her?"

"She don't count. She's a gavacha, not one of us. Plus, we got business with her, sabes?"

Norteñas? Who were they? San Bueno Youth Correctional was in the United States, El Norte. I was confused until I remembered my time at Centre. The gangbangers made up the rules. It didn't matter if they made sense. They expected everyone to follow their instructions or pay the consequences. Jester used a knife on other girls and laughed about it. She didn't care if she killed someone. I couldn't afford to mess up in this place. I still owed her a favor.

FOUR

"**P**repare for chow," a staff shouted in the hallway.

Ms. Montes unlocked several other girls and me. It was my first time out with the group. Curious, I turned to look behind me. Maybe I'd recognize someone from Centre Juvenile Hall.

"Eyes front, Ivanov," Ms. Montes shouted.

My heart leaped. I was only a few feet away from her. Behind me, in line, Jester snickered.

In the unit's dining room, small windows lined the tops of the brick wall. Scraggly curtains blocked out most of the night sky. It seemed mean to make them high up, reminding me that I couldn't reach them to see outside.

The room looked like an old cafeteria I'd seen on TV. I slid my orange plastic tray along the food line. Three girls in white wrinkly aprons and black hairnets stood on one side of the counter—each with a ladle or tongs. Gina stared at me from the other side. She pushed her hairnet back, exposing her thin brown eyebrows.

"Did you enjoy your dinner last night?" She dumped a pile of white rice in the largest section of my tray. "Gotta be fast."

The next girl scooped brown sauce on top of my rice. The salty smell pierced my nose as the mound of mushy vegetables spread out in the compartment.

Jester elbowed me. "Chinese day. Move it."

I stepped to the left. Another kitchen worker, an older girl who looked bored, handed me a slice of white bread and a plastic spoon with short tines at the top. The utensil looked like a fat fork.

"Don't lose your spork. Desserts over there." She pointed to the end of the counter with her tongs.

With my tray complete, I sat at the table where my room number was stamped on top. Jester sat across from me, bent over her tray, and dug into her food. I gave myself the sign of the cross over my chest and quickly mumbled a prayer, disrespecting God with my hurriedness. I didn't want to give Jester another reason to make fun of me.

Around me were tee shirts in shades of blue. Some washed out, and others were new. Young, older, chubby, skinny, white, black, brown, and in between. So many girls.

Mariana sat at the table next to ours, with three other girls. She took small spoonfuls of food from her tray, pausing between bites. Her back stiff against the chair, she stared at Ms. Montes, who stood at the open dining room door.

One of Mariana's table mates had her hair braided into several rows, the ends tied with blue rubber bands at the base of her thick neck. She ate like Jester, hunched over shoveling food into her mouth, one arm around her tray.

"Stop staring. Shit," Jester said, chewing with her mouth open. "That's Chantilla. She's a Crip. Calls shots for the mayatas."

My mouth screwed up at hearing the word mayata. It meant a black beetle, and Centre staff told us it was disrespectful to use the term to refer to people.

Jester pointed her lips to the table next to us. "Probably recruiting your Black friend, the one who speaks Spanish."

"Mariana? Why?"

"Bloods outnumber the Crips in San Bueno. Crips need more soldiers. We run this unit."

At Centre, the staff put me in an "immigration hold" section for my first month. The Black girls in my area were from countries like Somalia, Haiti, and the Dominican Republic. We didn't have gang problems and rules like Jester's until staff moved me to what they called the general population. But I didn't tell Jester this because she wouldn't care.

"How you get a job in here?" I asked.

"The jefa, Mrs. Shaffer, picks the workers for the juice jobs. Bunch of smackas. Now shut up and eat before I take your food."

I moved my tray closer to me, picked at the rice at the edge of the watery sauce. I was in a new place with new rules, and I needed to learn them quickly. I had to be friendly with Jester, so I could find out what to do in here, but I didn't want her to think I wanted to be a gang member either.

"Seconds," Ms. Montes shouted.

Gina came to our table, nudging Jester. "What's up? I gotta make the trays."

"Give Babydoll extra juice and this when you deliver her food. Tell her I'll kick her down more in the morning." Jester slid a piece of paper, folded into a triangle, to Gina.

"Fer sure." Gina grasped the paper and bounced away.

"Babydoll still sick?" I asked.

"Ask for aspirin at med call tonight and pass them to me."

"But staff checks the mouth."

Jester shook her head, blew out her breath. "Damn. Watch me."

She took a tiny piece of bread, rolled it into a ball, opened her mouth, and ate it, I thought, until she pulled her lip down. She hid the bread between her lip and gum.

I scratched at my neck. "Ms. Montes might catch me."

"Listen, paisa. You owe me a favor, and Babydoll's still detoxing. She needs pain meds."

Getting her the aspirins didn't seem to be a bad way to pay back Jester, but if I failed, Ms. Montes would write a discipline report on me. I couldn't have bad stuff on my record, not if I wanted to get out as fast as possible.

Someone behind me coughed. I turned and saw a husky, beady-eyed correctional officer enter the kitchen. He nodded to Ms. Montes. Gina eyed him with a slight smile as he strolled around the dining room.

"Who's that staff?" I asked. "Why's he walking around in here?"

"Pinche security. He comes by all the time because he's one of Gina's sanchos."

"Sancho?"

"Ee-ho man, you don't know jackshit, Mouse."

Jester had black letters on each finger spelling out XIII with three faded blue dots between her thumb and forefinger. Heat rose to my cheeks. I knew so little about this place, but I was trying to learn.

"Means 'mi vida loca.' I'm a gangster, baby." She leaned back in her chair, bobbed her head. "Where in Mexico you come from?"

"Santa Isabel, in Chihuahua. After my mamá died, I go to work in Mexicali, meet my—"

"Psst," she flicked her hand at me. "Did I ask for your life story?"

Blinking, I beat back the tears rising to my eyes. No one ever listened to me. I pushed my food around the plate. "Sorry."

Jester slurped her milk. "My jefita died too."

She lifted her chin to someone across the aisle and winked. Babydoll curled her index fingers and touched her thumbs together, making a heart sign.

"Jester," I asked, "where do I find paper and a stamp?"

"Staff give you your issue. In here, you make trades for everything. I trade for oranges, bread, noodles, whatever you got that I might want." She drained her cup and smacked her lips. "I draw pictures too. One of my foster mothers told me I could be an artist, work for Disney Studios. They're in LA, serio. There's a water tank with Mickey Mouse. I seen it once."

I was glad Jester told me her life story because she didn't seem so scary as before. The Polaroid photo of Katrina was small but the only remembrance I had of my baby. A larger drawing of her could help me remember every detail of her face.

"How much to make a picture of my baby and a stamp?"

"Four slices of bread for the stamp and two oranges for the drawing. I'm giving you a break cause it's your kid."

"Can I pay you later? I need the stamp right away."

Jester snickered. "Nah, Mouse. Pay upfront."

"Do I ask Gina for the bread and oranges?"

She rubbed her forehead and grinned. "Yeah, yeah, ask her when staff calls scrape."

The first table of girls got up to scrape their trays. They emptied their food into garbage bins and dropped their plastic forks into a bucket in front of Ms. Montes. I got up, moved to the food line, and asked Gina for bread and oranges. She snorted, shook her head, and told the other girls on the kitchen crew what I said. They pointed at me and brayed like a bunch of donkeys. I hurried back to my seat. Sweat wet my underarms while my face burned red.

That was the way Jester was. She played jokes on people and studied your face when you found out she lied. I couldn't afford to get on her wrong side, so I shrugged and kept my mouth shut. Jester pounded the table as she laughed.

Among the many things I need to tell my daughter when she's old enough is to figure out who's trying to use you for their benefit. I had so many examples to choose from that I was embarrassed to tell anyone.

"Everyone's on quiet while I do the spork count," Ms. Montes said. "And as a reminder, nothing goes out of this kitchen except ice."

She stood by the door, dropping the utensils into another bin with her gloved hand. "Fifty. The count's clear. Line it up by row."

All of us stood at our small tables and waited for the hand signal from Ms. Montes.

Jester slid behind me in line. "Get that aspirin today and drop the Black chick. She belongs to the other side."

FIVE

The cell door swung open without warning. I pulled the bed-sheet over my face, blocked the burst of hallway light into my room. Did staff find out I hid the aspirin in my mouth? Did they see me pass it to Jester in the dayroom earlier?

"Who is it?" My voice squeaked.

"Weekly issue. Two pieces of paper, one envelope," Ms. Montes said. "You can send out one unsealed letter a week without a stamp."

"Do I give you the letter when I'm finished?"

"Nope, going off shift." The lock clicked shut. "Give it to the night staff." Her voice echoed down the hall.

I jumped out of bed, grabbed the paper and my pencil, and began writing in the dark. I had to convince my sister to stay in Mexico with my baby.

Dear Lupe,

I understand you must do what your husband wants, but sister, you're pregnant. Crossing the border is too dangerous. I've heard many terrible things too many times when I worked in Mexicali. People die crossing. Women raped, and children kidnapped. Please, I beg you to stay in Santa Isabel with Katrina. I'll send you whatever money I earn from here.

How is my baby? Has she grown a lot? How is Papá's diabetes? When I leave here, I'll go to Mexicali, to Maribel's, and call you. I'll do everything I can to leave this place as fast as possible. I promise. Please write. Kiss Katrina for me. I miss her so much. Siempre tu hermana,
Juana

The sound of tennis shoes squeaking in the hallway echoed. I slid the unsealed letter between my doorframe.

"This letter in Spanish?" The night staff lady asked. "Translation's needed first, young lady."

"My sister don't read English. The letter is important. How long to send out?"

"I'll leave this off for a Spanish-speaking staff who'll pick it up in the morning. Who knows how long it'll take to translate and clear for mailing?"

Since I couldn't talk to Mariana in front of Jester, I asked Anaya how to find the bread and fruit to trade. She didn't want to tell me; she said I'd get in trouble. I figured it out myself. I hoped I wasn't making a mistake to trust someone like Jester, but I wanted another picture of my baby. Something to keep me going in this place.

It took me two days of lunches to save for the stamp and two more days to come up with the fruit. Before I gave the oranges to Jester, I rolled them back and forth across my cell floor, breathing in the citrus scent. They made me hungry, but they were too valuable to keep.

Jester passed me the drawing of Katrina at breakfast, where I flattened it under my shirt and hid it until I got to my cell.

I couldn't believe how beautiful Jester drew. Katrina's black hair had shades of brown in her curls. Glints of yellow in her eyes brought her to life. A ribbon with lettering spelling out KATRINA with tiny pink roses for a border were underneath her shoulders. Where did Jester buy the colored pencils?

"Psst, Mariana." I pushed out the old rusty window in my room until it hit the mesh screen in front of the bars. "Do staff give us tape to put photos on our walls?"

She giggled. "No, use toothpaste. Sticks pretty well."

With a glob of the white paste, I smeared the back of the drawing and the photo and stuck them to the wall at the foot of the bed. Now I could see Katrina before I went to sleep and when I woke up.

Her tiny mouth was open in the photo, her eyes wide while she looked up at Lupe. She was five months old, but I'm sure she recognized Lupe wasn't her mother. It hurt to imagine Katrina feeling how I felt in a place full of strangers.

She'll be almost seven years old when I parole. In school already. I worry she'll think of Lupe as her mother by that time. Maybe she's already called her mamá.

The thought depressed me so I made an effort to concentrate on better times at home. After Mamá died, my father,

Lupe, and I kept up her garden. Papá said this was out of respect for my mother.

I imagined Papá, Lupe, and Katrina in the vegetable patch with the squash blossoms and tomatoes surrounding them in fragrance. The sounds of chickens pecking and scratching for cornmeal. Perhaps Papá scooped a small handful of dirt in Katrina's hand so she could touch and smell the moist earth.

Why did I ever leave home?

The photo of Katrina made me think of Alek. Memories of him flooded my mind. Alek in Mexicali, Alek in Los Angeles, Alek on the last night I saw him alive.

"Are you alright, Juana?" Mariana tapped on her wall. "Sounded like nightmares. Like you couldn't breathe."

That bad dream again. Alek chasing me. I made it to the bottom of the stairs, my baby in my arms. Next, Alek's body crumpled on the cement. He pushed himself up, reached for me.

"I'm okay, Mariana." I took a deep breath to stop the thumping in my chest. "Go back to sleep."

"Juana, I didn't kill anyone like everyone thinks."

She killed a person? Her round freckled face looked so innocent. Her voice so soft and whispery.

"Ms. Montes said I had to talk about what happened in our next group, but I don't remember everything. That's the truth, but no one believes me."

"They don't believe me either," I said. "Sometimes the papers say you did something you didn't do."

"Wish Ms. Montes would let me tell her privately," Mariana

said. "Tomorrow, you want to practice your English? I could make you a list of words to learn."

I remembered what Jester said. I couldn't be friends with Mariana, but practicing English wasn't friends. She could be my teacher. If Jester said anything, that's what I'd say.

SIX

The new staff lady waved us up from Alpha hallway and into the dayroom. "Program time."

Everyone filed into the room and spread out, taking a seat. I didn't see Mrs. Shaffer or Ms. Montes, only a woman correctional officer at the desk.

Several girls moved to the TV rows, a few sat at the two small card tables, and the others in the seats along the brick walls. I followed behind Anaya, with Mariana behind me.

Anaya turned to us. "When Mrs. Shaffer's not here, sit with your back to a wall if you're by yourself. The dayroom's safer than the end of the hallways and showers."

I gulped. Mariana's eyes grew huge. I moved on stiff legs to a chair that faced the staff desk with Mariana and Anaya two seats away from me on either side. I hoped the staff who sat in the rolling chair at the desk paid attention.

"One of the female staff is from another unit. The correctional officer, the CO, Ms. Isadora, watches pretty well," Anaya said.

The CO was around Ms. Montes's age with black hair in a bun at her neck. She leaned against the wooden counter that separated the staff desk from the dayroom. Behind her, the older lady watched us from her chair.

My body relaxed a bit, but I glanced around and watched the other girls for a few minutes. The dayroom was like a fishbowl, where everyone kept track of the others, where they sat, who with, and when they got up from their seat.

I pulled out my list of words from the ward handbook that Mariana translated for me. A tee shirt and jeans landed on my paper, crumpling it to my lap.

"Mouse."

My shoulders tensed at the sound of Jester's hard-edged voice.

"From now on, you're on ironing duty." She stood in front of me and narrowed her eyes. "Got it?"

Next to her, a tall skinny girl with black marble eyes and a slash for a mouth stood like a wooden soldier. Her glance shifted from my face to my feet and back again. A lump clogged my throat.

"This is Bruja. Don't piss her off, or she'll give you mal ojo." Jester pulled the skin under her eye.

The name, witch, fit the girl well. Thin from her face to her feet, she wore a sour expression.

"Come with us," Jester said. "Bring my clothes."

"But I'm learning English for a good job when I leave here."

"Yeah, right," the witch laughed. "Get your ass over to the iron."

Her order made my neck cramp. I glanced at Anaya and Mariana who sat up in their seats, their faces frozen. Neither said a word. I followed Jester and Bruja across the room until they stopped at the empty ironing board.

"What're ya doing with that Black chick?" Jester said.

"Mariana? She knows Spanish. She's teaching me the English words from the handbook. Ms. Montes told her to," I lied. "I need to learn more to find a job when I get out of here, provide for—"

"TMI." Jester's hand flew up. "Business is okay, but remember what I said."

She'd told me her rules about mixing with other races on the second day I was here. I nodded though they were stupid instructions. There was no drinking at the water fountain after the Black girls, no sharing cups or food with them.

"Don't fuck up, or you'll be one sorry mousy," Bruja said. "And iron them good."

I hated to iron, but I didn't want to be on Jester's or Bruja's bad side. I'd never find a curandera here in San Bueno to roll an egg over me to take off the evil eye hex.

After ironing Jester's pants, I returned to Mariana and my English lesson. "Where's Anaya?"

"TV row." Mariana kept her eyes on the card table where Jester and Bruja sat. "They don't like the races mixing. I don't want to cause any trouble."

"Don't worry, she said business is okay," I said. "Hey, are you black or brown?"

Mariana turned from watching the card table and shook her head. "Does it really matter?"

"No, not to me. I ask because you speak Spanish. Not even Jester or her friends speak as good as you."

Her shoulders relaxed. "I'm biracial. My real father's Black, my mother's Puerto Rican. She taught me Spanish."

"Real father?"

"My mom remarried. I have, uh, had a stepdad."

Mariana glanced away from me and slid lower into her chair. I caught Bruja glaring at us. I didn't like how her eyes lingered, observing Mariana and me. She reminded me of my brothers who hid behind the boulders near the river, waiting to lasso iguanas with their ropes.

"That girl's staring. I don't need any problems." Mariana pushed the list of English words into my hand and moved to another seat.

Anaya left the TV rows, crossed the dayroom, and stopped at the card table. She reached her hand out to Jester, but she and Babydoll said something to her and turned their backs. Anaya's face creased. She shrugged and returned to the TV rows where she used her tee shirt to wipe her eyeglasses.

The girl had been nice to me, so I walked over to the TV row and sat a seat away from her, placing Jester's ironed clothes between us.

"Anaya, why did Jester call you an estrella, a star?"

"Don't call me Anaya like the staff. My name's Xochitl. Call me by my name." Her words snapped as tight as the long braid she wore.

"Xochitl? Qué bonita nombre."

She glanced at me, a hint of a smile at the corner of her mouth. "I'm her enemy now, but I don't bang. Never have, never will."

"Enemy? Why?"

"Jester says I'm a norteña because I'm from the Bay Area. You better not let her catch you talking to me."

The explanation didn't make sense, but a lot of things in here confused me. Xochitl knew how things worked in this place, and I needed to understand to keep out of harm's way.

I leaned forward, eager to ask her questions. "The officer who brought us here said 'welcome to Disneyland.' Why he say that?"

"Because this is a kiddy place compared to the woman's prison."

So not too bad, I guessed. I rubbed at my chin trying to remember the words Jester had used at dinner. "What's a smacka and a juice job?"

"Smackas are kiss asses. Juice jobs means the better ones like working laundry and kitchen. They pay more too. And Jester hates smackas."

"The blond girl Gina has a kitchen job, and Jester talks to her. Is she a skinhead girl? You're not a kiss ass, and Jester acts like she hates you."

Xochitl glanced around the dayroom before answering me. "Nah, Gina's not neo-Nazi. She's her own category."

Before I could ask her what a neo-Nazi was, she grabbed her papers, moved to a chair closer to the staff desk.

This place puzzled me. The staff had rules, the gangs had their own, and the other girls had rules too. Breaking the rules could be bad sometimes and good other times. I had to figure this out so I could keep safe.

SEVEN

The morning routine at San Bueno sounded like a bad song. The night staff banged on our cell doors, yelled "wake up, wake up" as they walked up and down the hallways. This was followed by the click-clack of steel sink buttons punched by dozens of girls trying to turn on the water which spurted out into the sink. The odor of rotten eggs filled up my room while I washed my face.

"Remember to turn in your work application to Grandma," Mariana called to me through the wall.

A few of the girls called Mrs. Shaffer "Grandma," and she'd say, "If I were your granny, you'd have sense enough not to be here." She made us laugh, but then I'd think how I didn't have an abuela or a mother, and I'd stop thinking about grandmas.

We filed past the front door of our unit onto the roadway and into the cool morning, where the damp odor of fertilizer from the surrounding fields enveloped us. The stink in the air stuck in my throat. Never had our chicken coop at home stunk so terribly.

Standing side by side on the road like girl soldiers, we waited. I listened to the murmurs of the fifty girls, the shifting of their feet and arms while Ms. Montes did another head-count.

"Hey, give this to Sadgirl. She's in your class." Jester held a folded note, a kite, in the palm of her hand.

Passing kites and aspirin made me sweat every time. The COs did random pat downs on the girls before and after class. If I got caught, I'd receive a discipline report and stay locked up in my room for the weekend. If I didn't take the kite, Jester would punish me today. Taking a breath, I remembered that Xochitl said the COs didn't touch the chest area, at least not in front of everyone. I reached back and grabbed the letter.

"Move out." Ms. Montes swatted the air with her hand.

As I slid the kite under my tee shirt, I noticed a heart drawn on the outside. Sadgirl was Bruja's girlfriend. I entered the class-room and took my seat.

Bruja and Sadgirl sat at the same four-seat table as me. With only eleven other girls in the room and the teacher turning her back all the time, there was a chance Bruja would see me pass the kite to Sadgirl. She could take it from me, see the heart drawn on the outside and punch me. But Jester might ask Sadgirl if I gave her the kite, so not passing it would be the same. If I dropped the kite and Bruja found out Jester sent it, there'd be a fight between them which was okay with me, but I'd be the next person Jester went after.

My fingers hurt from twisting them back and forth in my lap. The teacher turned to the whiteboard. I quickly slipped the note under Sadgirl's textbook. Bruja lifted her eyes off her work-sheet, searched my face, and stared at her girlfriend. Sadgirl didn't flinch. She kept writing on her sheet of paper.

41

"Watch it, Mouse. She's my hyna."

Sadgirl blew out her breath. "Bruja, what the shit are you talking about?"

"I don't like girls." My cheeks grew hot, the palms of my hand damp.

Bruja bobbed her head. "That's what they all say. At first."

"I had a husband."

"Ivanov, do you have a problem?" the teacher asked and stepped toward me.

I shook my head. Sadgirl bent forward, a curtain of hair covered her face. She grasped the edge of the kite and dropped it to her lap. Her hand didn't tremble one bit.

The lunch bell rang like a fire station alarm and made me jump. A CO came to the open door and signaled to the teacher.

"Pass your worksheets to the end of the tables and up to me," she said.

The girl with the cornrow braids, Chantilla, tapped the back of my hand and passed me a kite along with her worksheet. She winked at me.

"You're learning fast," she said, her voice hushed. "Give this to Mariana."

I tucked the kite into my pocket and rushed over to my section beneath the flagpole, the "quad," where rows of girls stood waiting for the signal from their staff.

"Don't run!" CO Wozinsky, the man who was Gina's sancho, shouted.

He stood in front of the groups, his hands on his hips, his broad chest puffed out as far as his hanging belly. His head swiveled left and right like a ranchero inspecting his herd. How did he see anything through those black sunglasses he wore?

Gina loitered in front of him, flashing him a big grin. Ms. Montes didn't notice Gina in the wrong area because she stood talking to another staff.

I slipped into the row where the Mariposa girls stood and waited. In the row next to me, a girl slapped the back of another girl's head, hard. She stumbled out of line, righted herself, her jaw tense. I winced. My shoulders tightened. Memories flooded back. My fingers clutched the bottom of my tee shirt. I had once stood there like the girl, my heart racing when Alek hit me. A cry stuck in my throat because there might be more anger if I made a sound.

The staff didn't see what happened to the girl. The others didn't want to be involved. I'd be invisible here, too, another faceless girl in blue. I clenched my fists, tried to stop shaking. I had no one to guard me and now I had another reason to be on friendly terms with Jester. I needed protection.

EIGHT

Xochitl flopped into the green dayroom chair next to me and stretched out her long legs. "You watch that crap, *The Young and the Restless*?"

I nodded. "The show reminds me of telenovelas. I'm studying the list of English words Mariana gave me. Want to test me?"

Jester shuffled over to us, her chin up with one hand in her jean pocket, gangbanger style. She squinted at Xochitl's face, scowled, and strolled away.

"Damn, she keeps mad dogging me." Wrinkles creased her forehead.

I pretended not to notice. "I like your name, means flower in the Aztec language. Are you Mexican?"

"Born here. My grandparents on Mom's side come from Zacatecas. My pops is Nicaraguan. I prefer to call myself a Chicana."

"Why in the United States, people who I think are Mexican call themselves Hispanics or Latinos or Chicanos?"

"It's whatever you think about yourself. Your identity."

I didn't understand what she meant. My education stopped after secundaria when I was fourteen, but I still liked learning. I added the word "identity" to my word list to look it up in the dictionary in English class.

"Ivanov." Ms. Montes crossed the dayroom, her clunky tennis shoes squeaking on the linoleum floor. She handed me a Spanish Translation Needed form and left.

"I've waited so long. The mail could be from my sister."

"Lemme see that paper." Xochitl wiped her glasses clean with her tee shirt.

"My sister writes in Spanish. I wait for staff to interpret it before I receive the letter."

"Up to a week for translation? Sounds illegal. You should complain. Go to the library, ask the librarian for the laws in California, " Xochitl said.

"They do this at Centre Juvenile Hall too. I don't want to make a big escándalo. Ms. Montes will think I'm a troublemaker."

"What if there's an emergency? How're you gonna find out if you gotta wait a week for a letter to be translated?"

"Ay, don't say that." I made the sign of the cross over my chest. "My baby is so far from me."

"We have a ten-minute phone call every week. I guess you can check on your baby by phone."

"It cost a lot to call Mexico, so I can't. My daughter stays with my sister Lupe, who takes care of my father. He had an accident at the railroad that left him without an arm. But I'm worried because Lupe's husband wants her to cross the border. I need her to keep Katrina in Mexico."

"Messed up." Xochitl shook her head. "You need to do something. Quick."

"Ivanov. Need to talk with you." Ms. Montes stood at the staff office door in the back of the dayroom.

"See you later, Xochitl."

"Have a seat." Ms. Montes sat on the corner of the desk. "The Corrections Board will meet with you in two or three weeks. They determine your time even though the judge gave you six years."

I flinched at the thought of so many days and months in this place.

"The board members will read the case report I write. If you do well in your program, you can earn time off at the end of your sentence. If you don't, we add time. Understand?"

Six years. I'd miss my baby's first words, first steps, so many birthdays, Christmases, and school days.

"Are you listening, Ivanov? This is important. You must acknowledge your crime, stay out of trouble."

"But Ms. Montes, I didn't kill Alek. He fell down the stairs on accident."

"This is what we go by." She waved a file in front of my face. "The judge already decided your case. You're convicted of voluntary manslaughter."

"But he was alive when I ran away. That's what I'm trying to tell you. I don't understand why I got six years and not—"

She flicked her hand up in the air and stood. "Just wanted to tell you about your hearing. Behave, or you'll end up doing more than six years. Now go back to the dayroom."

Words gurgled in my throat, but Ms. Montes waved me out the door like a pesky mosca. My file was like the Bible to her, and she wouldn't give up believing in the words of the report. My own counselor didn't think Alek had an accident. She didn't care what I said about that night.

I dragged my feet and moved over to the TV row. Xochitl

was nowhere around. Instead, Jester and Babydoll were in the seats at the far end of the row out of staff's sight. They held hands and leaned into each other. I laid my papers in a chair three seats away from them and sat.

Jester's eyes darted in my direction. "What did Montes want?"

"She explains the hearing."

Babydoll poked her head around Jester. "You should cry at your initial. Makes them feel sorry for you. They'll give you less time. Could work 'cause you look so innocent. No tattoos or nothing."

"Pfft. Don't believe what Montes says. The board does what they want," Jester said. "They'll give you *all* your time."

Six long years. I bit my lower lip to stop it from quivering. I wouldn't cry in front of Jester and Babydoll. Girls in jail hated crying, it made them uncomfortable. I had to go back to my room before my tears fell. I snatched my papers from the seat.

"Hey, did I say you could go?" Jester grabbed for my hand, but I pulled it away in time.

She laughed like it was a joke, but my pounding heart believed she'd hurt me.

"Órale, you're quicker than I thought. Sit down." She pointed to the seat next to her and moved close to my face, bringing her stinky breath. "You can't talk to Anaya. She's an estrella."

Her face twisted and made me gulp, but I wanted to know why I couldn't talk to Xochitl. "I don't understand. Why you call her estrella? San Bueno is the north."

"'Cause of the north star. A northerner, get it?" Babydoll said and giggled.

"Yeah, and this is the sur, pendeja. Sureña territory. Anyone past Fresno is a norteña." Jester's hands flew in front of her chest as she spoke. When she finished talking, she gave me her squinty eye stare. "Understand?"

"I'm not in a gang from the south or the north. Why can't I talk to her?"

"Stop asking questions, or I'll put you on the leva now instead of giving you a chance."

Babydoll put her thumb and pointing finger against her chest in an L shape. "That means none of us will talk to you. You'll be the enemy."

"Alvarez, iron," Ms. Montes's voice shouted across the dayroom.

Babydoll hurried to the ironing board.

"Al rato. Remember what I told you." Jester touched her middle finger to her temple, pointed it at me before she joined Babydoll.

The enemy? I glanced up to see Bruja glaring at me, and behind her, Xochitl kept her eye on me.

I moved to a chair facing the staff desk and thought about this leva thing. I added it to the rest of the rules Jester gave me.

"Program's over," Ms. Montes called out. "Alpha Hall first. The rest of you stay seated."

I kept my eyes and ears open while the girls lined up against the dayroom wall. I didn't stand near Xochitl or look in her direction. I felt like I betrayed her after she offered to help me. I didn't want to lose her friendship, but I had to keep away from her while Jester and her friends watched me. And they were always watching.

NINE

rs. Shaffer moved quickly around the dining room in her black grandma shoes that made no sound. She inspected the food bins and the kitchen workers. Girls sat up when she walked between the four-seater dining tables. Not because they were afraid of her, but because she usually stopped and asked us about our families or how we were doing.

She was one of the few staff who used our first names and told us when we did something right. She also told us when she expected better, so I guess she was like a caring grandmother after all.

"Okay, Juana Ivanov, Mariana Johnson, and Xochitl Anaya. You girls are the cleaning crew today," Mrs. Shaffer said. "Wait in the dayroom after dinner."

Bruja's unblinking eyes of stone followed Xochitl before they darted back to me. She'd tell Jester about me and the estrella working together, but that's a chance I'd take. I thought up a convenient excuse, just in case. I'd tell Jester I gained more ironing time to press her clothes.

Mrs. Shaffer unlocked the hall closet, handing me rags and window cleaner, the mop to Xochitl, and the push broom to

Mariana. She hauled out the short ladder, placed it in front of the dayroom windows, and returned to the staff desk.

I sprayed and wiped the countless squares of glass until a van drove up and parked at the curb. CO Wozinsky got out and stopped at the sidewalk to our unit. He pulled a comb from his pocket and ran it through his thin brown hair. I motioned to Xochitl and Mariana to come to the windows.

We spied on him as he pushed the door latch in, silencing the buzzer. Through the window in the front door, we watched him glance to his right toward the staff desk before he turned to his left and hurried into the kitchen.

"Gina's using the guy for smokes and stuff," Xochitl said. "He thinks he's her only man. Idiot."

"She has more than one?" I asked.

"One guy, but two malfloras on the other compas."

"Bad flowers?" Mariana asked.

"Geez, you guys. Malfloras means gay. Nobody bothers Gina. She has plenty of protection."

I'd heard the word gay at Centre, but never malflora. To call the girls bad flowers like something was wrong with them, or they were evil, didn't sound right. Especially coming from Xochitl. Before I could say anything, Mariana spoke.

"Gina's been here almost two years. For murder. I heard her boyfriend is in San Quentin."

"Yeah, he was supposed to shoot Gina's ex but missed him and shot the guy's wife," Xochitl said. "Check it out. Shaffer's going to the kitchen. Let's go see."

We took our rags, went to the hallway, and told the desk staff that the social worker's office windows needed cleaning.

We had a clear view into the hallway leading to the kitchen. The CO rushed out the door, his head lowered. Mrs. Shaffer followed.

"I swear I didn't hear the door buzz." She stood in the hallway outside the kitchen with her hand on her hip. "Did you?"

The staff lady at the desk glanced up from her paperwork and shook her head. Mariana strode into the dayroom, leaving Xochitl and me in the hallway.

"I did, Mrs. Shaffer." Gina came out of the kitchen, trailing behind her. "You didn't hear because you were busy."

"Young lady, I hear plenty well. Why was he sitting at the table with you?"

"Oh, my mom called. She can't visit this weekend." Gina dropped her chin, sniffed. "I miss her."

Mrs. Shaffer's forehead wrinkled. "The Communication Center phones the unit and tells the staff. A CO doesn't come to you personally."

Gina flashed her fake smile and played with her blond ponytail. "I don't know why Mrs. Shaffer."

"Stay in the dayroom with these girls. Help them clean." Mrs. Shaffer pointed at Xochitl and me.

"Can I deliver meal trays with you later?" Gina asked. "Please."

"We'll see."

Gina picked up paper towels and followed me to the dayroom. "If Shaffer asks you to take the trays, I have something for Jester." She patted her jean pocket before she walked away to clean our already cleaned hallway windows.

I moved over to the other side of the dayroom, where Mariana swept, and Xochitl held the dustpan.

"Gina asked me to give something to Jester," I said.

Mariana's eyes grew as wide as her mouth. "Are you going to do it?"

"What else can I do?"

"Everyone knows Shaffer has an eagle eye. She'll catch you if you pass anything during trays," Xochitl said. "Tell Jester you put the stuff in the tampon container in the shower. That way, you don't get into trouble for passing."

"Hey, why Gina don't ask you?" I asked Mariana and Xochitl.

"Really, Juana?" They both said.

"She must think my blackness will contaminate her contraband," Mariana said.

"And I'm the enemy," Xochitl said. "Idiots."

"More work, less talk, girls," Mrs. Shaffer said while she moved to the kitchen. "Gina, prepare the lock-up trays for the rooms."

"Sure, Mrs. Shaffer." Gina sprung up from her seat. "You got lucky, Mouse. You don't have to do me a favor after all. Not this time."

TEN

I sat in the cold, empty kitchen under the fluorescent lights on a plastic chair like I did when the police took me into the station. Ms. Montes flipped through papers in my file folder while tapping her pen on the table.

I chose to forget some parts of my life, but Ms. Montes kept asking me to talk about what I didn't want to remember. She insisted I tell her about that night with Alek. His last one. But I couldn't get the words out.

"Let's start at the beginning. How did you meet him?"

Her voice sounded softer than she usually spoke. She rested her chin on the palm of her hand like a friendly person who's interested in your story. The pinch at the bottom of my neck eased.

"Alek came to the restaurant, where I worked, with his friends for dinner. One time, he came alone, sat at the table in my area, and talked to me while I served customers. Back then, he worked in Calexico, on the other side of the border from Mexicali, where he did construction. We'd go to the movies after he finished work."

"Says in your file that he was nineteen. How old were you?"

"He just turned eighteen when we met. I was almost sixteen. We fell in love." I squirmed in my chair. "Six months later, I found out I was pregnant, but before I could tell Alek about the baby, he told me his construction job finished. He wanted to move back to Los Angeles."

"Did he ask you to leave with him?"

"Uh, not at first." I hung my head.

Ms. Montes scribbled another note on her paper. "Okay, so now you're in LA. How did Alek's family react to you?"

I wasn't about to tell Ms. Montes that my mother-in-law hated me. I wondered what Katrina would think of me if I told her the truth about her grandmother and father.

"He only had his mother, Anna. She came from Russia but moved to the US before she had Alek. His father died two years before we met. Anna acted excited when Alek told her about the baby."

"And your relationship with her?"

"Not so good. Anna threatened to call immigration whenever Alek and I argued. When we visited her, she'd make a big deal of cooking for him, talking to him in Russian, leaving me out of the conversation. She'd take Katrina from my arms and cuddle her, ignoring me."

"This report says you claimed Alek hit you. Tell me about the incident."

Sour fear flooded over my tongue. Which incident, the first, the last? I didn't like going over those times. I sucked in my breath.

"Was this the first time? Or did he hit you before the night of the crime?"

A headache gripped the back of my head. The heat of the memories choked my throat. I couldn't answer. I couldn't tell Ms. Montes, although she was a grown woman who probably heard hundreds of terrible stories in here. What would she think of me?

Ms. Montes drummed her fingers on the table. "Juana, did he break your nose?"

A spasm gripped my chest. Flashes of scenes traveled by me like a movie. I rubbed the hump on the bridge of my nose and pictured our apartment. Alek, the couch, our bedroom. The smell of whiskey, glass breaking, yelling.

"Anna said any arguments were my fault. I didn't know how to be a wife."

Ms. Montes stared at me, her pen bouncing against the table. "Ivanov, were these arguments, or did Alek hit you during your marriage?"

Now she sounded like the police officers who interviewed me, distant and impatient. I collected my memories like bundles of wood to take to the firepit at my father's house. Quick, say the words, I told myself. I squeezed my eyes shut.

"The first time Alek came home drunk. He yelled at me, 'Give me my money,' and yanked my purse off the table. Then he grabbed for me. I got away. He jerked me back by my blouse, shoved me against the wall. When I tried to get loose he threw me to the floor. I fell against the coffee table and hit my nose."

"Did you call the police?"

The lawyer, judge, and probation officer asked me the same question before I was sentenced. Like I could just pick up a phone and call right in front of him. What was I supposed to do afterward? Where was I to go? I shook my head.

"Why didn't you seek help?" Ms. Montes said.

Anger pushed through my stomach. "I didn't know anyone in Los Angeles. I didn't talk to anyone except the salespeople who spoke Spanish at the markets. I couldn't go anywhere without glancing over my shoulder, freezing whenever I saw the immigration agents."

"But it says here you had a green card. You could've called the police, filed a report." Ms. Montes pushed my file aside and sat back in her seat. "*If* the incidents are true."

The truth didn't matter to immigration. So many people were taken by La Migra right from their apartments, from their work sites. The police and many people thought every brown person could be a terrorist. Did Ms. Montes forget what happened a couple of years ago?

"Alek told me the police would send me back to Mexico, and they didn't care whether I had a green card or not. His mother told me that too. They'd keep our daughter if I got taken because she's an American citizen. They said I'd never see my baby again. I believed them."

"So no police report, huh?" Ms. Montes pressed her thumb and finger against her chin. "Didn't happen then."

I slumped into my seat. My caseworker in the juvenile hall told me that I was at a disadvantage without a police report of domestic violence because I couldn't prove it in court. At least that lady was nicer when she told me than Ms. Montes.

"It did happen, but I can't prove it to you."

"Why didn't you leave him if he hit you? Didn't you have a friend's place to go to? A family member to call? Couldn't you have taken a bus back to Calexico then?"

She sounded like the judge in juvenile court, punching me with questions quickly without emotion, pushing me into a corner.

Reliving Alek's threats twisted me up inside while a trickle of hot tears slid down my cheeks. Fear, shame, helplessness kept me quiet then and now.

Whenever the authorities asked me questions, I felt ashamed and stupid. Who'd understand I loved him? Who'd believe I kept hoping those instances were the last time?

Ms. Montes tapped her pen on the table. "Answer me. I need to understand why you didn't leave before the night of the incident."

"Alek was nice at first. He worked hard; he provided for us. We were a family."

I hung my head, expecting her to tell me how stupid I was.

She sighed. "So you didn't want to leave him even though he allegedly hurt you because you were family?"

Allegedly. I knew that word meant she didn't believe he hit me.

"He lost his job. He acted mad all the time, stayed out late. Drinking made everything worse. Things would be calm, peaceful for a few days until he started again. That's how I lived those last months. A few days at a time."

Ms. Montes shut my file, exhaled like she was more worn out than I. "Time's up. I have several other questions, but we'll talk again later."

"Miss, did you read my mail, the one in Spanish?"

"Tomorrow."

"Who is it from?"

She shoved her chair against the table. "Later, I said. Think about the question I asked. Why didn't you leave Alek when he first hit you?"

Ms. Montes didn't think my reason was good enough, or I was lying. Or she wouldn't ask me to keep thinking about that time. I walked out of the kitchen dazed with emotion and stopped at the staff desk. I needed to distract myself from all the questions.

"Mrs. Shaffer, can I borrow the sewing needle, please?"

"Sure, but in the dayroom only. Sewing is a lost art." She smiled at me. "Too bad I can't allow you to teach the others to sew. Needles are contraband."

I nodded, but teaching the girls to sew was the last thing I wanted to do. If I were permitted to go to my room with the needle, I'd hem and resize everyone's state uniform just so I could stay out of sight and busy.

Before I found a chair, I looked to where Jester and her friends sat. They were playing cards in the far corner of the dayroom. I took a seat two spaces from Mariana, who was a chair space away from Xochitl.

"What happened with Montes?" Xochitl asked, keeping her eyes away from me while she talked into the air space in front of her.

"Nothing. I don't want to talk."

"Okay. Whose pants are you sewing?" Mariana asked.

"Traded Jester for another drawing."

Mariana shook her head, her lips pressed tight like my mother used to do when I did something wrong or foolish. Xochitl shrugged and returned to reading her magazine.

Ms. Montes's question stirred in my mind while I sewed a hem in Jester's pants. *Why didn't I leave when Alek hit me?*

I thought about it the first time, but if I telephoned Lupe and said I wanted to go back home, she'd tell Papá. I'd prove him right. I couldn't make it in the US. I was useless. Worse, I was bringing another mouth to feed. I didn't tell anyone.

Thinking about Alek chasing me, his fists, the screams made me want to cry, but I had to stuff everything that hurt down inside and make it small to protect myself. I couldn't break down in front of the other girls. They'd tease me or hate me for showing my pain. I had to leave the dayroom.

My whole body shook. I staggered over to the staff desk to ask Mrs. Shaffer if I could go to my room, but she'd left to the kitchen before I got there, leaving Ms. Montes at the desk with a CO who had walked into the unit.

"Ms. Montes?"

"Can't you see I'm busy right now? Take a seat."

One minute she talked to me about personal things in my life, and the next, she ignored me.

Across the dayroom, Babydoll glanced up at me, waved me over, and motioned to Jester. I didn't want to go to their table, but Jester might come over to me if I didn't. I swallowed and tried to breathe as I shuffled over to their table.

"Why you keep talking to the norteña?" Babydoll asked. "You should be over here kickin' it with us."

"I'm not talking to anybody."

"Hunh." Jester slouched in her seat and slapped a card on the table. "You better not talk to norteñas, or you'll find yourself not talking at all."

The gulp in my throat was loud enough to make them laugh. I crossed the room on stiff legs to an empty chair, close to the staff desk, away from Xochitl and Mariana. Beads of sweat wet my neck like when Alek came home drunk, and I could feel something was about to happen.

ELEVEN

We didn't see many men staff in the Mariposa unit and no one as handsome as the one who stood at our kitchen door. He didn't wear a green and tan uniform, just jeans, a short-sleeved shirt, and a smile. He didn't look as intimidating as the COs.

His eyes scanned the four rows of girls at the dining tables before leaning his body against the doorframe, arms crossed. Strong forearms, curved with muscle, and his thick dark hair reminded me of Alek. I glanced away.

A few girls pointed at him, giggling as if we were on the outside at the mall and not in prison. The noise level rose with each minute until there was a loud buzz in the dining room. My chest tightened.

"Why he don't say anything?" I asked Xochitl, who sat across from Mariana and me.

"Newbie counselor. They don't know what to do." Xochitl twirled the wide soft noodles and lumpy brown sauce into her mouth.

Hungarian day.

Gina plopped her food tray down across from me. Mrs.

Shaffer assigned her to our table, and she didn't like it at all.

"For your information, he's not new. His name's Jay, and he's twenty-eight." She leaned her elbow on the table, her chin resting on the palm of her hand. "Still young."

"Ms. Montes is twenty-eight," Mariana said.

"Who cares?" Gina screwed up her red lips stained with cherry Kool-Aid powder from the commissary. She pulled off her hairnet, shook out her hair like the models in the commercials. "He's so fucken fine."

"Don't let CO Wozzy catch you staring at him," I said.

"Hah, I can handle Woz."

"It's getting so loud." Mariana jammed her hands under her armpits. She took a quick look to her left.

My eyes followed in the direction of her glance. Jester. She took her tray to the serving line even though it wasn't time for scrape. Her eyes tightened to dashes when she caught me staring.

"Young lady, sit down," Mr. Jay said. "I didn't call scrape."

"Pfft. Young lady?" Jester snorted. "Settle down, Rambo."

"Boo-yah," Bruja yelled.

"Rambo, ha." Babydoll screeched out a loud giggle while a few girls snickered.

Mr. Jay sprung away from the doorframe, took something from his pocket. "Lower the noise level, or I'll break in my new pen writing you all up."

The voices dropped to whispers because nobody wanted to be locked into their rooms for twenty-four hours.

"Scrape, counter row," Mr. Jay shouted.

The girls stood table by table and dumped their unwanted

food into the garbage bins near the serving line. Babydoll and Bruja stacked their trays, strode past Mr. Jay, following the other girls out into the hallway behind him. Once a few girls got in line, Ms. Montes would signal them to go into the dayroom and wait.

"Rambo. Good one." Bruja's snorts followed Babydoll's high-pitched laugh in the hallway.

"Quiet," Ms. Montes said, but they laughed and talked so loud I could hear them in the dining room.

"Stop it, Bruja," Babydoll yelled.

Mr. Jay turned away from us to peek into the hallway. A chair behind me scratched the linoleum, fast and loud. Jester ran to my table, reached for Xochitl's long braid, and yanked her backward off her seat. She tumbled to the floor. Her eyeglasses flew off her face into the air.

My mind moved to help Xochitl, but my body froze. Shouts came from the other tables. "Fight, fight."

"Code three, everybody down," Mr. Jay yelled. "Stop."

A hand grabbed mine. Mariana tugged at me until I squatted on the floor, covering my ears because of the falling chairs and shouting.

"Puro Sur!" Jester kicked Xochitl twice in the ribs.

Xochitl rolled away, struggled to get off the floor, her hand against the side of her stomach. "What the fuck?" She squinted at Jester, who punched her in the face. She staggered.

Jester raised her fist again. "You punk ass norteña."

"Stop." Mr. Jay grabbed Jester's shoulder, pushed her against the wall, and handcuffed her wrists behind her back.

Shoulder's heaving, Jester sucked in air. Xochitl's fists balled up, she huffed, moved closer to Jester.

"No, don't," I said.

She spotted me under the table and stopped. The door buzzer shrieked. Two security guards ran into the kitchen. CO Wozzy grabbed Xochitl's arm and whirled her to the wall.

The attack happened so fast I didn't believe what I saw. My stomach muscles tightened at the sight of the overturned chairs, the strands of brown hair on the floor, and bright red blood dripping from Xochitl's nose onto her tee shirt.

"Anyone see who started the fight?" CO Wozzy asked.

Jester's stony eyes locked on Mariana and me.

Silence.

Ms. Montes entered the kitchen and stood at my table, hands on her hips.

"Take them to seg."

Wozzy dragged Xochitl out of the living unit while another CO took Jester away. Ms. Montes bent down and stared at me under the table.

"You and Johnson wipe up the blood with bleach. Put everything back the way it was."

Although my heart pounded in my ears and my legs were wobbly, Mariana and I did what she asked. We picked up the overturned chairs, pushing them back four to a table. I found Xochitl's eyeglasses in the corner of the room. One of the lenses cracked.

"Why did Jester do that? Xochitl do nothing to her," I asked Mariana.

"Whatever she says goes, for you guys."

"What do you mean?"

Mariana shrugged. "You know, for the Latinas."

"I told you, I'm not a gangbanger, and I'm not Latina. I'm Mexican."

"Jester doesn't care how you identify. You're either with her or against her. She follows the gang rules, and sureñas aren't supposed to be friends with norteñas like Xochitl. You need to be careful."

My body tensed at her warning. The muscles in my stomach stretched while I walked back to my cell. I'd be next if I said anything about what happened in the kitchen.

The staff searched Xochitl's, Jester's, Babydoll's, and Bruja's rooms. A girl across the hallway from them laughed out loud, shouting "busted" over and over when staff found contraband pens, pads of state paper, and a tattoo gun in their rooms.

Later, a yelp like an injured dog sounded during my shower, followed by the muffled gurgling over the running water. The thin shower partition between our shower stalls shook. Bruja slid across the wet floor on all fours and glared up at me. I backed away.

The girl who had shouted "busted" came out of the shower, her lip and nose bloody. When the staff at the desk asked her what happened, she said she slipped on spilled shampoo, hit herself on the shower wall.

When you're in prison, you learn to see nothing and say nothing. Much like my life with Alek, I knew when to shut up. But living like that with one person was one thing. Surviving with forty-nine other people was a different story.

TWELVE

All evening I worried about Xochitl. I couldn't forget how she stood there, shocked, her nose and lip bleeding. Her chest rose and fell as fast as her hands curled and uncurled into fists. She was much bigger than me and still couldn't get a punch in. Jester snuck up on her, right in front of the staff. That could easily happen to me.

Icy air in my cell made me want to stay under my blanket, but I needed to get out of my jeans and put on my pajamas. I grabbed them from my locker and slipped off my pants. A hard knock sounded. The door swung open. I jumped back on my bed, sliding my jeans up to my thighs.

Mr. Jay stood there, a surprised look on his face. Quickly, I grabbed my blanket, threw it over my lap. He shouldn't have opened my door so soon.

I swallowed my spit to make myself talk. "Men are supposed to say 'Man in the hall' before they knock. That's what Mrs. Shaffer said."

Xochitl asked her to have the male staff announce themselves when they came through for checks. Mrs. Shaffer agreed but most staff did what they wanted when she wasn't around.

Several girls complained that the men stared through their window when they changed their clothes or used the toilet.

"Oh, yeah, sorry, but you didn't answer when I called your name." He stepped back. A blush covered his high cheekbones. "Ms. Montes said to ask you if you'd come out to clean."

My tongue twisted into a knot so I bobbed my head. Once he shut the door, I hurried to zip up my pants and put on my shoes.

I found Mariana in the dayroom already sweeping. She hurried to my side. "I heard Xochitl's brother called the warden and made staff take her to the clinic for X-rays. Her nose might be broken."

"She's lucky she has someone to call," I said.

At least Xochitl had someone who cared for her and would try to put things right. I thought of who I could call in similar circumstances. No one. I wiped down the chairs in the dayroom and overheard staff talking at the desk.

"Gonzales yelled out 'puro sur,'" Mr. Jay said. "There's a lot of that in Gaviota unit too."

"I'll call the gang information officer," Ms. Montes said, picking up the phone. "You did a great job controlling the situation. I'm glad you were here."

She spoke to Mr. Jay with a gentle voice I'd never heard her use before. She had a way of giving orders like a big boss, but now she showed her softness and even smiled at him.

The door buzzer sounded, and in walked Wozzy with Xochitl, her arms behind her back in handcuffs. Her eyeglasses sat crooked on her nose, one lens with a zigzag crack. Gina bounded out of the dining room, followed Wozzy up to the staff desk.

"Why are you out of the kitchen?" Mr. Jay asked.

"Oh. I need the mop closet unlocked." Gina leaned forward on the desk counter, inches from his face. "I'll wait."

"Backup, Jones."

She fluttered her eyes at him and grinned but didn't move away from the counter.

"I'll unlock the closet for you. Give me a sec," Wozzy said from the hallway. He pulled out his handcuff key, twisted it into the pinhole, and pushed Xochitl into the detention room.

"No, I got it." Ms. Montes motioned to Gina. "Be there in a minute."

CO Wozzy paced back and forth in front of the staff desk. "You guys need help? I can stick around for showers."

The girls said Wozzy liked to supervise showers, hoping one of their towels slipped off like Gina's had once before.

"No, we got it," Mr. Jay said.

"You're new, huh? Be careful 'round these bitches." Wozzy readjusted his black belt, dipping his chin up and down like the bobblehead bulldog I'd seen on the dashboard of the city bus. "You gotta let them know who's the boss." He walked away and poked his head into the laundry area in the corner of the day-room.

Ms. Montes cleared her throat. "Going in the kitchen."

"Those kind of staff make the job harder." Mr. Jay shook his head.

I kept my eye on Wozzy while he strolled around the day-room. The small walkie-talkie clipped to his shoulder crackled. "What's your twenty, Wozinsky?"

He pushed the side button. "Mariposa. 10-4. Gotta go." He strutted out the back door of the hallway like a big rooster.

"All done." Gina strode out of the kitchen, followed by Ms. Montes. She flipped her hairnet off and ran her fingers through her blonde hair. "So, you're from the Gaviota unit, huh? The girls said you're cool staff. Is your first name Jay or your last name?"

"It's *Mr.* Jay. Stand by your door with the others." He pointed to the hallway before crossing his arms over his chest. "Thanks for your help."

Mariana and I glanced at each other. He wasn't about to talk about his personal business. Gina wrinkled her nose, turned on her heel, and huffed. No one ever ignored her before.

"Stand by your door, Jones." Ms. Montes laughed as she locked Gina into her cell.

Mariana pushed the broom across the dayroom towards me, one hand pressed against her lips. We giggled softly at what happened with Gina.

"Watch out for her or any other 'flashers' during shower time, Jay," Ms. Montes said. "Write them up quick."

"Yeah, I got the rundown on Gaviota the first night. Booked five girls for slippery towels. Haven't had a problem since."

Ms. Montes grinned, making her whole face light up. Her eyes changed to the color of canela sticks, a bright amber brown. Wozzy had the same excited expression when Gina nodded to him in the kitchen.

Shower time was noisy, but this gave us a chance to yell out the windows or talk to our neighbors without staff hearing our business.

"Xochitl, how are you?" I said out of my cell window.

"Damn malflora blindsided me—punk move. Raza fighting each other is so stupid. I don't gangbang. I like to skate and shit."

"Maybe the fight is over now."

"I can't have a disciplinary on my record."

"I'll tell staff she grabbed you from behind, okay?"

"Ssshh, no. They'll call you a rata. Worse for the both of us." Xochitl closed her window with a punch.

The word rata echoed in my ear. I couldn't tell anyone what I saw. A girl laughed at the room searches and got punched by Bruja in the shower. Something more harmful would happen if I told on Jester.

Xochitl and Jester had been friends. Now Jester attacked her just because she came from a different city, a place that was okay last month but not okay today. But Jester didn't care about people. You were either with her or against her, no in between. Next week, she could choose not to like me anymore. Either way, I wasn't safe.

THIRTEEN

The sweet scents of Kool-Aid and red licorice floated through the dayroom. Everyone who was out had their hair fixed and clothes ironed like for Sunday church. Voices rose into an excited wave while we filed into the room. The chairs were assembled in a big square with Mrs. Shaffer standing in the middle.

"You ladies look very nice. Remember, best behavior for the monthly birthday celebrations. Work crew?" She pointed at me. "Sit here in the front. I'll need you to clean up when this is over."

Xochitl, Mariana, and I rushed to our seats. I spied Gina wrinkle her nose out of the corner of my eye. She didn't sit with us. She and Bruja moved a few seats away. Mrs. Shaffer didn't know it, but she gave me the best seat in the room, and she gave me a chance to sit with my friends without the other gang-bangers bothering us.

Six volunteer ladies entered the living unit. They took their seats across the room. Some were about Ms. Montes's age and others older than Mrs. Shaffer. The blue and white nametags pressed on their pretty blouses said "Birthday Ladies." One carried a cake and the others carried colorful paper sacks. They smiled at us.

"They come from a church around here," Mariana said. "Look, they have cute gift bags."

For once, her voice sounded light and eager instead of whispery.

"Don't get all excited." Xochitl slouched into her chair. "They only bring stuff like a toothbrush, candy, lipstick, or brush."

I hadn't had any candy or worn lipstick for months and had nothing but a small comb, which kept losing teeth in my long hair. "Really? I need all those things," I said.

"Pfftt," Xochitl blew out her breath. "Dollar store stuff."

"Why are you so pissy?" Mariana said. "You're out of seg, and Jester's still there."

"Because I want to be out of here before my eighteenth birthday, but the fight might add time to my sentence."

"But Mr. Jay can tell Mrs. Shaffer that Jester was out of bounds. She started the fight." Mariana nudged my shoulder. "So, you're gonna be seventeen or eighteen?"

"Tomorrow, I turn seventeen, but I feel older."

"Yup, same," Xochitl said. "Jester turned eighteen in seg. Wish they'd keep her there till she maxed out of this place."

"Girls, we have some music for you," one of the younger Birthday Ladies said. She took a black and silver boom box out of a box, set it on the card table, and plugged it in the socket.

The girls shouted, "You got Alicia Keyes?" "What 'bout Brandy?" "No, put on some oldies, yeah?"

"Don't they know they only play church music?" Xochitl said. "Dummies."

"There's a lot of modern church music. Music to dance to," Mariana said. "Ma'am, can you play some Toby Mac?"

Xochitl stared at her. "Who?"

"A Christian singer. I grew up in the church."

I tapped Mariana's shoulder. "Ask the lady if she has Mexican music."

She asked, but they didn't have any. "Ah, too bad, Juana. I love cumbias and salsa."

"Really?" I said. "I haven't danced cumbias in so long a time."

Music started playing, like a rap song but with no cursing. Mariana moved her shoulders as she sat in her chair and hummed.

"Hey now," Chantilla yelled as the music beat faster.

She stood up, moved her feet heel to toe and apart, jumped back, and snapped her fingers. She glided over the floor like it was freshly waxed.

"Alright, cuz," her friend shouted.

Mrs. Schaffer stepped closer and wagged her finger at her. "Ms. Chantilla."

"My bad," she said and clapped her hands. "That music's fresh."

"She was Crip walking," Xochitl said. "Told you Mrs. Shaffer had eagle eyes."

Chantilla waved Mariana to the floor. She and two other girls stood and joined her. All of them were smiling and twirling around.

"Check her out," Xochitl pointed, "she's a different Mariana."

She bobbed her head, singing the words out loud. The church volunteers clapped to the tune. "Yes, girl, you got the spirit," one said. I cheered Mariana on too.

Gina and Bruja slumped into their seats, leaning their chins into their palms, while the rest of the girls clapped. The song finished, and the dancers dropped into their seats, grinning.

"That was nice." It had been several months since I smiled so much my cheeks hurt. "You made it a fun birthday, Mariana."

"How did you celebrate last year?" she asked, fanning herself with her hand.

"Alek surprised me. We spent the day at Venice Beach."

I closed my eyes, remembering when he came into our bedroom and woke me. His wavy hair still wet. The scent of soap on his skin.

"He put a grocery bag stuffed with food on the bed and told me to change into my nice maternity clothes. I forgot about my tiredness, my six-month stomach pressing into my back, and rolled out of bed."

Mariana's head drooped like she remembered something too. "That's sweet."

"We took three buses to Venice Beach. Alek spread our towels on the sand, took out ham sandwiches, cupcakes. He sang happy birthday to me right there in front of the other people. A lady clapped. Someone else said "happy birthday.""

I sat back in my seat and remembered when he held the lit candle on the cupcake up to my lips. The scent of chocolate, melted wax, and saltwater made me recall Alek's face. How he used to look at me before he changed. He had kissed me, brushing my hair back. "Make a wish," he'd said. I wished we'd love each other for the rest of our lives.

"So you used to have good times with him?" Xochitl asked.

"Huh?" I forgot she and Mariana were sitting next to me for a few seconds. "Sometimes. Last year's birthday feels like someone else's memory, now."

"Yeah." Mariana's voice lost its bouncy sound. She sighed.

"Birthday girls, please stand," Mrs. Shaffer said.

"Ms. Ivanov, happy birthday. God bless you." The smiling lady handed me a bright purple bag with "Juana" written in black marker.

"Thank you, Miss."

Inside I found a small pink hairbrush, pages of lined paper, and a lip gloss. "Look at this." I held up the brush and gloss to my friends. "Says Berry Nice." I opened the top, sniffing the strawberry scent.

Xochitl cleared her throat. I glimpsed Gina and Bruja moving toward us.

"A pink brush, ooh, and a lip gloss." Gina reached her hand toward mine.

I stuffed the gloss in my pocket, but she grabbed my brush, sliding it under her tee shirt.

"This can't find its way through your mess of hair," Gina snickered. "Always tangled, like you don't care how you look."

"Hey," Xochitl said.

"What the fuck you gonna do?" Bruja came up behind Gina and threw her chest and chin out.

We remained quiet.

"That's what I thought."

They left as fast as they had appeared.

"You're going to scratch the floor the way you're throwing around the chairs," Mrs. Shaffer said. "Tomorrow, you'll have to use the buffer."

I crashed the seats into each other, the way I wished I could have thrown Gina when she took my hairbrush. All the favors I'd done for Jester didn't mean anything.

The door buzzer rang, and in walked a CO with Jester in handcuffs. Before she stepped into her cell, she yelled over to me in the dayroom. "Bring my stuff out, Mouse."

She wasn't there two seconds before she began ordering me around again. I had more than enough of her and Gina's treatment.

"Get your things before I call the hall out for program," Mrs. Shaffer said.

I rushed to my room, grabbed Jester's unfinished sweatshirt, and took it with me to the dayroom. Xochitl and Mariana sat a couple of spaces away from me so no one would think we were together, but we still talked to each other without turning our faces.

Xochitl's eyes narrowed. "That sweatshirt's too big for you. It's gangbanger style. Montes might bust you."

"Why are you doing favors for Jester when her friend took your brush?" Mariana asked.

"Because I want another picture of my baby." I put the sweatshirt down. "Did you get a behavior report for the fight, Xochitl?"

"You mean the attack. Montes gave me Jay's report. He made it informational. Luckily, he told the truth but don't you tell anyone. If Jester finds out, she'll be pissed."

"Why? She started it."

Her leg bounced up and down while we sat. "Because she'll fight me again. Whoever wants to get in good with Jester will line up to jump me, or Mariana, or you, Juana."

My breath caught in my throat. Mariana's eye twitched.

"Xochitl, you can't fight. You don't go home on time," I said.

"What else am I supposed to do?" She bit at the side of her ragged fingernail. "I gotta watch my back every time I'm out of my room now. Jester doesn't care if she gets disciplinary reports. On her twenty-first birthday, she maxes out of here unless she catches another case and gets transferred to the women's prison. I gotta fight or lock it up, like a PC case."

"This PC is bad?" I asked.

"Yeah, you're marked. If you tell staff someone's picking on you, you'll end up hiding out in your room, in protective custody. A pesay." Xochitl glanced around the room, squinting. "My damn glasses are still broken and I can't see right. I gotta call my brother again."

"Why do you call him and not your parents?"

"He's in law school, almost graduated. I don't want to bug my mom and dad. They have enough problems."

Across the dayroom, Jester and Bruja laughed out loud. Bruja put her pointing finger and thumb in an L shape against her chest, a reminder to me about the leva.

They already started in on Xochitl. Gina gave her only half a scoop of food when she served meals and told the girl who gave out the bread to give her one of the broken end pieces. Xochitl ignored them and wouldn't touch the prefilled cups of juice.

"If I PC up, promise me only you guys will serve my food and deliver my tray."

Mariana nodded. "You guys would do the same for me, right?"

"Promise. But, Xochitl, I don't think you should do the proer custody thing. If they know you're afraid, they'll pick on you more."

"You still have to go to school," Mariana said.

"School movement's the worse." Xochitl shook her head. "Don't say shit if staff ask you questions about the attack."

Xochitl tightened her fist and uncurled her hand, over and over. She chewed on her bottom lip. I recognized her fear. I didn't like living like that outside, and I hated having to live like that inside.

A balled-up piece of paper flew in the air, landed on my feet. I glanced up to see Babydoll motion to me. She mouthed, "Come here," and pointed to the card table where Jester, Bruja, and Gina sat.

"Jester and her friends are mean. I'm not going to do anything for them anymore." I picked up the sweatshirt and marched over to the card table.

Jester scowled at me like she was my boss and I was nobody. "What did I tell you about talking to norteñas?"

The words came out of her mouth tight and scolding while her finger jabbed the space near my stomach.

"She thinks she's somebody," Gina said.

"You have lots of brushes and things," I told her. "Why did you take mine?"

Gina burst out laughing. "Because I could, stoo-pid."

Everyone except Babydoll snickered. The hair on my arms and back of my neck rose. Embarrassment and shame grew in my chest. I had to do something, anything to make them stop treating me like a worthless dog. I glanced back at my friends, then over to the staff desk. Good. They weren't watching us. I held Jester's sweatshirt over the tabletop and let it drop from my hand like trash.

"Here. I'm not doing any more trades." The shirt knocked the cards out of Jester's hand.

"Holy crap," Gina said. "Are you fucking crazy?"

Jester grabbed her sweatshirt, inspecting the collar. "Take it back and fucken finish."

Babydoll pushed back her chair, her eyes and little bow mouth frozen in an "o" while Jester's lips stretched into a snarl. She flexed her shoulders. I wanted to run, but I drew in a deep breath.

"Jester, I am friends with everybody. I'm from Santa Isabel, Mexico. I'm not in a gang." I tapped my chest while I said the words, wanting her to understand I wasn't like them.

"Finish. My. Sweatshirt." Jester picked up her playing cards, glared at me.

Gina scooted her chair back away from the card table. My legs swayed like they'd go out on me. My heart sped up, making a whooshing sound between my ears.

Bruja half rose in her chair. "Fucken paisa."

My breath rattled in my throat. Jester kept her eyes on mine, her face motionless. Her cards dropped onto the table.

"Ms. Ivanov," Mrs. Shaffer called out. "Return to the TV rows."

I made myself stare at Jester for two more seconds, trying to stop my hands and knees from shaking before I stumbled back to my seat.

"What the hell?" Xochitl gnawed at her fingernail again.

I exhaled all the breath I'd kept in my throat.

Mrs. Shaffer came to my seat, stood over me. "What's going on?" She glanced toward Jester at the card table.

"Nothing, Mrs. Shaffer." I shook my head. "I'm fine."

All night I worried I made the wrong decision. I didn't want Jester as an enemy or a friend, but I needed to get along to get through this time.

"Juana," Mariana said through her window. "Remember the kite you gave me?"

"From Chantilla?"

"She's the shot caller for the Crips," Xochitl said from the next room over.

"She's a gang member?" Mariana asked. "No wonder she asked if I was Black or Mexican. I told her what I told you. I'm half Puerto Rican and half Black. She said that meant I'm Black, and I should kick it with her friends, not the Mexicans."

"She's gonna make you pick?" I asked.

"I told her I want to get along with both groups."

"Wrong answer. Means you aren't choosing her group," Xochitl said.

"What do I do?" Mariana asked.

"You gotta do what you gotta do," Xochitl said. "I'll understand."

"Ssshh, Jester's talking." I tried to hear her conversation, pressed my ear against the window screen. "Listen."

Voices bounced up and down from Jester, Bruja, and other gangbangers. "The staff gonna have an intervention . . . that norteña better not snitch. You need a shank next time."

Chantilla shouted from her window, "You eses better take care of yo' business on the down low. You messing up our program."

Other voices joined in, "Yeah, you messin' with our hair time, gurl. You know how long the list is for the hot comb?"

"Fuck your hot comb," Jester said.

"Boo-yah," Bruja said, laughing like a crazy woman.

"Bitch, who said that?" Chantilla shouted.

"No hot comb's gonna make you any prettier. Chantilla the gorilla," Bruja yelled.

"Fuck you, you wetback."

Voices burst through the walls. "Tacos, border bandits," and "chanates, pinche mayatas," and a bunch of other words I didn't understand were exchanged. I shut my window.

My skin tingled like tiny bees stung both arms and legs. I sat on my hard bed while angry voices filled the air. Squeaky shoes and jangling staff keys rang down the hallway while staff thumped on doors and yelled, "Quiet."

The hallway became silent, but I knew Chantilla and Bruja hadn't calmed down, and their argument hadn't ended.

FOURTEEN

Nightmares came one after another that evening. Alek was chasing me. I looked back, but it was Jester and Bruja. I kept running until I saw Lupe ahead of me with Katrina in her arms. "Wait, wait," I screamed. They disappeared.

I wiped the sweat off my forehead and felt my way to my locker. Searching through the pockets of my jeans, I pulled out the plant leaves I found near a shady wall at the Catholic chapel.

The herbs reminded me of the home I'd left behind in Santa Isabel. The yerba buena leaves, curled and dry, still had the sharp scent of mint when I sniffed them. I tore the leaves into tiny pieces, dropped them into my plastic cup. Mamá used to brew yerba buena for stomachaches and serve it in her favorite ceramic mug. I always felt better afterward.

Xochitl made me a thing she called a stinger from the wires in an old headphone. On one end was a broken nail clipper wrapped with tape on a piece of a pencil. The other end was a piece of cord she said she found. I kept the tool on braided strands of thread like a long keychain and hung it inside my wall vent as she told me. When I pulled on the line, the stinger came out of the vent—a good hiding place.

I dropped the metal end into the cup of water and plugged in the cord. Xochitl told me not to touch the wires. Sometimes, a girl yelled out "Ay, cabrón," or another bad word, and I knew she burned her fingers from using a stinger.

Once the tool dropped inside the cup, it took a few minutes for the water to become hot enough to make tea. During that time, I tried to imagine I sat in my kitchen, taking a break from cleaning the apartment while Katrina slept in her bassinet.

Thinking about our home made me miss cooking. I liked buying groceries, smelling the melons, choosing tomatillos. I yearned to hear onions sizzling when I tossed them into my iron pan and the smell of corn tortillas frying in oil. My favorite memories were bathing Katrina, dressing her, even changing her poopy diaper. From when I awoke until I fell asleep, I had a purpose.

Now, my only reason for getting up in this place was to use up the day. I busied myself with school, volunteering, group, and church, but I still had many hours left. Lonely hours.

My tea ready, I pulled my composition book from underneath my mattress. Five months passed since the accident with Alek and six weeks since I arrived at San Bueno Correctional. I wrote 24 February at the top of the page.

After my first group, Ms. Montes gave me an assignment, "*What I should have done before and after my crime.*" I didn't want to go back to that time, but I had to do it soon because Ms. Montes would question me again.

When my father had too much to drink, which happened a lot after he lost his arm and my mother died, he'd walk outside, talk to the rooster, or listen to old songs on the radio. He never hit me, but he yelled at Lupe and me for every little thing, whether he drank or not.

What if I'd fought back when Alek hit me the first time? Would he have stopped or hit me more?

Alek was a different man than my papá when he drank. The meanness buried underneath his sweetness came out. He'd shout about things I didn't understand, using Russian words or cussing me out in English. Sometimes it seemed he wasn't talking to me but someone else in the room, someone he hated. Safer to keep busy cleaning the kitchen or go to the bedroom until he fell asleep. The following day he'd be irritable. When I told him what he did and said, he'd say I exaggerated or hang his head and not talk to me.

Once, we argued about something that had happened the night before. I told him I'd move back to Mexico with Katrina unless he stopped drinking.

"Go wherever you want, I don't care, but you better not take Katrina." He stood over me, his finger in my face. "If you do, I'll track you down in Calexico, Mexicali, Santa Isabel, whatever it takes. Don't ever threaten to take my daughter."

I never brought up leaving again, but I thought about it. Many times. But where would I go? How could I leave? I didn't have any money. Would a safe place take me without being a citizen?

Laying on my bunk, I made myself think about the first time Alek hit me. It was late one evening. I tried waiting up for him but fell asleep on our couch. The slamming of the refrigerator, the clanging pots and pans woke me up. I'd saved his favorite enchiladas for him, the ones with tomatillo sauce, but he didn't care. He shouted, "Where's the money," over and over. The day before, he gave me part of his paycheck. An allowance, he called it, for two weeks. Money I spent on groceries and diapers in one hour.

"The baby needed—"

"The baby, the baby," he imitated my voice.

He threw open the cabinets, flinging the spice bottles to the floor, cursing at me. His voice sounded panicked more than drunk. Squatting on the floor, he tossed cleaning bottles underneath the sink over his shoulder.

"Where's my fucking money?"

Katrina cried in her bassinet. It was time to nurse her again. When I turned away to go to the bedroom, he ran after me, grabbed my arms, and pulled me up close to his face, my feet dangling in the air. His once handsome face, now red and ugly, stared into mine.

"You're hiding it. Where is it?" He slapped me when I didn't answer.

Breaking free, I ran to the bedroom, scooped up Katrina, and locked myself in the bathroom. He hit the flimsy door until his fist smashed right through, slid his hand in, and unlocked the door. I cowered in the shower as the baby wailed.

"Alek, she's afraid." I rocked Katrina against my shoulder.

He stopped for a few seconds, stared at us, and left the bathroom. I came out of the shower, my heart beating against Katrina, tiptoed to the bedroom door, and peered into the living room. Alek was gone.

I thought of picking up the diaper bag and running back to Santa Isabel, but Katrina nuzzled my neck. Her mouth opened and closed like a little fish. Baby sounds gurgled up from her tiny perfect lips. Pressing my face into hers, I breathed in her baby shampoo and walked into the kitchen. I found the money I hid in the freezer, wrapped in white butcher paper. There wasn't thirty dollars yet. I couldn't leave that day.

In my notebook, I wrote that I saved money so I could leave Alek, but it wasn't enough.

"Ivanov," the night staff called from outside my door. "Mrs. Shaffer said to give you this." She slid an envelope between the doorframe.

Finally, the letter I'd waited to be translated for several days. Would it be good news or bad?

Delicias, Chihuahua, the return address said, the city where my older brother lived. I hadn't talked to him in over three years. My hands shook as I unfolded the paper.

Dear Juana María,

José Luis wrote to me and said you had a child and were in prison in the Estados Unidos. He gave me this address. I couldn't believe this, but why would anyone make up such a thing? I called our father right away, but he wouldn't talk to me about this serious situation.

My father still hated me. I shamed him so much he wouldn't talk about me.

José Luis wants Lupe to join him in Arizona. He says he can't wait six years to see Lupe and his own baby. It's a mistake to go to the United States, too many problems. It is too dangerous for her to cross, but José Luis insists. He asked us to take in your baby.

This is difficult for my family and children. I am sorry I can't help you, but I lost my job. If I don't find work soon, I don't know what we'll do. I hope you can find someone else to care for your daughter. I will try to convince Lupe to stay in Santa Isabel.

Sincerely, your brother, Miguel

My heart beat hard against my chest. This wasn't fair. How could José Luis push my baby onto my oldest brother? How could he push his wife to go over the border, pregnant? I had to convince Lupe to stay with my father, but how?

FIFTEEN

My mamá used to tell me many dichos. Sometimes they were words of wisdom and other times funny sayings. No hay rosas sin espinas was her favorite. With the roses come the thorns. This morning I felt all the thorns without seeing any flowers.

Moving through the chow line like a robot, I listened to the clacking of the serving ladles against metal containers, the mumbling voices, the sound of the oatmeal when it plopped onto my tray. I slid to the left until I arrived at the end of the counter, dragging my feet to my table.

"What's wrong?" Mariana asked.

"No one in my family can take care of Katrina. How can I beg Lupe to go against her husband's wishes and stay with my baby until I leave here if I can't talk to her?"

"I'm sorry, Juana. After last night with Jester, you don't need all this stress."

"Thank you. I don't know what Jester will do to me, but maybe she forgets about it."

Mariana's eyes sank to the tray in front of her. She knew as well as I did that what I said was foolish. Jester never forgets.

"Window row," the new staff lady at the kitchen door called out.

Jester rose from her table in front of mine when I stood. My eyes followed her until she stopped in front of Bruja's table in the middle row, where she wasn't supposed to go.

She always tested the new staff. I walked to the ice bin on the other side of the kitchen and reached inside for the ice scooper. An elbow hit my back, hard. I fell face first into the opening, my nose stuffed against a mountain of ice cubes. I struggled to pull my body out of the bin. My feet slid from under me. I hit the floor. I scrambled onto my hands and knees, sprang upright. Out of the corner of my eye, I watched Jester stroll back to her chair as if nothing had happened.

The girls near me scattered. They laughed, pointed at me. Ice cubes stuck to my hair. My face grew hot as cold water dripped down my cheeks.

"Sit down, sit down. What happened? You okay?" the staff lady yelled to me.

"She's clumsy, must've slipped," Jester yelled from her seat.

I moved quickly to my chair. The pounding in my ears was so loud I pressed my hands over them, my elbows on the table. Mariana sat hunched, her arms around herself. Xochitl chewed on her bottom lip; her cheeks flushed.

"Did she hit you?" Xochitl asked. "I couldn't see with the crowd at the food line."

I hung my head, trying not to cry or call attention to myself while water pooled at my neck. "Yeah."

"Everyone line up," the staff said. "Utensil count."

Row by row, we dropped our spork into the containers in front of her and returned to our seats.

"Anyone forget to drop their utensil into this bucket?"

No one said anything.

The staff counted them again. "Spork count is off, Ms. Montes," she called out at the desk.

"Tell the kitchen crew to search the sterilizer, the food trays," she said. "Keep them there. I'm calling for backup."

"Hands on the table, no one move," the staff shouted to everyone in the kitchen.

"Oh shit," a couple of girls murmured.

Gina and another kitchen girl ran to the mop closet, behind the sterilizer, ignoring the staff lady.

Two men COs strode into the kitchen. "Line it up, ladies," one said. "Against the wall."

Ms. Montes stomped into the room, glanced around. Her eyes rested on Jester, darted to Bruja. She walked over to the ice machine and eyed the puddle of water on the floor. Turning to us, she scanned the wall of girls until her glare fell on me.

"Ivanov, your hair's wet. Don't tell me you had an accident."

I didn't move or say a thing.

"Jones, get a mop." Ms. Montes clicked her walkie-talkie button. "Need some strip searches done. Send me a female CO. Yeah, missing fork."

"Gonzales, Alvarez, you're up first. Stand over there." She pointed to the wall on our left, near the ice machine.

"Why me, Montes?" Jester said.

Babydoll sniffed, sauntering over to the area. "Whatever."

The rest of us watched while the COs pulled apart the kitchen, moved the ice machine, and searched the garbage cans. Their racket echoed in the dining room while we pressed our backs against the bumpy brick wall.

Ms. Montes patted down both girls. "Stay here. Next two."

"Fuckin' messicans. Give them the fuckin' fork," Chantilla said. "I got shit to do."

"What the hell did you say, pinche mayata?" Jester yelled out.

One of the COs spun towards Jester. Bruja bolted from the line we were in and landed a punch on Chantilla's face. Her head bounced back, but her fist came up and hit Bruja under the jaw, knocking her to the floor. Girls scattered. Bruja jumped up and hit Chantilla again. I flattened myself against the wall, my heart pounding through my chest. My jaw hurt from clenching my teeth, from pushing down the scream in my throat.

Ms. Montes ran across the dining room and helped the CO grab Chantilla and Bruja as they shouted at each other. More COs ran into the kitchen.

"Take them to seg," Ms. Montes said. "The rest of you, nose against the wall, arm length apart. Step out of your shoes. When I get to you, lift your tee shirt to your neck, shake out your bra."

"But there's male staff in here," a girl's trembly voice said.

"Just do it." Ms. Montes huffed. She grabbed hold of the girl's shoulder and whipped her around. "On the wall."

The sound of heavy breathing surrounded me as another woman CO and Ms. Montes patted the girls down. Mariana wrung her hands. Xochitl jammed hers into her armpits, her face in a frozen stare. My insides vibrated against my ribs, my throat tight and dry. I turned and touched the tip of my nose to the rough brick.

"Ivanov, I know you were involved," Ms. Montes whispered in my ear as she moved her hands from my damp shoulders to my waist, down my hips and sides of my legs.

My body stiffened. I closed my eyes.

"Who was it?" Ms. Montes asked.

There was no way I was saying a thing.

"Everyone turn around now," Ms. Montes said. "No fork's going missing on my watch. Strip down to your underwear."

No one moved.

"Now! Spread your legs, pull out the waistband of your panties and bras."

"Oh, fuck no," someone said.

"This is illegal, Montes," Xochitl said.

"Shh," I turned my head to tell Xochitl to stay quiet.

"Another word, and you're in seg three days," Ms. Montes shouted.

We stepped out of our jeans, took off our tee shirts, and stood there almost naked. The two women staff made everyone yank open the waistbands of our underwear. This was almost as bad as when I first got to Centre, and they made us all strip while they filled out a sheet of paper.

A whimper, sighs, and muttering filled the air. My chin pressed against my chest while a chill and goosebumps ran over my back and legs.

After all the searching and our humiliation, the staff didn't find the missing spork.

"Get dressed, file out." Ms. Montes dismissed us to the hallway. "We're on lockdown until we find the missing utensil."

I lined up behind Xochitl. "What happens if they can't find the fork?"

She turned to me. Her mouth twitched. "It'll show up in someone's back."

SIXTEEN

You live another life in prison. Your old life you visit in your head. The lockdown went on for several hours, inching by like when it's three in the morning and you can't sleep.

Breakfast in paper bags slid through the opening at the bottom of our doors: a stiff granola bar, milk carton, and two cheese squares. I lifted the bag to my bed and returned to studying Katrina's picture. Her fine baby hair was only long enough to tie a pink ribbon around a feathery curl. In the photo, she had her chubby arm upright, trying to reach the ribbon, a wisp of a smile on her lips. She looked like she waved hello—or goodbye.

I wondered what Katrina did during the long days. Did she still take an afternoon nap? Was she warm enough in the cool evenings? Did she wear shoes yet?

When she was an infant, I swaddled her in soft baby blankets, snug and secure, with the ends tucked under her chin. She'd gurgle and make baby sounds. The memory of her pleasant heaviness warmed me in my chilly cell.

The day we returned from the hospital, Alek held her swaddled body in the striped baby blanket. He rocked her in his arms. "She's a baby burrito," he said, and we laughed.

Anna always took off one of the coverlets before she picked Katrina up. "Too many blankets. Not good for the babies to be so warm."

Holding Katrina against her shoulder, she'd take her to the window, point out the people and cars below our third-story apartment. She'd cradle her and sing a song with words I couldn't understand, but Katrina enjoyed the sounds.

My eyes heavy, I moved under the scratchy blanket to get warm. I grabbed my pillow and placed it against my chest as if I were filling the emptiness. This didn't work. I needed to think of other memories.

I imagined the river and mountains near Santa Isabel. I used to throw rocks with my brothers, gather sage with Lupe, and pick tunas from nopales with Mamá. Everything around us green, blue, yellow. So many colors, scents, birds, butterflies, and bees. The colors swirled around me as I drifted off to sleep.

"Ivanov, wake up."

I lifted my head. Ms. Montes had her body halfway into my room.

"Come out to the office." Her voice was in a whisper, unusual for Ms. Montes.

Something was wrong. My skin prickled. Was Katrina okay? Did something happen to my family?

At the staff desk, Mrs. Shaffer pointed me to her office across the empty dayroom. I glanced at the wall clock. Nine thirty-five. No one was out, not even the laundry girl. Ms. Montes stood in the office and waved me inside.

"Take a seat, Ivanov. I need to talk to you about something. Staff saw your little tiff at the card table the other night."

My brow wrinkled at the word "tiff."

"Between you and Gonzales." Ms. Montes blew out her breath. "Don't lie to me. Did she push you into the ice bin?"

"What?" There was no way I was going to tell her the truth. The image of Jester stabbing people—stabbing me—with the missing fork was all I thought about for two days.

"No, Miss, it wasn't Jester, uh, I mean Gonzales. I bend over too much and fall in."

"Juana, when will you stop making excuses for people who hurt you?"

Did she think I liked getting hit? Or that I thought it was okay for Alek and Jester to hurt me? I turned away from her scowling face and kept my mouth shut, although I wanted to explain why I couldn't tell her the truth about Jester.

She didn't know what it was like when someone had power over you and could abuse it. To her, I wasn't standing up for myself, but I tried and look at what happened. There was nowhere to run and hide in San Bueno Correctional. No safe place.

"I slipped and fell."

Ms. Montes shook her head. A knock sounded on the staff door, and a CO walked in, his uniform pressed and crisp. His shirt had a patch on the upper part of his tan sleeve. His smile was gentle, his eyes friendly. He lifted a chair and sat across from me.

"Juana, right? My name's Sergeant Cuellar."

Mrs. Shaffer joined us in the office and sent Ms. Montes to the desk in the dayroom. She gave me one last glare before she left.

"I'm the gang information officer for the facility," Sgt.

Cuellar said. "I'd like to ask you some questions. Do you understand English or want me to speak in Spanish?"

"English is okay with me," I said because I wanted to practice.

"We're asking several girls if they've heard about problems between the norteñas and sureñas. You know, the northern and the southern inmates."

"I'm not a gangbanger."

"Yes, I understand you don't bang, but even so, there are rules that gang members want the others to follow. I'm sure you're aware who the leader of the sureñas is, right?"

If I answered yes, he'd think I knew more, try to make me talk and get me confused, the way those police did when they asked me questions about Alek's accident. I made my eyes blank and shook my head.

Sgt. Cuellar leaned so near to me I saw the glistening gel on his short thick hair. "I know you want to keep out of trouble, but the more information we have on who's disrupting the units, the better."

I glanced up at Mrs. Shaffer to see if she'd say anything.

"Ms. Ivanov had a slip and fall before the fight. Called it an accident, said no one else was involved. Is that right, Juana?"

"Yes, Mrs. Shaffer."

"Seems like accidents happen a lot around here," Sgt. Cuellar said. "Juana, my job is to collect information, prevent violence from happening, and keep the units safe. For you and staff. Anytime you want to talk, you write me or ask Mrs. Shaffer to call Sgt. Cuellar. Okay?"

He translated what he said into Spanish, perhaps to make

sure I understood. When he finished, he gave a bright white smile.

"And if any of your friends want to talk, let me know."

He pushed himself off the desk and stood. He wasn't very tall, but he was well built and carried himself with the type of confidence Alek used to have when we first met.

When he left, Mrs. Shaffer stood. "Juana, you're between a rock and a hard place."

Both things are hard. I sucked my bottom lip and thought about her words. Maybe it was a dicho. "I don't understand."

"I mean this is a difficult situation."

"Mrs. Shaffer, I just want to do my sentence and go back to my daughter, but too many things stand in the way."

She nodded. "I guess all I can say is to do the right thing for you and your daughter. You can return to your room now."

I passed the staff desk, went into the Alpha Hall, and stood by my door. Ms. Montes locked me back in my room without saying a word.

The right thing wasn't easy to do in this place. I tried to keep myself safe each day, but that was getting harder. If the girls caught me giving staff information, like the Sergeant requested, they'd say I'm a rata, and everyone in prison knew what happened to rats.

SEVENTEEN

Mrs. Shaffer stood at the front of the hallway. She peered over her eyeglasses at the girls lined up by their room door. The odor of sweat and dirty hair soaked the warm air. Staff skipped our shower time the night before, and we'd been in our rooms for almost three days.

"Everyone to the dayroom for a large group," she said.

Sgt. Cuellar and two COs including Wozzy stood guard over us while we took a seat in the large circle of chairs. Each CO was in a corner of the room while the Sargent stood in the middle. Ms. Montes leaned against the staff counter. Her arms crossed.

Mrs. Shaffer strode to the middle of the dayroom and swiveled her head left to right, scanning our faces. "We've had two fights. Two too many."

"Yeah, knock it off, or you'll stay locked down longer," Ms. Montes said.

Mrs. Shaffer frowned at Ms. Montes and turned back to us. "The group needs to get it together. The only reason the two who fought aren't in segregation is that the unit's filled up."

"But keeping us all down is group punishment," Xochitl said, followed by grumbling from other girls. "Not fair."

"When are we getting off lockdown?" Gina glanced at CO Wozzy.

He smiled at her, lifting his chin. Sgt. Cuellar caught Wozzy's move, arched his eyebrow for a second, and swung his gaze back to Mrs. Shaffer.

"Not today. Too many unsolved questions."

"What about visiting? We already missed today, that's not—" Xochitl said.

"Get yourselves straight, and you'll visit next weekend," she said.

The gangbangers with Jester and those in Chantilla's group slumped in their seats and yawned. They looked like big alley cats in the sun resting after having their fill of food from trash cans.

They didn't care how their fight made us miss school and visits. The girls who had their kids come from far away couldn't see them. Their grandmothers or mothers and babies rode the bus for hours to San Bueno, but those things didn't matter to the gang members. Only their rules counted.

"Some of you will come out for dinner after I finish up with the next large group," Mrs. Shaffer announced. "The rest remain on lockdown. Back to your rooms."

As soon as my door clunked shut and the lock turned, I pushed open my window. Girls shouted across the wings of the building and rooms. "Mrs. Shaffer's being a bitch," "Sgt. Cuellar's fine," "Damn it, it's Italian day, no seconds if we have dinner on trays."

Babydoll called out Jester's name several times, but there was no answer.

"Mariana, I don't hear Jester answering Babydoll," I whispered through the gap in my door.

"I'll tell you in the kitchen."

"Need you both to serve dinner." Ms. Montes passed a hairnet to Mariana and me before returning to the kitchen entrance.

All the black, brown, and white gang members remained locked in their rooms. About half of the girls took their places at their assigned seats. I looked around at the empty spaces at the tables and wished the kitchen was half empty all the time. Except I wished Xochitl were out.

"So what happened between Babydoll and Jester?" I asked Mariana as we stood behind the serving counter.

"Heard them from my window. Gina told Babydoll she passed *it* to Jester, but I don't know what they meant."

Someone in the dining room made kissing sounds, the sound they made for smackas, kiss asses.

"Oh God, they're starting already." Mariana's eyebrows raised to her hairline.

"Ignore them," I said.

Mariana removed the cover on the large serving dish. A spicy aroma of tomatoes, garlic, and onions escaped from the pan. "Look, lasagna." She scooped a big gooey piece with her spatula. We had enough food for everyone to get seconds.

"Ivanov, when I take the group out, prepare the room trays," Ms. Montes said.

Mariana and I loaded up the metal wagon with trays. I pushed the wobbly cart out of the kitchen and followed Ms.

Montes to the hallway, where she stopped and keyed open Xochitl's door.

Curled up on her mattress, Xochitl held her stomach. Her face was paler than usual.

"You sick?" I asked.

"Cramping bad. I need more tampons and aspirin."

"You buy tampons at the commissary," Ms. Montes said.

"I finished my box, Montes. Canteen doesn't come in for two more days." Xochitl held her abdomen and winced. "Can I have a few state-issued ones and aspirin?"

"We'll see. I need to deliver the trays." She shut the door with a bang.

"I give her some of mine."

Ms. Montes ignored me and moved on to the next room. I couldn't understand how staff could leave someone in pain, not give her pads for her period. If she didn't give Xochitl aspirin, I'd ask another staff myself, hide them, and slide them under her door. Sometimes the staff made you break the rules.

We stopped in front of Jester's cell door. Ms. Montes flicked on the light, glanced inside the wicket. "Gonzales, wake up."

No answer. She unlocked and pulled on the door. Something stopped the door from opening. A rolled-up towel came loose. Ms. Montes kicked it away and swung open the door. "Gonzales!"

Sprawled on her bed, Jester's arms hung off the mattress. A sharp vinegary smell rushed out of the room, making me gag. I gulped, the sour taste rising in my throat. Ms. Montes pinched her nose.

"Gonzales, wake up," Ms. Montes said.

She didn't move.

"Mrs. Shaffer, Code 3. Call Com Center for a nurse." Ms. Montes waved me away from the door.

I crouched down against the wall in the hallway, but I could still see into Jester's room. Newspaper covered the upper part of her wall window. Colored pencil drawings of Winnie the Pooh, Tigger, and Mickey Mouse filled her locker door from top to bottom. An ink portrait of Babydoll, with the words "Always and Forever" beneath her bare shoulders, hung above the bed.

"Gonzales," Ms. Montes yelled again.

A gurgle came out of Jester's mouth.

"What's happening? Why's she yelling?" Excited voices traveled throughout the hallway, bouncing off the walls.

Babydoll pounded on her door, pressed her face in her wicket. "She okay, Mouse? Tell me."

I shook my head. Jester made the same gurgling sound as Alek when he passed out from being drunk.

A nurse and two COs rushed down the hallway and into the room. The nurse picked up Jester's wrist and put two fingers on her neck. "She's alive but intoxicated. Needs her stomach pumped."

The lady CO clicked on her radio. "This is CO Isadora. We need a stretcher to take a ward to the clinic. Possible alcohol OD."

The nurse and another CO left with Jester on a stretcher, passing me in the hallway.

Ms. Montes entered the room, sniffed a plastic cup, and pulled her head back. "Whew, powerful pruno. Isadora, hand me your flashlight."

"I'll come back for it later, gotta run." The young CO jogged out the back wing of the hall.

Tapping against the wall behind the toilet bowl with a small handheld mirror, Ms. Montes found a loose panel and pulled out a clear garbage bag. Pieces of rotten oranges and swollen slices of what looked like bread floating in yellow liquid. She took the bag down the hall to the staff desk. I followed her.

Mrs. Shaffer sniffed the bag. "Whew, cookin' for a while. How is it we didn't find the pruno before? Either someone's not doing their room searches, or Gonzales had this stashed somewhere else."

"Like in the kitchen," Ms. Montes said.

Mrs. Shaffer waved her hand at me. "Ms. Ivanov, go stand by your door."

After I was locked in, I pulled open my window, where I knew I'd hear more information.

"I told her not to do it. Too much stuff for one person," Babydoll said.

"We were gonna share at backyard time. I took it out of the kitchen two days ago and passed it to her, but we had the lockdown," Gina said. "Probably had to drink some or it would've exploded."

"She looked dead, Gina," Babydoll said. "What if it's too late?"

"They'll pump her stomach. She'll be okay."

Babydoll sighed. "She better."

I didn't want Jester to die, but I hoped she got sick—real sick. Maybe she'd start thinking about her own life and leave me alone.

EIGHTEEN

"Ivanov." Someone tapped on my door until I sat up in bed. "Mrs. Shaffer left a log note saying you're on the kitchen crew. And you have mail."

The sight of the slanted writing on the envelope made my heart beat faster. Lupe. I pulled out the letter.

Dear Hermana,

I hope you are doing well so you can come out soon. Juana, I'm sorry I didn't tell you I'm going to have a baby. But now you can understand why I want to join José Luis in Arizona. I need to leave before summer arrives, but I can't find anyone to care for Katrina, so I must take her with me.

What? No. My fingers gripped the edges of the paper. My mind raced back to when I saw men and women waiting to cross the border in Mexicali. They lingered near the restaurant where I worked, eating their last meal huddled near the trees, waiting for their coyote to arrive. She couldn't take Katrina on the journey.

*Our brother, Miguel, will move back to our house in Santa
Isabel. His family will take care of Papá. Please understand
I have to try to make a better life for my family, just like you
did when you left Santa Isabel and Mexicali for Los
Angeles. I will write to you after we arrive in Arizona.*

Love, Lupe

The letter dropped from my hands. Didn't she understand
how dangerous crossing into the United States could be? How
could she do this? She couldn't just walk over without documents—she had to go through fences and the river, run across
fields and deserts, hide during the day, and wait for José Luis to
show up who knows when.

No, Lupe couldn't go. I had to convince her to stay in Santa
Isabel. I was trying my best to keep out of trouble here to go to
my initial hearing and get less time. I needed to call and beg her
to reconsider.

The door swung open. "Ready to work?" said the staff lady.
"Ivanov?" She snapped her fingers, tapped her shoe on the floor.
"Ivanov, hey." She slammed the door shut.

Time froze around me like I was there but not there. Lupe's
handwriting filled my head: *I can't find anyone to care for Katrina.*
No one wanted my baby.

"Ivanov," Ms. Montes said from my doorway. "I need you in
the kitchen. Get a move on."

The impatience in her voice brought me back to my cell. I
nodded but didn't move from my bed.

"What's wrong with you?"

"My daughter. Can I use the staff phone to call and check if she's okay?"

"Emergencies only."

"She's in danger. I mean, she's very sick."

Her shoulders heaved up and down. "After breakfast, for a couple of minutes. You have to use the payphone."

That's all I needed, two minutes—enough time to beg Lupe not to cross the border.

"Ooh, you guys will get a beat down for telling on Jester," a girl said to Mariana and me at the serving line.

"Ms. Montes smelled the stinky pruno from the door." I dropped the lumpy oatmeal on her tray, waved my ladle at her to move on.

"Nah, you and this porto rican chick told on her." She pointed a stubby finger at Mariana and me before she scooted down the line.

Mariana wrung her hands. "She's going to take the rumor and run with it."

"We can't act afraid. Tell the truth. Ms. Montes searched Jester's room and found the bag of pruno."

She was scared. So was I, but I wasn't going to get in trouble over something I didn't do. I had worse things to worry about.

How would I convince Lupe to stay in Santa Isabel? What if I called home and Papá refused to talk to me? Calling Maribel's house would be better.

After breakfast, Ms. Montes waved her hand to the payphone on the wall. "Two minutes."

With sweaty palms, I lifted the handle. "Collect call to Mexicali, Mexico, please." I rubbed my fingers against the brick wall and held my breath. The sound of the dryer in the laundry room rumbled over and over while I waited. I gave the operator the phone number to Maribel's house.

"¿Bueno?" a man's voice in the background said to the operator. "¿Quien habla?"

The operator switched to Spanish and asked if he'd accept a collect call from inmate Juana Maria Ivanov at San Bueno Correctional Facility.

"Tio?" I said over the operator's voice. My uncle didn't respond. "Tio, es Juana."

The harsh click of the phone sounded. He hung up. I gripped the phone handle tighter and tried not to give in to my tears, not there in the hallway. The sound of a dead phone buzzed in my ear.

Horrifying thoughts crowded my mind. If my baby or Lupe got sick, the coyotes would leave them behind in the desert. They didn't care if they ran out of water and died. Someone could hurt Lupe, kidnap Katrina. Separate them. What if Lupe couldn't find her husband in Arizona; how would she survive?

I hung up the phone.

"Won't accept the call, huh?" Ms. Montes said. "Let's go then."

The muscles in my stomach stiffened like I was having cramps. I willed myself to leave the phone and wondered if Ms. Montes saw anything in my eyes. She didn't even look at me when she unlocked my cell and shut the door. The only sound was the lock clicking into place.

What was I going to do? I was so tired of worrying, writing, and begging for help. Tears slid down my cheeks. I fell on my bed and let myself cry.

I had to write to Maribel, tell her about Lupe leaving, and that her father wouldn't accept my collect call. I couldn't give up on keeping my baby safe.

My hand shook as my pencil made squiggling marks across the sheet of lined paper. Guilt and regret flooded through me. How could I ask for Maribel's help when she's the one who told me not to return to Los Angeles? If I had listened, I wouldn't be in this awful situation. Why didn't I listen to my papá years ago?

I had made so many mistakes, but what was done was done, and I only had now to think about. I wiped the tears off my face and took a deep breath before pouring my fears, my nightmares, into the letter to Maribel. I begged her to call Lupe and convince her to stay in Santa Isabel. I explained that getting back to my daughter was my only chance at enduring in this place. I had to have someone to hope for. That was the only way I'd survive.

NINETEEN

Ms. Montes opened my door, hooked her thumb in the direction of the dayroom. She continued down the hallway, making her headcount while I sat in an empty dayroom and waited.

What did she want from me now? Everything she told me to do, I did. I stayed to myself, worked, volunteered, and attended groups and school.

She strode into the dayroom and pointed to the back office. I followed.

"Juana, we made you part of the kitchen crew, permanently. Several girls will want you to do favors for them—don't. If you do, we'll fire you, like Gina Jones. Entiendes?"

"Yes, I keep to myself, Ms. Montes."

"I don't want to amend your initial hearing report." She handed me some papers. "Read and sign this. Your signature proves I gave you your case report."

I held up the papers and began reading the first page:

"Juana Maria Ivanov ran from the scene after her husband fell down a flight of stairs, leaving him to die of his injuries. She neglected to call for emergency services. She maintains her innocence."

The report sounded like I knew Alek was injured badly and didn't call someone on purpose. That wasn't true.

"Ms. Montes, I didn't leave Alek to die. He lifted himself, yelled at me. I kept running because I thought he would stand up and come after me."

"But he died, didn't he? Your signature doesn't mean you agree with the report, only that I gave it to you. You can read the rest in your room."

I hesitated. She wasn't going to change her mind. I took her pen and signed the paper.

"You can go now." She waved me out of the office.

In my room, I sat on my bed and read the rest of the report:

"Ward Ivanov claims she endured domestic violence, the threat of deportation, and the removal of her child on a regular basis from her husband. Even with these mitigating circumstances, if true, Juana needs to understand the gravity of her negligent actions and develop the appropriate decision-making skills needed to become a mature and law-abiding person."

I wrote 1 March at the top of my composition book and copied all the words I didn't understand: endured, domestic violence, mitigating, gravity, and negligent. All those hard words. More words to look up in the dictionary or ask Mariana to translate.

Information about my progress in school and volunteer work was listed on the report, too, which sounded better than I expected from Ms. Montes.

On the last page under "Recommendation," it said, "If Juana continues showing progress in all treatment areas and fully understands the seriousness of her crime, she may be ready for a parole consideration hearing before her maximum time of six years."

Before, Ms. Montes said *before*. There was hope for sooner. I had to tell Lupe this news. I prayed she'd wait for me to get back home.

"Hey," I tapped on my wall. "You come out for our group tonight, Xochitl? I need to borrow a stamp."

"Sure, Jester's still in the hospital, so it's cool."

Being on the unit was better than ever with Jester gone. I hoped she'd stay there for a long time or at least long enough for me to attend my hearing.

"Group time." Ms. Montes walked out of the staff office and stood in the dayroom among the chairs. They looked like someone tossed them across the room. "Ivanov, straighten these up." She instructed me like I was the maid of the unit. I didn't like the sound of her voice, but I did what she told me because I couldn't get on her bad side. Not now.

Mariana helped me put the seats in a circle while the other girls crossed their arms and waited for us.

Bruja dropped into her seat, using her elbow on the armrest to prop her head. Next to her sat Gina. A new girl with dry-looking orange-brown hair and nervous fingers sat across from Xochitl and me. Scabbed-over scratch marks dotted her arms. Mariana took the seat next to Ms. Montes, who pointed to the new girl.

"Introduce yourself."

"Lauren Lopez. Kay? But you can call me LaLa. I'm part

Mexican and white. I'm a dope fiend and a call girl," she said, snorting out a loud laugh. "No shame in my game."

Bruja reached over, slapped Lauren's hand in the air, and sunk back into her chair.

"Doubt she's a call girl." Gina made a face like she smelled a carton of sour milk.

"Calling me a liar?" LaLa leaned forward, tilted her head up at Gina.

"Save it, Lopez. We have things to do here." Ms. Montes turned away from LaLa. "Listen up. Some of you have initial hearings coming up, and a couple of you have hearings for time adds." She jerked her eyes sideways at Gina. "Tonight, we'll listen to Anaya and Johnson's presentations for their hearings next week."

"Pfftt," Bruja hissed.

"You go first, Anaya," Ms. Montes said.

"*Ms.* Anaya." She glared at Ms. Montes, who wrinkled her nose. "This is what happened. I went to a protest for immigration reform because the cops stopped people and asked for documents to prove their citizenship. Immigration cops were raiding businesses, houses, leaving kids without parents. So unfair. At the demonstration, a peaceful one, hundreds of people came. Everything was cool until someone started throwing things at us.

A bunch of skinheads and people with signs saying *ILLEGALS GO HOME*, stuff like that, ran toward us. Things got rough, cops shoving us around. Some white supremacists got up in our face. Next thing I knew, the tear gas came. Everyone's running. My eyes watered so bad I couldn't see. Someone grabbed me, we fell, and I kicked him off. I end up flat-faced on the ground, hand-cuffed, and dragged away."

"What is your committing offense," Ms. Montes said.

"Assault on a cop," Xochitl said. "But he grabbed me first, punched me in the back. It was a lawful protest. We're appealing."

"What do you mean a lawful protest?" I asked.

"For the illegals, like you." Gina flicked her wrist at me.

"You don't know anything," Xochitl said. "A lot of kids had parents bring them over here. They didn't have a choice. My brother was three when my dad fled Nicaragua. His wife died over there. My brother's an American. As much as you are."

"Pfft, getting welfare and shit, living off the government," Gina said.

Xochitl blew out her breath. "Forget you. Your mom's probably on welfare."

"Nope, Gina's people make big money," Babydoll said. "Don't you?"

"Shit, my mom's on welfare, so what?" LaLa said.

"Let's get back on track." Ms. Montes snapped her fingers. "Why did you appeal when you admit you kicked the police officer, *Ms.* Anaya?"

"How did I know it was a cop who grabbed me? For all I knew, it was one of those neo-Nazis with a baseball bat. What would you do, let him wail on you?"

"We're not talking about me. I didn't commit a crime."

"My dad sought asylum here. Now the government's pulling all this crap because of what happened on 9/11," Xochitl said. "What if they try to send him back to Nicaragua? What about the Dreamers who've been here most of their life?"

"We're not here for a political debate," Ms. Montes said. "You broke the law, and you have to do your time. It's only six months."

"Six months? It's a felony on my record." Xochitl's eyes moistened, she tilted her head up. "You don't understand."

Ms. Montes cleared her throat. "Ms. Johnson, you're next. Tell us about your crime."

Mariana hands twisted together in her lap. She stared at her fingers. "I was at school when my stomach started cramping, so I went to the bathroom. And, I must have fainted. When I came to, I saw a paramedic standing over me." She took a long breath while her fingers drummed against her thighs.

"There's a big gap in time. Go on," Ms. Montes said.

"He, the paramedic guy, said a, uh, a newborn drowned in the toilet." She pulled at the hem of her tight tee shirt. "The cord wrapped around its neck. On the floor, I saw something small covered in a towel."

"Yew, in the toilet, how gross." Voices from the group rang out. "Ugh, how sick. Drowned?"

A baby drowned? Sickening waves churned my stomach.

Mariana's head hung down to her chest, her eyes focused on her lap. "The man said I gave birth. They took me to the hospital."

My mind pictured a dead baby in a toilet. I turned away from Mariana, noticed Babydoll cradling her abdomen.

"Settle down. She's not finished," Ms. Montes said. "Go on."

"I swear I didn't know I was pregnant. I didn't have my period, but not having one happened to me before. I've been heavy for a long time, so I didn't think missing my period meant anything."

Three hands shot up, waving in the air.

"If you were having sex, didn't you think you'd be pregnant?" Gina asked.

"I wasn't having sex," Mariana said in a tiny voice.

Several girls hissed.

"You're not the Virgin Mary, so what happened?" Babydoll said.

"You were raped, huh?" LaLa said.

Mariana's eyes blinked several times while her mouth sucked in a breath. She gazed at Ms. Montes like she was drowning.

"We've had individual sessions already, Mariana. The Corrections Board expects you to discuss your crime and answer any questions. Speaking in the group will help you."

"My father, uh, stepfather, he, you know, um—"

I moved forward in my chair to hear Mariana's whispered words.

"Your dad molested you, didn't he?" LaLa sat at the edge of her seat. "I know firsthand about that shit. My stepfather raped me, the fucken bastard. No one believed me, so he got away with it. That kind of shit happens all the time."

Everyone shifted away from her in their chairs. At the staff desk, CO Isadora stood up.

Mariana glanced at me, fear clouding her eyes. I couldn't help her and glanced away. Bruja sat, her arms crossed, staring at the clock on the wall. Babydoll had her head down, stroking her thumbs against her stomach. What Mariana said seemed impossible to believe.

"Did you report him?" Xochitl asked. "Isn't he a preacher or something like that?"

"An elder. That's why I didn't tell anybody. No one would believe me, so I stayed out of his way," Mariana said. "He'd touch me or try to bother me, but during my sophomore year, the other thing happened."

I bit at my knuckle. "He's an evil man."

"Are you saying the crime isn't her responsibility?" Ms. Montes asked.

"Fuck no, it's not her fault," LaLa yelled, her eyes angry and wet. "These fuckin' pervs get away, and we're stuck with the babies, or gotta get an abortion. Or we get arrested for stabbing their ass."

"But the baby didn't commit the crime, Lopez," Ms. Montes said. "Do you have something to say, Ivanov?"

I shook my head.

"You sure?" Ms. Montes asked. "Speak up."

She must have seen the confusion on my face. "Mariana, when I had the labor pains with my daughter, it hurt so much for hours before I had her. Why you don't call for help at your school?"

Mariana sucked in the bottom of her lip and held it there. I almost felt sorry for her, but what if she meant to drown her baby?

"Answer the question," Ms. Montes said.

Tears slid down Mariana's cheeks. The squeaking sound of girls squirming in their chairs filled the dayroom.

"Assholes," LaLa said. "That guy should be in prison, not her."

"Mariana, you're not prepared, and you don't have much time before your initial hearing." Ms. Montes wrote something on her clipboard. "Juana, the question you asked is something I want you to think about. Why didn't you call for help?"

Once my door was locked, I couldn't stop thinking of Mariana's crime. She seemed so gentle and quiet. She couldn't have hurt a baby. Could she?

I had to stop thinking of helpless babies. I knocked on my wall adjoining Xochitl's. "How are you appealing? Do you have a lawyer?"

"My brother's in law school. He's helping me. I'm hoping he gets ahold of a video showing what happened at the protest. I swear I didn't know it was a cop who grabbed me."

"Can anyone appeal their crime?"

"There are certain rules. It's kinda complicated, but my brother's handling that."

The muffled sound of tennis shoes came down the hallway and we stopped talking. I peeked out my door window. Ms. Montes called out Mariana's name. A few minutes later, Mariana began crying.

I pushed my window open. "Hey, what happened?"

Her cries turned into loud sobs. The sounds, like howling wind, gave me chills. Over and over, she cried. Her moans rang out like La Llorona, the scary woman who drowned her children in the river. I shivered with the thought of dead children. I had to make her stop crying.

"Mariana, talk to me. Please."

She didn't answer me. "Talk to me," I shouted over and over.

"Shut the fuck up," someone yelled out.

"Juana, stop yelling," Xochitl said. "Leave her alone."

The sounds of despair that Mariana made became piercing wails. Sounds that cut me with their harshness, causing my insides to smash together. I shut my window, pressed my pillow over my head to keep the cries from squeezing my heart dry.

TWENTY

The sky sagged with heavy gray clouds while we lined up for the school movement on wet asphalt outside our living unit. Our hands in our pockets, we waited for the signal to move ahead. Damp cold crept under my sweatshirt and thin jeans, making me shiver.

Someone nudged my elbow and slipped a kite into my palm. Ms. Montes wasn't watching, so I unfolded the half sheet of paper.

"You're so cute," signed "watching you" with a smiley face. I clutched the kite in my hand and stared at the girl behind me.

"Wasn't from me." She shrugged. "Passed it from the back."

"Tell whoever gave you the kite that I had a husband. I don't like girls that way."

"Yeah, right. Husband. Pfftt." Her sharp laugh made me cringe.

The day before, someone threw a kite under my door with the exact words, in large print, the same "watching you." I didn't want anyone trying to be my girlfriend. I needed to stay out of trouble and get out of San Bueno quickly. I stuffed the paper in my pocket.

The COs rushed us to our classrooms, their voices booming

instructions, "move it, move it. Eyes forward. Classroom one step out, classroom three step out," until our line disappeared into the brick buildings.

My body dropped into the hard chair in English class. I flipped open my workbook, copied the words from the whiteboard, and wrote the definitions. They were easy words like write, right, sight, site. I finished filling in the blanks on my worksheet and opened the small dictionary the teacher gave us. I still didn't know what the words meant in Ms. Montes's report.

Domestic abuse: Any incident of violence, threatening behavior, or abuse (psychological, physical, sexual, emotional, or financial) between adults who are or have been intimate partners or family members.

That is what happened to me. My leg jiggled against the table. I shut the book.

"Psst. What's wrong," Sadgirl whispered from beside me.

I shook my head and pushed my knee down with my hand.

"Guess what. Jester cut Babydoll loose last night. We're really together now." A smile spread across her small face like she had won a big prize. "Didn't you know?"

I didn't care, but I needed to take my mind off the words I read in the dictionary.

"Me and Jester talk through her window whenever I'm in the backyard," Sadgirl said and sighed.

None of the window gossips mentioned the breakup, but when Jester stayed in seg for a week, Babydoll grew gloomier, sometimes twirling her hair in endless motion while she sat in the dayroom. Xochitl caught her sucking her thumb while she sat in the TV rows.

Sadgirl's living unit, Gaviota, sat across from the segregation building, separated by a tall chain-link fence, higher than the one around our backyard on Mariposa. The wings of their buildings weren't very far apart, so she wasn't lying.

"That skonka." Sadgirl made a *psst* sound, cutting her eyes at Bruja, who had her stony eyes on us. "Busted her in the library last week, making out with a gavacha, that damn rich girl. The one who pulled those jewelry robberies."

"Quiet down," the teacher said.

"Don't me and Jester make a better couple?" Sadgirl whispered. "You should find somebody. Makes the time pass."

I shrugged, wanting to avoid the telenovela of prison life. I didn't want to find a girl or a staff member, but that kite in my pocket had me wondering who was watching me.

TWENTY-ONE

"Prepare three dinner trays," Ms. Montes yelled to me from the kitchen door. "Two for detention rooms, one for Alvarez. She claims she's sick."

Fish sticks and broccoli stunk up the air as I pushed the squeaky cart out of the dining room and into the hallway. We stopped at Babydoll's room. Ms. Montes peeked into the wicket, moved her head to the left and right of the narrow window in the door.

"Mrs. Shaffer," she shouted, "did Alvarez go to an appointment while we were in the kitchen?"

"No. Present at last count."

Ms. Montes pulled her keys from her belt. "Alvarez." She tapped on the door. "Answer me."

Nothing.

"Alvarez." She pounded on the door, her voice echoing in the hallway. Her forehead wrinkled. "I can't see her."

I plopped the dinner tray back on the cart and knocked. "Babydoll, come to the door."

Ms. Montes put her hand up in a stop sign. "Step back."

"Ms. Ivanov, come up here to the desk," Mrs. Shaffer said.

"What's happening?" Several girls yelled through their doors. "What's going on?"

Ms. Montes flung open the door. Her face went pale, her eyes widened. I glanced up at Mrs. Shaffer but decided Babydoll might need me and stepped back against the opposite wall.

"What's wrong?" I asked.

"Oh my God. Mrs. Shaffer!" Ms. Montes jabbed the alarm button on her belt with one hand, reached out to grasp something with the other hand.

I moved closer, saw Babydoll's chair tipped over on its side. Her small bare feet dangled next to her locker. She hung from the ceiling vent, shoestrings tied around her neck. My breath caught in my throat. Hard footsteps rang in my ears.

"Push her up, take the weight off her neck," Mrs. Shaffer shouted. "Check her pulse."

Both staff held Babydoll up and against the side of the locker. Her heap of hair covered half her face. Her skin, the color of milk, looked cold. The side of her locker wore a big dent like someone kicked at it.

Ms. Montes grabbed her limp wrist. "I can't feel a pulse."

Stretching her arm up, Mrs. Shaffer struggled to reach the braided laces tied to the ceiling vent slats. The knotted shoestrings held tight.

I grabbed the overturned chair, pushed it under Ms. Montes. She jumped on it, supporting Babydoll's body in her arms. From the edge of the chair, I leaped onto the top of the steel locker and worked the knot until it fell against Babydoll's limp shoulder.

Mrs. Shaffer grabbed the radio from Ms. Montes's belt,

clicking it on and off. "Dead battery. I'll run to the phone, tell them we need a nurse and an ambulance."

The sound of boots slapping on the hallway floor came closer. The COs might think I wasn't supposed to be inside Babydoll's room and take me to seg, so I dove onto the bed and slipped out of the room, pressing myself against the wall.

Two COs and Sgt. Cuellar stopped at the doorway while Ms. Montes and Mrs. Schaffer carried Babydoll out and placed her on the floor. Sgt. Cuellar checked her wrist. "Beginning CPR."

He lifted Babydoll's neck, her chin jutting out, and placed a plastic piece over her purplish lips. With his mouth over hers, he puffed air down her throat and clasped his hands, one on top of the other, at the bottom of her ribs. His hands pumped up and down as he counted out numbers.

I slid down against the brick wall, making the sign of the cross from my forehead to my chest. "Por favor Dios, help Babydoll. Please, help her stay alive."

"No time to wait. We've got to get to the clinic," Sgt. Cuellar said.

They lifted Babydoll and jogged out the back door.

Ms. Montes bent over and took a deep breath, her hands at her waist. She ran her fingers through her hair and stared at me when she stood up. Without a word, she walked me back up the hallway, where I glanced at several girls' faces pressed against their wickets. All of them asked what happened, but Ms. Montes said nothing and locked me in my cell.

A frightening stillness came over the hallways. I didn't know if Babydoll was alive or dead. I pictured every girl on her bed, like me, staring at the dingy ceiling, thinking about their life inside this place. Maybe they imagined the faces of their loved ones beyond the bars and fences of San Bueno and dreamed of someone to comfort them inside these walls.

What if no one on the outside waited for me? No Lupe, no Katrina, no Papá, nobody. Grief squeezed at my heart. Hurt, disappointments, and the fear of an empty future shoved at the ache. My heart, an open wound, stung. I didn't know if I could live through the torment anymore. What if Babydoll thought the sureness of death, the end of pain, would be easier than the harshness of living?

I used to think the girls in San Bueno were so unlike me. They grew up in the US, were in gangs, or took drugs, but I realized they weren't so different. They had sisters, brothers, and children they worried about too. Some of them had the names of their kids etched on their cups, in drawings, or tattooed over their hearts. They didn't want to forget them even if their children never saw them again.

Most of the girls had grandmothers who took care of them; some had mothers, a couple had their fathers. All of them had stories, even if they didn't share them. Stories buried deep. Like mine.

Hard, stinging loneliness overtook me. I moved away from the feeling and made myself study the photos of Katrina on my wall, made myself remember her small warm body, the touch of soft searching hands on my face. Closing my eyes, I pretended her pudgy baby fingers traced over my lips and cheek. I imagined bathing her in her little yellow tub, her hands splashing water, the suds of baby shampoo. I remembered Alek's body next to mine when we slept and I kissed him goodbye before work.

My heartache deepened until I fell in, lost myself in the anguish of memories that floated out of my head, spilled into the hole in my heart, and came out in hot tears. The emptiness too much to bear. When would this nightmare end? I was buried under my thoughts until I couldn't breathe anymore. Then I understood why Babydoll did what she did.

TWENTY-TWO

rs. Shafer's voice drifted down the hallway. When the unit was quiet, we could hear bits and pieces of the staff's conversation when they talked at the desk. Sometimes the information was important and other times only gossip. Xochitl said it was a way to keep up with the happenings in the facility, so I pressed my ear against the doorframe and listened to Mrs. Shaffer.

"Clinic said Paula Alvarez is gonna make it. We need to transfer that child to the mental health unit."

"But, there's a long waiting list," Ms. Montes said.

"We could move a bunk into Juana Ivanov's room. Put them together."

"Can't. Ivanov's here for a violent crime, Alvarez isn't."

"Oh, I'd forgotten the specifics of her offense," Mrs. Shaffer said.

"Yeah, she plays innocent."

Ms. Montes is afraid I'll be a bad influence on Babydoll because of a crime I didn't commit? She's made up her mind about me. I need to make staff pay attention to the truth. But how?

"Imagine wanting to end her life over a breakup with a career criminal like Gonzales," Ms. Montes said. "What about moving her in with Xochitl Anaya?"

"Ms. Alvarez is a follower, and now that we have north-south issues, that won't work."

I called over to Mariana. "You hear Mrs. Shaffer and Ms. Montes?"

Mariana didn't answer.

"Xochitl, you hear Mrs. Shaffer about the mental unit for Babydoll?" I said through the wall.

"Yeah, the Thorazine Queen unit."

"What is the queen unit?"

"No, Thorazine's a drug the doctor gives the girls. That med makes them look like zombies."

"Babydoll doesn't need meds. She has her heartbreak."

"You mean a broken heart. Yeah, I bet Babydoll feels like shit with her business out on front street. But girls like her fall in love all the time."

"After Jester cheated, her eyes had so much hurt. They shouldn't give her drugs."

"She needs therapy, not drugs. You could try talking to her, yeah?"

I sat back on my bed. "Okay, I'll tell her what my mamá used to say. La vida es dura, but the hard life makes for a strong person."

Mamá repeated the dicho many times after the accident at the train yard that cut my father's right arm so severely the doctor amputated it above his elbow. She urged Papá to ask the railroad company where he worked to pay for a fake arm so that he could return to his job. He wouldn't talk to them. My mamá didn't give up.

We took the bus to Delicias, where his job used to be, and

Mamá marched to the foreman's office, demanding to see the boss. He called security instead.

They made us leave. Mamá gripped her purse to her stomach on the bus home, her lips pressed together.

"What'll we do now, Mamá?"

"We'll work extra days at the market and save money to buy your father the fake arm the doctors recommended."

"He hates the empty sleeve hanging off his shirt," I said.

"A reminder that he can't provide for us the way he used to. But he can still learn to do things. We can too." Mamá's face relaxed into its smoothness. "The boys are old enough to work, and we have our garden. We won't go hungry."

The following year, my two brothers, who were fourteen and sixteen, left for other cities to make money to send for my father's medications and to help Mamá buy the prosthetic arm he needed. She let me help at the weekly mercado, but my father didn't believe a ten-year-old girl could contribute anything.

In a way, he was right.

In Santa Isabel, the buses painted with yellow flowers and leafy vines looked like the surrounding hillsides in early summer. Lupe, Mamá, and I carried boxes of squash, chiles, and tomatoes on our lap while happy accordion music blared from the bus radio.

That was the day I ruined everything. We unloaded our boxes at the mercado and set up our vegetable stand.

"Who picked the squash blossoms?" Lupe peered into one of the covered boxes. "Mamá?"

"People like them for soup," I said. "We can make a lot of money."

Mamá examined the inside of the carton, shook her head. "These are too young, too small. You cannot pick the blossoms before they're ready."

"Now, all the squash in the garden is stunted," Lupe said. "I'm telling Papá."

When we returned home, with little money, my father became furious. "You stupid, worthless child."

Even today, I hear his voice ring in my ear. Maybe Babydoll hears the same thing.

Ms. Montes unlocked my door. "I need you and Mariana to set up the dayroom for a large group."

Mariana dragged her feet like she had leg irons on her ankles. She didn't talk or look at me while we arranged the chairs in a large circle. There were times she became silent, disappeared into her thoughts, and I let her be although I wanted to hug her. Sometimes we needed to be in our feelings here.

The girls streamed into the dayroom from the hallway, one group at a time, until all the seats were filled. The social worker, Mrs. Snow, who the girls called Snowball because of her round body, white hair, and pale skin, waddled into the circle and took a seat next to Mrs. Shaffer.

CO Isadora stood at the staff desk directing everyone to fill in the seats according to our room number.

When everyone was seated, Mrs. Shaffer stood. Her eyes focused on us, her lined forehead more prominent. "I want you to know the facts. Paula Alvarez attempted suicide. She's in the hospital."

Gina stroked her ponytail while Bruja stared out of the day-room windows, her face unmoved.

"Talk to your counselor or request to see Mrs. Snow if you're unhappy or sad. Better than hurting yourself."

A few girls smirked because everyone in prison felt unhappy or sad most of the time, even if we didn't show it on the outside.

Mrs. Snow shuffled papers on her lap. "These are the signs of depression. . . ."

Her voice rumbled on while a girl yawned, others slouched in their chairs, their eyes closed, and some, like Xochitl and Mariana, picked at their fingernails.

She continued, "Sign the list on my office door if you need to talk."

Several girls rolled their eyes because Mrs. Snow rarely came to her office in the unit.

"Any questions?" Mrs. Shaffer asked.

"When do we program?" Chantilla slumped in her chair, her thick legs sprawled in front of her. "We've been down too long."

So disrespectful. I stared at her until she leaned forward, glared at me, and lifted her hands. "What?" Her eyes changed from a mud color to a flashing brown.

My body jumped before I could turn away from her. How the girls acted in the large group made me think no one cared about Babydoll. It pained me that she was so depressed, so alone.

In our group counseling, she told us of her arrest for theft and being under the influence of heroin. She'd been a drug addict for two years—and only sixteen.

I should have been friendlier. When Babydoll returned to the unit, I'd tell her stories about Santa Isabel, about our vegetable garden at home, the winding river beneath the sage-covered hills, the giant iguanas my brothers caught. I'd ask her about her family and her life before she got to San Bueno Correctional. Talking about the outside could help her on the inside.

TWENTY-THREE

The staff member's footsteps squeaked up and down the hallway every thirty minutes. All day. All night. Each screech brought me closer to the time of my hearing. I sat on my bed and reread Ms. Montes's case report.

I hoped talking about my crime in group counseling prepared me for this day. None of the girls acted mad at me or yelled like they did when Mariana talked about her offense. They let me talk. I told them I found out what domestic violence meant and gave them the definition. Everyone nodded, and LaLa said I was a victim of domestic abuse, and what did people expect victims to do, just take it? That started a whole other discussion.

Every girl except Mariana said guys had chased them in anger, and if the guy fell, they deserved whatever he got. I don't believe Alek deserved to die, but I didn't say anything about that in the group.

During the last three days, Xochitl gave me consejos about the hearing, and I needed all the advice I could get. She'd been to her board appearance weeks before and didn't receive more time on her sentence.

"Read your report ten times and practice saying, 'Good afternoon, yes sir, no sir' when they question you. Remember to look at them instead of putting your head down," she said.

"If I look them in their eyes, they will think I'm arrogant. It's a sign of disrespect. They are people of position."

"Listen, this is the United States. If you don't look them in the eye, they'll think you're lying. And talk loud enough for them to hear you. Speak up for yourself."

At the beginning of our practice sessions, my feelings grew inside me when I relived that night and interrupted my words, causing me to mumble. Sweat popped up under my arms and the back of my neck, but Xochitl made me start over.

"Again. You need to tell your story in a way where the board members can hear what you're saying. Understand?"

"Okay." I shook out my hands, cleared my throat. "Xochitl, why do you help me?"

"'Cause you're the only one who talked to me, even if it was on the sly after Jester told the rest of the Chicanas not to. You're a real friend."

Her comment helped me relax. A person could make mistakes in front of a real friend, and they still cared about you.

"Makes me mad we can't be amigas, like on the outside," I said. "And talk wherever we are and in front of anyone."

"Yeah, I know, it's bullshit. I think Jester's going to go easier on you now since you didn't tell anyone about the kitchen incident and helped save Babydoll."

I kept the shove into the ice bin and threat from Jester a secret, lying to staff about it so I wouldn't be hit harder next time, by her or any of her friends. But every time someone argued or a chair screeched across the linoleum, I tensed, stopped breathing.

Images of that day filled my thoughts. The fork was still

missing. What if Gina hid it in the kitchen, ready to give to Jester or Bruja when they wanted to use it? Staff searched Jester's room after she pushed me and never found it. They searched Bruja's and Gina's rooms, too.

Maybe no one had it, and the fork fell into the drain underneath the ice machine. Better to imagine it there and not aiming for my back.

I reread my report again. I practiced deep breathing. A knock on my door startled me.

"Board hearing, Ivanov. Meet Mrs. Snow in the admin building," Ms. Montes said. "Check in with the CO at the desk."

Staff rushed in and out of the small offices in the brightly lit administration building. A woman in a floral dress pushed a rolling cart filled with stacks of green files down the hall. The fragrance of jasmine perfume and burnt coffee lingered in the air.

I checked in and sat in a chair near CO Isadora. Her uniform shirt and pants were always clean and pressed. Even her black boots shone like the smooth bun at her neck.

"Ms. Gonzales went into the hearing room. You're next," she said.

Was Jester inside the room nearby? I hadn't seen her since the COs took her to the seg unit for threatening to kick Ms. Montes's butt. She had made fun of Jester's many tattoos by asking if she ran out of scratch paper.

When Jester comes out of the hearing room, she'll be right in front of me, irritated at the additional time they'll give her for the discipline reports. What if she takes her anger out on me?

You could never tell with her. One minute she told jokes, laughed, and the next, her face froze into a glare so intense you had to turn away.

My eyes wandered to the brick walls in front of me and the shiny floor. I picked at the nubby material on the chair and then rubbed my moist palms against the knees of my jeans. *Speak up, look them in the eyes, yes sir, no sir.* The advice ran through my mind.

Minutes went by, each one bringing me closer to the people who would decide how long I'd stay at San Bueno Correctional. The officials in the hearing room might let me go once they realized they made a mistake by sending me here. At least I prayed that they would.

I flinched when the phone rang.

"No, Paula Alvarez was scratched from the list. She's still in the clinic," CO Isadora said to someone.

"Ms. Isadora, you know when Babydoll, I mean Alvarez, will be back?"

"No, I don't. Hey, you're a bundle of nerves, Ms. Ivanov. Try to relax. Go in, tell the truth. Simple."

I couldn't tell the whole truth or risk getting more time, but I would tell them what happened with Alek.

The door cracked open, Mrs. Snow's hand on the knob. Jester, dressed in a yellow jumpsuit from the segregation unit, strolled out in handcuffs, wearing a smirk on her pasty face.

"Six-month time add," Mrs. Snow said. "Maxed out."

CO Isadora made a mark on the list of names she had on her desk. Jester looked as unconcerned as if she was taking a walk through her neighborhood park.

"Qué pues, Mouse?" She lifted her chin towards me, smiling with her one dimple showing.

"The transportation van will be here in a minute." CO Isadora pointed to the chair next to me. "Wait there, Ms. Gonzales."

Jester might have been in handcuffs, but she could hurt me if she wanted. Only six inches separated us from each other. If the CO glanced away, Jester could jump up, kick me, knock my chair over before the CO could grab her. She didn't look angry, but that didn't mean anything. She didn't look angry the minute before she shoved me into the ice bin, either.

I had to stop the fearful thoughts, or I'd mess up my board hearing. Taking another breath, I thought of the vegetable garden back home. *Go out to the garden with Mamá. Stay calm*, I told myself.

Jester leaned towards me. "Tell Babydoll I love her."

Another CO walked up and took Jester's arm. She stood, winked at me as she headed down the corridor and out a side door.

Whew. I released the breath I held inside. I didn't have to worry about the missing fork anymore.

The phone rang again. My knee jerked in response.

"A break? Thanks," the CO said.

"I go back to the unit, Ms. Isadora?"

"No, sit tight for ten minutes. Use the time to think about what you're going to say, okay?" She clicked on her radio and spoke to someone.

Think about what I need to say. I'd say the truth of what Alek did, what I did, and tell them what my mother-in-law did. The problem was whether they'd believe me or not.

TWENTY-FOUR

The hearing room door opened. Mrs. Snow poked her head out and lifted her huge round glasses. "Juana Ivanov," she shouted like she couldn't see me sitting six feet away. "Ms. Ivanov?"

"Here." I wiped my damp hands against the sides of the chair.

My legs trembled when I entered the hearing room. Overhead lights shone on the polished narrow desk, which filled most of the space. The air conditioner blew cold air over my sweaty face. I stood there until Mrs. Snow tapped the back of an empty chair.

Two older men and one woman sat on one side of the long table. Behind them a picture of the President of the United States, Mr. Bush. The flags of the US and California stood on poles on either end of the room. The place reminded me of the juvenile court hearing, but with three judges instead of one.

In this room, my future would be decided by people who did not know me. Or Alek or about my baby far away. They didn't understand what my life was like after I left Mexico or before coming to this place. Their only knowledge of me was what was written in the court papers, Ms. Montes's report, and what I would tell them.

The man in the dark grey suit had an unfriendly stare and sharp features. Next to him sat a woman in a navy-blue suit with a slender gold bracelet on her wrist. Her clear polished nails flipped through the pages of the file in front of her. An older bald man sat next to her and smiled at me. Mrs. Snow, two others, and I were on the other side of the table.

"These are the Correctional Board members, Mr. Axel, Ms. Maxwell, the Chairperson, and Mr. James." Mrs. Snow pointed at them left to right. "At the end of our row is the Supervising Parole Agent, Ms. Palomarez, and our clerical staff, Ms. Cobos."

They nodded. The heat of their eyes were on me. I remembered to swallow and placed my hands on top of the table like Xochitl told me to do.

Ms. Cobos pressed a button on a tape recorder while the parole agent wrote something on a long sheet of paper.

"Do we have an interpreter?" Ms. Maxwell asked Mrs. Snow.

"No, I don't think we need one. Ms. Ivanov knows enough English."

"We need to ensure she understands us, and we understand her. Please find us an interpreter."

"Ms. Maxwell, this will delay the hearing. We're already behind." Mr. Axel, the sharp-featured man, glanced at his clunky watch.

"I'm certified to interpret," Ms. Cobos said.

"Wonderful. Tell Ms. Ivanov we'll begin in English, but she can ask you whenever she doesn't understand something," Ms.

Maxwell said. "When we ask a question, translate it for her. We'll start with Mr. James."

Ms. Cobos repeated the instructions in Spanish while Mr. Axel rolled his eyes and leaned back in his black leather chair. The lines on his face reminded me of grooves in the canyons near Santa Isabel weathered from years in the sun.

"You told the arresting officer your husband hit you twice before the night of the offense," Mr. James said. "Why didn't you return to your family or seek help?"

I cleared the nervousness from my throat. "I wasn't sure if his drunkenness is what made him hit me. Always he was sorry afterward. I hoped things would get better and—"

Mr. Axel leaned forward on the desk, his hands outstretched. "But, why didn't you tell the police the first time your husband allegedly beat you?"

I hesitated. Could I tell him I didn't want him arrested? I'd just had the baby. I loved Alek. I didn't want to leave him. Where would I go? If I told Mr. Axel these reasons, he'd think I was stupid, crazy, or both.

Ms. Cobos repeated the question.

"We had a new baby. I didn't want him to go to jail. This is the way I thought then, but not anymore."

Ms. Cobos kept her eyes on me as if she expected more of an explanation. My hands shook. I took them off the table, burying them in my lap.

"*If* he hit you," Mr. Axel said. "There's no evidence to support your statement."

Mr. James cleared his throat. "Ms. Ivanov, tell us about the events before the crime."

This is what I've waited to tell Ms. Montes and Mrs. Snow, but they always stop me. They don't let me finish.

"After I came back from the laundromat, I saw Alek throwing things in our apartment, tearing up the room. He asked me for money, but I said I took what we had for our wash. He called me a liar and ran through the apartment like a crazy man turning over the sofa cushions, screaming at me." I paused to suck in another breath. "I went to the bedroom and put my baby in her bassinet, but he grabbed me and pushed me against the wall. His eyes looked wild like a dog when it has the disease."

I was out of breath again, my tongue thick, my mouth dry from the rush of words. It hurt to swallow. Closing my eyes, I remembered Xochitl's advice: breathe.

"Take your time." Ms. Maxwell sat back in her chair. "What happened next?"

"The baby, her name's Katrina, she started crying. Alek ran to the bassinet, picked her up, and threw her on our bed. He never did that before." I wiped my sweaty forehead. "He threw her blankets and the mattress, kicked them to the wall. That scared me more. I grabbed her, my diaper bag, and ran outside, down the steps. Alek followed me, yelling for me to give him the money. Then I heard a thumping sound and turned to see him on the cement. He fell down the apartment stairs."

"What money? Why did you leave your husband at the bottom of those stairs?" Mr. Axel said. "You must have had a telephone in your apartment. Why didn't you call for help?"

Each question slapped my face. I rubbed at my neck and glanced at Mrs. Snow. She wasn't looking at me. She ruffled the pages of my report. Ms. Cobos asked me the questions in Spanish.

"I, I don't know."

Mr. Axel lifted his hands in the air. "You don't know? Of course, you do. Didn't you want him dead? Isn't that the real reason? You pushed him down the staircase."

"No es cierto, yo no hice eso."

"It's not true. I didn't do that," Ms. Cobos translated.

Mr. Axel's thin lips pressed together. He exhaled out of his big nose like he didn't believe me. He acted like he saw me push Alek.

I knew the truth. I lifted my head, gulped in some air. "When my husband threw the baby, I had only one thought, to run for my life and hers. After he fell, he pushed himself off the ground, yelled at me again. I was scared. I ran to the bus stop down the street and took buses until we got to Calexico. My cousin, Maribel, lives across the border in Mexicali. I phoned her, and I gave her the baby when she came. I could have stayed there, I should have stayed, but I returned to our apartment. I thought if I talked to Alek, he'd promise to stop drinking. But when I got there the next morning, he wasn't there. The police told me he died."

The creases in Mr. Axel's forehead squished together in two lines as he glared at me. "I don't buy your story. Once he was incapacitated on the concrete, your husband wasn't a threat to you. You took your daughter out of the country because you knew you did wrong, not to keep her safe." He pointed his thick finger at me. "You absconded instead of contacting authorities."

He spoke so fast I turned to Ms. Cobos. She repeated what he said to me in rapid Spanish.

"No, no." Shaking my head, I opened my mouth but couldn't find the words and looked down at my hands. I wanted to cry, and it wasn't for sympathy.

"You killed your husband and left the country to escape prosecution," Mr. Axel shouted.

The anger that came from him made me shrink into my seat, but he was wrong.

"No, no, I didn't leave the country. I went to Calexico, and I came back." Then I remembered what I read in my report. "I ran from domestic violence."

Ms. Maxwell tapped the desk with her pen. "Mr. Axel, ward Ivanov is not here for murder but voluntary manslaughter. Now, Ms. Ivanov, why didn't you call the police the first time your husband hit you or on the night of the offense? Take your time."

Her voice was gentle, almost comforting. I glanced at her smooth brown face, her clear eyes, and knew she'd listen.

"Alek took my green card and hid it from me many weeks before this happened. He told me if I called the police, they would deport me. He would tell them that Katrina must stay with him because she's an American citizen. His mother could help raise her, he said. I didn't want to lose my baby, Miss."

Ms. Maxwell flipped through the pages of my life in the United States. Pages that told only one part of my story.

I pushed myself to tell her more. "I swear, after Alek fell down the stairs, he tried to stand up. He yelled at me again for money. I thought he was going to keep chasing me. Hurt the baby and me."

Ms. Maxwell closed the file and leaned back in her seat. The room became quieter as I grew more nervous, sweat covering my head and chest.

"I move to follow the correctional counselor's recommendation to give this young lady a hearing date before her maximum time of six years," Ms. Maxwell said. "I motion to set her parole date at the midterm of her sentence. Three years."

My eyes watered, my shoulders unwound. I thought I'd faint—three years, not six.

"Let's not be hasty." Mr. Axel thumped the desk with his hand and frowned at Ms. Maxwell.

"Mr. James, how do you vote?" she asked the other man.

"She's discipline free. This young lady can benefit from the counseling and education within the time you've stipulated. I agree with your motion."

Mr. Axel pointed to Ms. Cobos. "Tell her I disagree. She should have a maximum term of six years. She's lucky she's enjoying the privileges of the United States of America."

Ms. Cobos told me what I already understood.

"Motion carries, two votes to one," Ms. Maxwell said.

"Thank you, Miss. Thank you, Sir," I said to the Correctional Board members.

Mr. Axel turned away from me and mumbled something.

Mrs. Snow tapped my arm. "You can go now."

"Tell her." Mr. Axel's sharp voice cut through my happiness. "Translate what I said. She needs to understand."

His voice sounded so rough that I sat up straighter and glanced at Mrs. Snow, then to Ms. Maxwell in front of me, who wrote notes on their papers.

"I want her to know exactly what I said." Mr. Axel leaned across the table.

I drew myself back into my chair, swallowing the lump growing in my throat, while Ms. Cobos glanced at me.

"He says he wants us to investigate your green card status."

TWENTY-FIVE

*I*nvestigate her green card. Mr. Axel's last words stayed in my head. He said it with so much hate, looked at me with disgust. He didn't believe a word I said.

In juvenile hall, a girl told me the authorities would find out, eventually, that my documents were fake, and the transportation officers would leave me at the border in Tijuana. I had no idea how I'd find my way out of there, but I couldn't think about that now. My cousin Maribel's home in Mexicali was almost two hundred kilometers away from Tijuana.

The trouble I'd get into with a fake card could lead to another charge. That worried me.

How did my life go so wrong when I tried to do the right things? I hoped for a new life, a better one, here in the US, with Alek, a home, and a family. Now, the only piece left of my dream was Katrina, but every day I spent in San Bueno became another day she moved further from me.

I crossed the prison grounds and back into my unit. The staff locked me back in my room. With less time to do here, maybe that would convince Lupe to stay in Santa Isabel.

Dearest Lupe,

I still haven't received a letter from you. The hearing officers gave me three years instead of six years. I thank God, they believed me.

I understand I am asking you for a great favor, to be separated from your husband, but I pray you do not go to Arizona, it is too dangerous. The desert is merciless. Both you and Katrina will be in much danger. Don't risk crossing while you're pregnant.

When I finish my sentence, the authorities will take me to Tijuana, but I'll find my way to you. If you leave for the United States before I parole from here, I won't be able to cross back and pick up Katrina legally.

If I cross illegally, the Migra can arrest me and I'll go back to prison for a very long time. I miss Katrina so much I ache. I promise to try very hard to get out of here sooner. I go to school, do what they tell me, and stay out of trouble.

Please, show her the picture I've enclosed, every day. Tell her I will be with her in the garden soon.

With much love, Juana

I had made a trade for another picture of Katrina by sewing Jester's sweatshirt collars tight last month. Luckily, she gave me the drawing before she got mad at me.

Jester drew me holding Katrina in my mother's garden just as I described. She colored the squash blossoms the right shade of orange, the tomatoes bright red, the sunflowers a deep yellow with shades of brown. I folded the drawing and carefully placed it inside of the envelope to send to Lupe.

I dropped my letter into the mailbox, bolted to the wall near the staff desk, and walked into the dayroom.

"I understand your hearing went well," Mrs. Shaffer said.

"My sister Lupe will be happy. She takes care of my little girl Katrina."

"It's important to keep in regular contact with your child. Keep out of trouble and you can earn three months off each year if you make significant progress in counseling and achieve high scores in school and the unit. The good time credits can amount to nine months' time off in three years."

Nine months off? Her words made me smile. "Oh, much better news, Mrs. Shaffer, thank you."

I wanted to hug her for telling me this, but I couldn't or I'd get in trouble. I hurried across the dayroom to find Mariana or Xochitl but didn't see them anywhere. I sat alone facing the staff desk.

Bruja slid in front of me. Her black marble eyes swept over my face. One thick eyebrow rose over her penetrating eye. "Hey, heard you went to Board. Did Jester send a message?"

I shook my head. She pulled her hand back. I flinched. Bruja pushed her hair behind her ear, snickered her witchy laugh, and strolled across the dayroom to sit with Gina at the card table.

Xochitl came into the dayroom and motioned to me to go to

the TV rows. She flopped into the first row, and I took a seat two spaces away.

"What'd Bruja want?" she said.

I kept my eyes straight ahead pretended I wasn't talking to Xochitl since Bruja might report to Jester that I was talking to a northerner.

"She thinks Jester had a message for her, but she didn't. Jester told me to tell Babydoll she loved her."

Xochitl glanced over her shoulder. "Bruja's been trying to get next to Babydoll, the backstabbing bitch. Heard you got three years, maybe you can leave in a little over two."

"Yes, Mrs. Shaffer explained. I am very happy. You see Mariana?"

"Hard-timing it in her room. Ms. Montes gave her a bad hearing report, recommended she do all her time. Someone's putting notes under her cell door, calling her a baby killer."

"That was an accident."

"How do you know? You weren't there. Even if she didn't do it, no one believes her because she never tells people off, never defends herself."

What Xochitl said was partly true. Mariana never denied she killed the baby, only that she didn't remember. When the girls in group questioned her, she slouched lower into her seat, flustered. I understood how she felt, but when I tried to get her to talk to me more about her crime, she wouldn't.

"It's a good idea she stays in her room," I said.

"No, not a good idea. If you hole up in your room, the staff think you don't have interpersonal skills. The other girls will think you're PC-ing it up."

The words Xochitl used often confused me. "What do you mean?"

"Staff takes points off for hiding in your room. They expect you to get along with the other girls, learn how to deal with problems. But if you're a pesay, in protective custody, the girls pick on you more. Either way, you can't hide and you can't win."

Ay, Dios, now I had to figure out how to be out in the dayroom without the gangbangers bothering me so I could make it out of San Bueno in two years not three. I already attended school, church, and volunteered to clean, but there were other times when everyone came out into the dayroom, especially on the weekends when Xochitl and Mariana had visits and were gone from the unit. No one visited me or Jester or Bruja.

There had to be something I could do on the weekends, something useful, and someplace away from the gangbangers.

"Xochitl, you think Mrs. Shaffer lets me teach a few girls to sew?"

"Nah, I don't think she wants a bunch of girls with needles and thread. Jester or Bruja would steal the needles or make one of the other girls take them."

"What about a garden for our compa, a little one? My mother taught me how to take care of flowers and vegetables and grow things."

"Never heard of a garden in prison. And we don't have any shovels or the special dirt you need or seeds. But that's something one or two people could do."

"We could work on it together. I'll teach you."

"Ivanov, iron," Mrs. Shaffer said.

"Sounds like a plan." Xochitl passed her pants to me. Someone kept scratching her name off the list, so I began ironing her clothes.

First thing tomorrow morning I'd tell Mrs. Shaffer about the garden idea. I had to get away from the snoopy eyes and ears of Bruja, Gina, and their friends. They told Jester everything.

At the ironing board, I sensed someone's eyes on me. I glanced up, saw Bruja glaring at me. What if she saw Xochitl pass her jeans to me?

TWENTY-SIX

Xochitl and I finished cleaning the dayroom while the rest of the girls were locked in their cells for the night. We had five minutes alone before Ms. Montes finished her paperwork and sent us to our rooms. Eager to jot down my gardening plan, I held my pencil over the back of one of my old worksheets.

"What were those words you used before?" I asked.

"Tell Mrs. Shaffer a garden can help inmates stay busy and out of trouble. The staff like to hear that kind of stuff. Say, the garden is ecological, good for the environment. Especially since we won't use pesticides."

"Those words are too big," I said. "You write it down."

"No, you need the practice. Write 'organic vegetables and flowers help inmates gain skills,'" Xochitl said slowly. "What are we going to plant?"

"Let's ask for tomatoes, chiles, some herbs, calabazas. Sunflowers, marigolds." I recorded the names of the seeds and plants. "Those are easy to grow. We need a water hose and bucket too."

"Finish up in your room, and I'll look at the list at breakfast."

"I'm glad for your help and that you believe I can grow vegetables here." I tucked away the paper in my pocket.

Xochitl shook her head. "Who would have thought that rocky dried-up ground in a prison yard could produce anything. But if anyone can make it happen, it'll be you."

Her words made me grin as wide as I did on my birthday. Xochitl believed in me and that made me trust in my idea. Now all I had to do was present the plan to Mrs. Shaffer and convince her I could grow a garden.

Staff locked us in, made their evening count, and dimmed the hallway lights. The excitement I felt about a piece of the ugly backyard made into a garden, full of vegetables and flowers, carried me into sleep. Colors other than faded blue, gray, and the officers' uniform green would be at San Bueno Correctional. Well, at least in the Mariposa unit.

A tap on my door interrupted my dream of picking huge red tomatoes. I couldn't see who it was in the dark, but I heard the door vibrate. I jumped and grabbed the edge of the envelope and pulled it out. A sealed letter with a Los Angeles return address. Only letters from an attorney or the state were allowed to be unopened. I unfolded the thick white paper.

Mrs. Anna Ivanov, mother of the deceased Alek Ivanov, petitions for full custody of her granddaughter Katrina Anna Ivanov.

My fingers gripped the sides of the letter.

Insomuch as Juana Maria Flores . . .

They used my real name. How did Anna find my real last name?

> *. . . incarcerated at San Bueno Youth Correctional Facility,*
> *is an imprisoned alien, she is unable to care for her child.*
> *The petitioner requests the court for guardianship of*
> *Katrina Ivanov. You may respond to this petition, by letter,*
> *to the address listed below.*

The paper shook in my trembling fingers. Anna couldn't have Katrina. She was the only thing I had left in this world. What kind of cruel mother-in-law would do such a thing?

"Miss. Come here, please." I banged on the door until the night lady appeared in my wicket, her wrinkled face angry.

"Ivanov, what the hell is wrong? Stop knocking."

"I want to talk to Ms. Montes. I want to—"

"It's ten thirty. No one's here. Talk to your caseworker in the morning."

"You don't understand, I—"

The staff walked away. I leaned my back against the door and slid to the floor.

"*Imprisoned alien, unable to care for her child.*" I read the letter over and over while I sat on the cold concrete, my stomach twisted up. Every time I read the word "alien," I thought of creatures that weren't human. Not a person, but a thing. Things that frightened people. That is what Anna thought about me even though she was once a stranger to this country too.

I always knew she didn't like me, but to take away my baby? She hated me. My life already torn apart could only be kept together by having my daughter. I had to do something, quick.

What if Anna called San Bueno Correctional, told the authorities my real last name? The investigation the board member asked for would be over before it started. They'd give me another charge. Could I tell Ms. Montes the truth?

My sentence was six years, then three years, but now the possibility of getting out in two years was disappearing fast. The pounding of my heart filled my chest. I crawled over to my bed, wrung my thin blanket in my hand.

The staff would learn the truth. There was no marriage, just a fake green card giving me a life in the US, a married life, a life as Alek's wife. An existence I made up to cover the shame of my pregnancy for my father and family. I told Ms. Montes the truth about how Alek and I met at the restaurant where I worked, but I didn't tell her how our relationship almost ended in Mexicali.

Alek came to meet me at the café after he finished his construction job, his clothes dusty, his attitude irritated. We went outside to the tables on the small patio, away from the big ears of the manager and other waitresses.

"One more week before I split from this boring town," Alek said when he sat. "I won't miss the miserable heat."

I pushed the ice-cold bottle of soda over to him and thought of not telling him the news. I had missed two periods in a row. If I didn't tell him, I'd probably never see him again. But maybe, he'd want to stay if I told him what I suspected.

"Alek. I'm going to have a baby."

His hard hat hit the cement floor. "What the hell?" He swept his hand through his thick hair. "Juana?"

"We need to get married right away."

"Maybe you made a mistake. Did you go to a doctor?"

I shook my head and reached across the table for his hand. He pulled it away and wiped his forehead. "Go see someone to take care of it."

I knew what he meant without him saying the words. "Alek, that's illegal in some parts of Mexico."

"Damn, Juana, I don't know what to do." He rested his head in the palms of his hands, rubbed his temples. "Find a place. I don't want to get married or have a kid. I'm nineteen."

Nausea rocked me until I thought I'd vomit. I closed my eyes, rubbed my hands on my jeans. My thoughts swirled around his words. "Find a place. I don't want to get married . . ." Alek didn't want me. He didn't want our baby. I turned away from him, bit my lip so I wouldn't cry right there in front of him.

"I'll see a doctor to make sure if I'm pregnant. I need to go back to work." I struggled to my feet. "Don't worry."

He planned to leave me.

Later that day, in my desperation and heartache of never seeing him again, being alone with a child, facing my father and the relatives I stayed with, I searched for a person who made fake documents.

My entire savings, the money I kept to buy my father his fake arm, came to the amount to purchase a phony Resident Alien Card, a mica. The card had my fingerprint and a new signature, Juana Maria Ivanov.

A couple of days later, Alek met me again at the restaurant. "The baby is yours," I said. "I'm not getting an abortion."

He rubbed his forehead, sighed. He scratched his head and glanced at the street, the sky, everywhere but me. I waited in silence.

"He needs a father." I took Alek's hand, wanting to connect myself and our baby to him.

He turned his face to me, gripped his fingers over mine. "A boy?"

"Your son. I bought a green card. We can go to Los Angeles together." I pushed the mica across the table, sliding it under his hand.

He picked it up and turned it over. "It says, Ivanov." His snicker, part laugh and part interest, gave me hope. "Okay."

We left for Los Angeles the next day.

The morning staff unlocked my door to work the kitchen. I dragged my feet out of my cell like a walking dead person, stooped over with the weight of the petition for custody letter.

"Look." I thrust the letter at Xochitl after we finished cleaning the kitchen. She took off her glasses, still cracked in one lens, and read the letter.

"You're shitting me. You're not married?"

I shook my head.

"Your green card is counterfeit? Why?"

"I got pregnant."

She scratched at the back of her head. "Damn, I thought you were all innocent."

"I don't know what to do. If I tell Ms. Montes, she'll report me to the Correctional Board. If I don't tell her and my mother-in-law calls here, things could turn out worse for me. The custody hearing's five weeks away."

"You're lucky this was legal mail," Xochitl said. "The staff doesn't know what you got, but I bet the lawyer sent a copy to Mrs. Snow or the warden."

"She wants full custody of Katrina."

"Alek's mom must be crazy to think you're going to give up your baby."

Xochitl's words pushed me upright, gave me energy. "I won't give her up, not without a fight."

"All right," she said. "And I got a plan."

TWENTY-SEVEN

The librarian waved Xochitl through the door. When I stepped forward, she pulled her eyeglasses down from the messy bun on top of her head and inspected my pass. Several silver rings decorated her fingers.

"Haven't seen you here before. Welcome. I'm Ms. Dillon." She waved me through, the bracelets on her wrists tinkling.

The place didn't look like the library in Mexicali or any library I visited in Los Angeles. It was just another classroom with steel shelves full of smelly paperbacks and old books. The beige linoleum was the same as the one in the living unit, but a colorful braided carpet lay in front of the first bookshelf. Across from the shelf was a table with stacks of books, and a few opened to show their colorful covers. They reminded me of butterflies with open wings.

Xochitl stopped at two bulletin boards covered with posters that brightened up the brick wall. She bent closer to a flyer pinned to the board. "Spring books coming out soon. Lots of promising novels."

"You never tire of books, do you, Ms. Anaya?" Ms. Dillon said. "A real reader."

"Did those new titles by Sandra Cisneros or Ana Castillo

come in like I requested?" Xochitl asked. "Oh, and the idea I had about getting us some of the newer authors like Michele Serros?"

"Still on order. I expect them sometime next week. We can hope."

"When they come in, you should check one out, Juana. I love Michele Serros, she's so cool."

"She is a Mexican author?"

"Latina, from the United States." Xochitl pointed to the poster where the author's face sat in a little square. "One day, I'm going to write a book."

"I believe it," I said. "When you do, you have to tell me, okay?"

She smiled so much her eyes squinted. "Deal."

"Can I help you with something in particular today?" Ms. Dillon asked.

"Would you read this and let us know how to research custody?" Xochitl pointed to me. "Juana needs to do something about this issue."

Ms. Dillon read the petition. "Hmm. I'd say start by researching the facility manuals and law books on child custody. They're on the top shelf in the back. You can work there." She pointed to a table a few feet in front of a smaller glass-enclosed area. The door said, "Librarian," with stickers of books on the window.

"Can we have a couple of sheets of paper?" Xochitl said and followed Ms. Dillon to her office.

Gina poked her head through the open front door, wearing fresh pink lip gloss that she probably stole from someone. She glanced to her right and left before stepping inside.

"Mouse, tell Dillon I'll be in the back, doing a report." Her thick ponytail bounced sideways when she rushed down the short hallway to the tables.

Xochitl returned. "We've only got thirty minutes left, so we need to work fast. Go find the manuals labeled "Facility" in the reference section. They're on the right side of the table, up top. Bring me the binders, I'll look up the laws. After I find what we need, you take the books back to the shelf, okay?" She pointed to the middle of the room.

Rows of bookshelves surrounded the table where Gina sat, head down, drumming her fingers against her folder. I didn't want her to see me, in case she was meeting Jester or Bruja. There was a back door across from the table so someone could sneak in if they wanted. I tiptoed behind a tall shelf and made my way around to the right side. A short rubber step stool was on the carpeted floor.

Only six feet and one bookcase stood between Gina and me. I stepped on the stool to reach the top shelf, lifted one thick book, and pressed it against my chest. I found the three-ring binder marked Facility Manual and picked it up. The back door creaked open. I froze.

Between the open spaces on the shelf, I watched the door open slowly. CO Wozzy poked his head between the opening like a big turtle. Gina sprang from her seat, grabbed his hand, and led him to the table.

My palm gripped the binder. I gulped, tried not to breathe, but my legs and arms quivered.

Wozzy sat next to Gina, shoulder to shoulder. Gina's long bangs fell forward when she brushed her fingers against his forehead and leaned against his rumpled tan uniform shirt.

The book grew heavier by the second. If they knew I saw them together, they could make my life more miserable than it already was in San Bueno. I didn't even want to imagine how much more. But I couldn't turn away.

Wozzy unzipped his heavy jacket and slid a manila envelope out of his pocket. He placed it on the table. Gina grabbed it and slid it onto her lap while she kissed him on the cheek. Then she pulled away and checked inside the envelope, which disappeared underneath her sweatshirt.

Wozzy's face relaxed into a dumb droopy smile. He moved in to kiss Gina, but she drew her head back, took his hand, and put it on her lap.

The book, solid against my inner arm, grew weightier. Dust from the shelf danced before my nose like a mosquito waiting to bite. I blew it away in soft puffs, terrified I might sneeze.

Gina's hand disappeared into Wozzy's lap, but her arm moved faster and faster. He slouched into the chair. My arm trembled from the load of the book. I pressed myself against the shelf, held my breath.

Ms. Dillon's shoes thumped across the floor. Gina jerked her hand to the top of the table, moved her chair away from Wozzy.

"CO Wozinsky, I didn't see you come in." Ms. Dillon adjusted her eyeglasses. "Nor you, Gina Jones."

He cleared his throat. "Oh, came through the back door. Just looking around, making sure everything is okay."

"Why would you come in through the back door and not look for me?" Ms. Dillon crossed her arms and gave him a look like my mother did when she scolded my brothers for telling lies.

Wozzy rose from the chair and lumbered out.

Gina smiled her bright teeth up at Ms. Dillon. "I didn't see you so I told Ivanov to tell you I was here."

"Exactly who I'm looking for, Ms. Jones."

Ms. Dillon moved in my direction behind the first row of shelves. I braced the book and binder against my stomach while my legs shook. It was too late to hide anywhere.

"There you are. I think we found something to help you with your letter."

Gina darted behind Ms. Dillon, glared up at me. "How long you been there, Mouse?"

TWENTY-EIGHT

"Hey. How long were you spying on me?" Gina asked.

"I didn't spy." I licked my dry lips while I waited at the doorway to leave the library. "I had to put away a book."

Gina's blue eyes narrowed. "Yeah, right."

"What're you talking about?" Xochitl said.

Gina's lip curled. "Mind your fucken business."

The class bell rang long and shrill. Gina darted out the door and into the quad. Xochitl handed me a sheet of paper with page numbers and another pass.

"We'll come tomorrow and look these up," she said as we stood by the door. "What's up with Gina?"

"Move it out," a CO shouted from outside the building.

I rushed to Mariposa's line. Gina stopped in front of CO Wozzy and pointed at me. He stretched his neck to the right to look. I prayed Gina believed me. If she didn't, I knew she'd take revenge the way she did with all her victims.

Gina must have told him I saw them together. What if she got CO Wozzy to make something up so he could lock me in the seg unit? Or worse, he could lock me in a room with Jester and Bruja, let them beat me up. My neck tightened into a cramp just thinking about what he could do.

"Juana." Xochitl pushed into my shoulder. "What the hell's going on?"

"I tell you later."

Wozzy reminded me of the leering men in the restaurant when I worked in Mexicali. The manager, a vulgar older woman with jewelry that clanked louder than her shoes, didn't care I was fourteen years old as long as I worked fast. The drunken men thought nothing of pulling me onto their lap. They'd ask me how much I cost with their foul-smelling breath and slurred words.

When I complained to the manager, she glanced at me up and down and said I could afford better clothes and shoes if I made a few men happy. Other waitresses flirted and let the drunks rub their butts for extra tips. I quit and worked at another restaurant.

There was no way to get away from Gina and CO Wozzy. I couldn't quit San Bueno.

Gina joined the line and stood next to Bruja. They were three girls away from where I stood. I had to return to our living unit, back to my depressing but safe room.

Our line moved forward until we passed the Gaviota living unit. A radio crackled with Sgt. Cuellar's name. I glanced back and found him a few feet behind me. My shoulders tensed. He better not ask me about anything in front of the other girls.

A van zoomed to the front of the line and blocked our path. Two COs jumped out of the front seat. One signaled to Ms. Montes to move us over to the curb. CO Isadora jogged toward me. My body went rigid, but she passed me, stopped at Sgt. Cuellar.

"Sit on the curb," Ms. Montes told the group. "Now."

"Ms. Gonzales," CO Isadora said to Jester. "Come over here. Need to pat you down."

"Oh, hell no." Jester stepped back. "What'd I do?"

"Cooperate, okay?" CO Isadora motioned to another CO.

"No way." Jester crossed her arms.

"It's a simple pat down," the man CO said and put his hand on her arm.

She twisted away from him. In two seconds, he shoved her to the ground, put his knee on her back, and pulled her arms behind her to put on the handcuffs.

"Take your fucking hands off me," she yelled.

Sgt. Cuellar called Gina's name. "Come here, Ms. Jones."

"What's happening, Sgt. C?" Gina clutched the book in her hand. Her eyes fluttered. "What's this about?"

"Stand over here and put the book on the ground," CO Isadora said.

Gina glanced at Jester struggling on the ground, pebbles of asphalt dotting her cheek. She dropped the book. CO Isadora picked it up and shook it out.

"Nothing here, Sarg."

"Cuff her and pat her down."

The curb full of girls craned their necks to take a closer look.

"Oooh, busted," Xochitl said in a low voice.

"Gina's gonna get it now, fucken smack, thinks her shit don't stink," a few other girls said.

CO Isadora patted Gina down, starting at her head, then under her arms, down and around her waist, hips, legs, and ankles. "Pull out your bra and shake it."

Gina cocked her head and crossed her arms. "I'm not gonna shake it out here. You can do that in my cell."

"That's fucked up," Bruja yelled and stood up from the curb.

Ms. Montes strode over to Bruja. "Sit down." She unbuckled her can of mace.

Everyone got quiet. Ms. Montes would use her mace without a second thought.

CO Isadora stepped closer to Gina. "Turn away from the male staff and pull the front out, or I'll have to do it."

Gina stood there until CO Isadora pulled at the front of her bra. An envelope floated to the ground. CO Isadora passed it to Sgt. Cuellar.

He opened the envelope, glanced inside. "Put Jones in the van."

Gina hung her head, her ponytail swaying to the side like a broken branch. Whatever was in the letter wasn't a secret anymore.

While the CO escorted her to the van, I noticed Sgt. Cuellar looking back at Mr. Jay near the Gaviota living unit. He tilted his head toward where CO Wozinsky stood stretching his neck to see what had happened.

"Everyone up, the show's over," Ms. Montes said. "The first group of ten girls go in and stand by your door."

Nervous laughs and whispers traveled up and down the hall. I said a silent prayer that Bruja wouldn't attack me while we stood in the hall waiting to be locked in our rooms.

Mrs. Shaffer locked everyone in except me. "Ivanov, I need you for cleanup." She pointed to the dayroom.

My whole face drooped. The dayroom was the last place I wanted to be.

The next group of ten girls, including Babydoll, marched past the staff desk. They glared at me. I grabbed paper towels and wiped down the chairs, but I could feel their questions. Why is she the only one out? Dayroom cleanup is after program time, not before.

Why didn't staff think about those things? It was dangerous for me to be out in the dayroom right after the incident on the roadway. Bruja knew I saw Gina in the library with Wozzy. She was probably thinking up ways to make sure I kept my mouth shut.

Once everyone was locked into their cells, Ms. Montes gestured to me to follow her into the back staff office. "Sit down." She pointed at the chair while taking off her jacket. "Sgt. Cuellar wants to talk with you. I'll be sitting in since I'm your counselor."

"Why me, Miss?"

The door buzzed like a squawking crow. Sgt. Cuellar crossed the dayroom into the staff office. He smiled, pulled a chair around, and sat on it backward. His chest leaned against the back of the seat.

"Ms. Ivanov, how're you doing?"

"Fine."

"Listen, I need to talk to you about Gina and CO Wozinsky. Ms. Dillon mentioned that both of them were in the library today. You were there too."

The mint of his chewing gum wafted towards me as he moved closer. "What did you see?"

"I'm there to find out about custody things." My hand touched my pocket where my letter sat.

"What custody?" He put his hand out. "Let me see."

My hand twitched. How would I explain the letter using my real last name, Flores?

He took my letter, without unfolding it, and passed it to Ms. Montes.

"We can talk about that later." She tucked the letter into her pocket.

I sighed from the close call.

"Sergeant, you were saying?" she said.

"We found contraband on Gina and need to know where she's getting the stuff from." Sgt. Cuellar turned to me. "Any ideas?"

I shook my head while staring at the patch of brown flooring between the Sergeant and me.

"Did you see CO Wozinsky sit next to Gina in the library today?"

"Tell him what you saw, Ivanov," Ms. Montes said.

Mind your own business, keep out of staff's way, stay out of trouble, ratas get beat up and put on the leva. I heard the rules in Xochitl's and Jester's voices.

"Listen, we know Gina Jones deals in contraband," he said. "She sells narcotics throughout the facility. She rarely has visitors, so she must be receiving the stuff from someone within the place. See anything unusual between the CO and ward Jones?"

My face warmed. My upper lip broke out in a sweat; I wiped it and folded my hands in my lap to keep my leg from jiggling.

Sgt. Cuellar crossed his arms in front of his chest. "Why're you nervous?"

It was dishonest not to tell him what I saw, but I just wanted to do my time and leave as fast as possible.

"Ms. Ivanov, were you aware that Paula Alvarez not only attempted to hang herself but took pills too? Probably the ones Gina brought into the facility," Sgt. Cuellar said.

"Babydoll took pills?"

"Showed up in her blood test. Ask her, she's coming back to the unit tomorrow."

"She is? She's okay now?"

"You don't want drugs in the unit, do you?" Sgt. Cuellar said. "What if other girls end up like Paula and aren't so lucky? They could die."

"This is serious," Ms. Montes said. "It's important to tell us what you saw in the library between Gina and the CO."

What if someone found out I gave staff information? I needed to get out of this place as fast as possible, but I had to live here. I had to keep myself safe, so I could keep Katrina safe. I remained quiet, hanging my head.

"If you want to talk later, ask staff to call me," Sgt. Cuellar said.

Didn't he realize what giving him information meant for the rest of my time here?

He walked out of the staff office. Ms. Montes shut the door behind him.

"You know more about Gina and CO Wozinsky, and I wonder why you don't want to talk about it."

She's going to yell at me, tell me I'm not fooling her. She'll read the custody petition and say she knew I was a liar all along.

She swung open the office door. "Mrs. Shaffer, sending Ivanov down."

I rushed out of the office, across the dayroom floor to the staff desk where Mrs. Shaffer spoke on the telephone.

"Take a seat, Ivanov."

Now that no one was out in the dayroom, I thought about

asking her about the garden idea, but she didn't look too happy. It would be better to wait though I yearned to be outside, feel the sun on my back, watch the clouds without bars in the way. I longed to see vegetables grow, anything, even the weeds. I just wanted out of these walls.

From my seat, I could see down Alpha Hall. Two COs came out of Gina's room, one of them carrying a full paper bag.

Ms. Montes came out of the staff office and stood above me, the letter from Alek's mother in one hand, my case file in the other. "I don't have time to read this now." She slid my letter into the folder.

"Juana, I want you to remember something," Mrs. Shaffer said. "There are staff rules and inmate rules. You have to decide which ones you want to live by. When you figure it out, come and talk to me. Deal?"

I nodded just so she'd let me go. If she and Ms. Montes read the letter from Alek's mother, they'd ask me about the name "Juana Maria Flores." If I didn't tell them the truth, the question of whose rules I'd follow would be answered. Either way, I was in deep trouble.

TWENTY-NINE

Mrs. Shaffer placed the living unit on lockdown because of the drugs and contraband they found in the first few rooms. On the second day of lockdown, the girls shouted out of their rooms that the searches took too long. Staff yelled back, and Mrs. Shaffer acted angrier than I'd ever seen before.

No one except the work crew was allowed out to clean and make trays. Bruja and LaLa were on room restrictions. Jester and Gina were in the segregation unit, which was fine by me because I could talk freely with Xochitl and Mariana.

I watched the van park on the curb outside of our unit from the dayroom windows. The CO slid the door open, and Jester stepped out in handcuffs. I stopped sweeping. She was back. I rushed to find a seat in the TV rows, hoping Jester wouldn't see me from the hallway.

"New room assignment, Ms. Gonzales," Mrs. Shaffer said to the CO escorting Jester. "Take her to B hall."

"What the hell, Shaffer," Jester said.

"If you don't like it, the CO can take you back to your room in seg."

"Psst. Whatever."

"Are you done yet?" Mrs. Shaffer turned to me. "Take it down to your room too."

Jester yanked her elbow away from the CO, turned around to see who Mrs. Shaffer was talking to, but the CO was faster than she was and pushed her down the hall. I loitered a couple of minutes near the TV rows, pretending to pick up trash.

When her cell door locked, I moved down Alpha Hall and waited for Mrs. Shaffer. Once inside, I opened my window to listen to the daily gossip. Jester's friends called out to her from their windows eager to find out the news in the seg unit.

"Check it out; the Sarg put Gina at the end of the detention wing. She's incommunicado."

Leaning closer to my open window ledge, I listened to Jester.

"Asshole Wozzy got busted too. Fucken fat fool. He's on admin leave. They got him dead to rights." Her howling laugh came out in snorts. "Stupid ass."

"You know what that means," Bruja said.

"Yeah, means you shoulda got rid of everything."

"We need another connection."

"Got it covered. The staff find anything?"

"They tossed our rooms yesterday. Didn't find nothin' important in ours 'cept in the norteña's room. She had a stinger."

"Wachala, making stingers like a banger," Jester said.

I thumped on Xochitl's wall. "You no tell me staff searched your room."

"They tossed it when you were *cleaning* the dayroom."

"Why you say it like that?"

"I'm sending you a kite."

Whenever we had something to say that we couldn't talk

about through the windows we sent notes to each other. Within a minute, Xochitl's kite, attached to a long piece of string and a paper clip, slid under my door. I crouched down and slid the note off the hook.

The COs searched seven rooms down this hall—all the Chicanas except yours. I didn't see you in the dayroom while I sat cuffed on the floor, but I saw Sgt. C and Ms. Montes in the staff office. I'm sure you were in there too.

I scribbled on the other side of the kite: *I didn't tell them anything. No one asked me about you. Te lo juro.* I tugged on the string so that she could pull the kite back to her room.

"Swear on your daughter?" Xochitl said.

"Si, te lo juro."

"What did they talk about?"

Could I trust her? If the information I had made its way to staff, I'd need to go into protective custody, be a pesay, stay behind this locked door, staring at bricks, always watching my back.

The kite hit my door again. *I'm facing a time add for the stinger, Juana.*

We talk tomorrow at the library, during second period, okay? I sent the kite back and thought about a plan.

Hidden between bookshelves, we sat on the floor, hunched over and whispering. Even then I was scared someone might hear us. I leaned over to Xochitl and told her what I saw between Gina and CO Wozzy.

"Sergeant C and Ms. Montes wanted me to tell them what I

saw. They said Gina sells drugs and Babydoll took some. They said they found them in her blood."

Xochitl shook her head. "If you tell, you'll have Gina, Jester, and crooked staff coming after you."

"Mrs. Shaffer told me I need to decide what to do. And Ms. Montes asked me again about Gina. I need her help to find out how to stop Mrs. Ivanov from taking Katrina." I rubbed the sides of my face. What was I going to do?

I had not felt so helpless since the day I went looking for Alek after I returned to LA from Calexico. He wasn't at our place, so I went to Anna's apartment. She screamed when she saw me, "My son, my son. You killed him."

When I asked where he was, she slapped me. Neighbors gathered near, everyone talking, trying to calm her as she cried. Until the police came and arrested me, I didn't know what was going on.

"Xochitl, Ms. Montes will find out I lied about being married to Alek and had a fake card. She won't help me if I don't help her. What should I do?"

"Let me think." She leaned her elbow on her knee.

Silently, I prayed while Xochitl tapped her fingers against the side of her head. What had I gotten myself into? I didn't want to see Gina and Wozzy rubbing on each other. I didn't want to know about gangs, drugs, fights, the crooked staff, but I couldn't avoid them, not in San Bueno.

"Got it," Xochitl said. "Tell Sgt. C you didn't see anything except Gina and Wozzy sitting at the table. Tell him *I* told you about the envelope she received and them stroking each other."

"No, you'll be in trouble with Jester and her friends."

"Look, she already hates me because I'm a norteña. She doesn't care what happens to Gina now, she's busted. And she'll be happy Wozzy gets fired."

"But, you have only two months left. Why you do this?"

"I'm facing a thirty-day time add to my sentence if I'm found guilty for having the stinger. I have information the staff wants, so I can trade the info for my infraction. They can drop it to a minor violation. You know, tit for tat."

"I don't understand."

"Tit for tat means this for that, like 'I give you this if you give me that.' Check it out. I was here in the library too. I'll say I went to the bookcases to look for something and saw Gina and Wozzy.

"Sgt. C will have three witnesses who saw them sitting next to each other and me saying I saw them doing nasty stuff and passing an envelope. Better yet, I'll tell them Wozzy snuck into the kitchen one time to see Gina, tell them Mrs. Shaffer knows too." Xochitl sat back, crossing her arms. "Anyway, I'm sure Gina's going to give him up in return for a lighter sentence. She's not stupid."

Gina and Wozzy would be punished, I wouldn't need to be involved, and Xochitl would receive a lesser violation for her stinger.

"You are a good friend, Xochitl, and so smart."

"This will work, but it's gonna take a lot of talking to explain your fake name and green card to Montes."

She was right. That was my next problem.

THIRTY

The sound of tennis shoes padded down the hallway. I peeked out of my wicket. Mrs. Shaffer. Babydoll walked behind her. They stopped at the empty cell across from Xochitl's room. She stared at her shower shoes while Mrs. Shaffer unlocked the door.

As soon as the cell door shut and Mrs. Shaffer walked away, the chatter of chisme began outside my open window. Girls wanted to know why Babydoll wasn't in the mental health unit.

"Babydoll," Jester called out. "I'll never hurt you again. Te lo juro."

There was no response, which was a relief. I didn't want to hear her give Jester another chance. I shut my window and sat on my bed remembering how Alek made me the same promises the first time he hit me.

After we moved to LA, he spent more time with his friends. His drinking got him fired from his construction job. He was always angry about one thing or another and every day he couldn't find a job, he got worse.

The first time Alek pushed me he said he was sorry, swore he would never hurt me again. Tears shone in his eyes. Afterward he brought me a bunch of pretty flowers. A month later, he slapped me. He swore on his mother and all that was holy he wouldn't lose his temper again—but he did. After the third time, he said if I didn't nag so much about his drinking and spending, he wouldn't have to hit me.

Always my fault, or the job, or his mother's demands. I began to tiptoe around him, trying to be silent, keeping Katrina quiet. Alek was now two people in my memory. The Alek from Calexico and the Alek from Los Angeles. The sweet one, and the violent one. One who loved me and one who hurt me.

I needed to convince Babydoll to stay away from Jester so she wouldn't get hurt again. Then I remembered my mother's dicho after my friends argued at school. "Consejo no pedido consejo mal oido." Advice not asked for is advice poorly heard. Why would Babydoll listen to me?

There had to be a way I could let her know I cared. I'd feel terrible if she hurt herself again. I flipped over an old worksheet and began writing.

Dear Babydoll,

I am glad you are back. I pray for you and hope you are well. Please do not hurt yourself again. Talk to someone instead. Sinceremente, Juana Maria Ivanov

I wasn't good at drawing, but I put a happy face on the paper and folded it into a kite. I'd pass it to her at school movement.

"Can I go, please?" I asked the unit cook. "I can't be late this morning." I rushed to finish my work behind the kitchen counter.

"Sure, Juana. Go on, I'll take care of the rest."

I ran to join the school movement line in the front yard.

"Where you going so fast?" Jester grabbed at my hand and missed.

Babydoll stood next to Xochitl in line, in the order of room assignments. I slipped into my spot behind her, whispered to her to watch for staff, and tapped Babydoll on the shoulder. She turned. Weariness filled her eyes, dark circles underneath.

"This is from me." I pushed the kite into the palm of her hand.

"Montes," Xochitl whispered.

Babydoll dropped her hand to her side, with the kite clutched inside. I clasped my hands behind my back.

"Move it up," Ms. Montes shouted at the group.

When we arrived at the school area, we stopped and waited while the COs directed everyone ahead of our line. The girls looked like blue streams flowing from the black asphalt onto the grey concrete and disappearing into brown buildings.

Sgt. Cuellar stood near the flagpole in the school quad and nodded to me when I walked by.

"What's up Sgt. C?" Xochitl asked him as we passed.

"Ms. Anaya, Ivanov."

Babydoll turned to us. Her eyes narrowed at Xochitl, glancing over to me before she left the line to shuffle to her class.

Sgt. Cuellar moved alongside me. I looked straight ahead but he bent towards my ear. "Need to talk to you later."

My insides shuddered. I moved on stiff legs to my classroom.

Could I make him believe the lie Xochitl gave me when he called me in for questioning again? He had to believe me. My baby depended on my story.

If any of the girls found out I talked to Sgt. Cuellar, they'd mark me a rata. My remaining time would be like playing dodgeball, watching out for everyone's moves. They could jump me during shower time, chow movement, or hit me in the school line. I had to be extra careful. Someone still had the missing fork.

I stood outside of the classroom door with my English teacher, shaded by one of the few trees among the rows of school buildings. Two COs stood on the narrow patch of grass which separated the two facing classrooms. They watched us when we left our classes, making sure no one stepped off the concrete onto the strip of dried-up lawn.

Another CO strode towards our classroom, calling the teacher over to him. She nodded and then turned, bending a finger at me. My heart flinched. I moved out of line, stood next to him.

"Medical appointment. Follow me," he said.

I hadn't received any movement pass for the clinic, but I followed him to a van parked at the curb near the school's flagpole. It reminded me of the one I sat in for three hours when I came to San Bueno. My stomach fluttered. It must have remembered too. I stepped on the running board and curled into the seat, chewed at my fingernail.

"No one will see you talking to Sarg."

He must have received more information about what happened in the library. I let out my breath and ran the lines through my head once more. *I saw Gina and Wozzy at the table. I stood behind the bookcase while they sat close to each other, their shoulders touching.* Those were the only words I'd say.

We walked up a small stairway behind the clinic building. Dim lights glowed in the hallway. Disinfectant hit my nose and stuck in my throat. The CO tapped on a door. Ms. Montes opened it.

"Come in, Juana. Let's talk," Sgt. Cuellar's voice said.

He sat behind an old metal desk and pointed to a folding chair in front.

"You know more than what you've told me. What did you see in the library between CO Wozinsky and ward Gina Jones?"

I repeated my lines. "Xochitl Anaya was with me in the library. She saw more than me."

"Ms. Dillon said you were at the bookshelves near Gina and she left Xochitl at the front table," Ms. Montes said.

I shrugged, struggling to keep a smile on my face. "She says she sees more." I hid my quaking hands between my knees.

"Hmm." Sgt. Cuellar leaned back in his chair, "Juana, is it true CO Wozinsky visited your unit one day and Mrs. Shaffer found him in the kitchen with Gina?"

"Yes, I worked in the dayroom and saw him outside the unit. He combed his hair before he came inside. He pushed the door lock in so the buzzer didn't go off. Xochitl and Mariana seen too."

Ms. Montes shook her head, her lips in a flat line. Sgt. C pushed the walkie-talkie button on his shirt and called for a CO to take Xochitl out of her classroom.

"When Anaya gets here, the CO will take you back to class. Thanks for your help, Juana."

"It's okay, Sgt. C."

Tit for tat, I remembered.

"Oh, before I forget." Ms. Montes opened her black duffle bag and pulled out an envelope.

The custody letter. I held my breath. She'd find out my real name and question me in front of Sergeant Cuellar. They'd find out I lied then, think I lied to them now.

"I haven't read the letter yet. We can go over it during our counseling time tomorrow."

THIRTY-ONE

The dismissal bell screeched like the lechuza who sat in our old cedar tree back in Santa Isabel. I missed watching the owl, hearing the morning crow of the rooster, and the chickens scratching for food. No birds lived around San Bueno.

I left my classroom and joined the school movement line for my unit. I searched for Xochitl but didn't see her anywhere in the quad. Maybe she was still talking with Sgt. Cuellar. If so, that was a sign her plan worked.

"Move out to the roadway," a CO yelled to the girls in our group.

Babydoll rushed towards me. She moved so fast, I braced myself. Had she seen me leave the school area with the CO? Did Bruja send her to fight me?

She stopped in front of me. I stepped back.

"Hey." Her mouth curved into a smile. "I can help you with your English worksheets. If you want."

I exhaled. Even though I had help already, I nodded so she'd know I appreciated her offer.

"Firme." She bobbed her chin and tucked a strand of hair behind her ear.

I didn't know why she was so friendly with me until I remembered she must've read the kite I gave her. My words must've cheered her up. I walked all the way back to the unit more relaxed than I had been in days.

Ms. Montes and Mrs. Shaffer sat at the staff desk when we came inside with the escorting staff. We stood at our cell doors waiting to be locked in and counted.

"The unit lockdown's over," Mrs. Shaffer said. "I expect you all to behave when you come out later."

Babydoll stood across from me and mouthed, "dayroom," before smiling at me again. I thought about the questions I'd ask her so she'd know I was interested in her life.

A few minutes later, Xochitl's door unlocked with a noisy click. She thumped on her wall. "Incoming."

I jumped off my bed and waited at the bottom of my door. A kite slid under the narrow opening.

Check it out, the plan worked. I told Sgt. C I'd take a polygraph to prove what I saw. So what if I flunk, he already reduced my violation.

"Gracias a Dios," I said out loud.

"No, gracias to me."

I laughed at her joke but still made the sign of the cross over my chest. "Go to your window."

"What's up?" she said.

"Babydoll said she'd help me with my worksheets in the day-room today. Is that okay?"

Silence. I repeated my question.

"Do what you want, but why do you want to be friends with her anyways?"

"She needs help. Sometimes she's like that baby duck Ping I read about in a storybook at the library."

"Oh my god, a duck. She plays the jailhouse games and she's not Miss Innocent, you know."

"But she wanted to die, and she's so young. You and I are friends forever. I can be friends with her too."

"Friends forever? Really?"

"Si, por vida."

"Program," Ms. Montes yelled into the hallway. "Get ready."

"Now's the time to ask Shaffer about your garden idea," Xochitl said.

I grabbed my list of reasons for a garden, my worksheets, and a sweatshirt before I stood at my door wicket. Remembering the photo of Katrina, I lifted it carefully off my locker door, brushing off the dried-up toothpaste glue.

Mr. Jay, the staff from Gaviota, stood at the desk at the top of the hall. I didn't see Mrs. Shaffer. Now I'd have to wait for her to come back to tell her about the backyard garden idea.

Whispers and giggles from the girls in the back of the hall floated to the top of the line. "Oooh, Ms. Montes's man is on duty. She'll be nice tonight," someone said.

"I'd flash him my tits if he played like that," one of the girls commented while a few others said all the other things they'd show him.

"Knock it off," Ms. Montes said.

These girls always talked about sex, boyfriends, girlfriends, and partying. Whenever the girls talked about those things, I thought about all I had missed.

I skipped years of my life, from age twelve when Mamá died

to meeting Alek three years later. During the time in between I struggled, along with my family, to keep a roof over our heads. I didn't have time to do the things teenagers did.

Alek gave me my first trembling in the stomach feeling, my first kiss, my first everything. Anytime my cousin Maribel invited me to quinceñeras, shopping, or dances, I said I had plans somewhere with Alek. It was always Alek.

Sometimes I think about sex, too, especially when I dream of him and our days together before we moved to LA, but I miss the hugging, kissing, and lying in bed part with him more.

San Bueno Correctional had rules like "no handholding, no hugging, no kissing." It was one of the harder ones to follow because as a child, I held my parents' hand or my brothers', or Lupe's. At school, I held hands with my friends. Later, I hugged and kissed Alek and Katrina. It's natural to touch other people.

Brushing or styling someone's hair was the closest thing to touching we could do without getting into trouble with the staff. Many of the Black girls liked to use the flat iron and made their friends' hair pretty or made tight braids over their heads in different patterns. Mariana let me do her hair when Jester and the Latina gangbangers were on room restrictions. She liked when I wove her thick wavy hair into French braids.

The best hairstylists on the unit traded canteen or other favors with the girls. Mariana started styling some of the girls' hair after Chantilla mentioned her curled hair looked "dope," which I didn't understand, but Xochitl said that meant the best.

"Alpha hall, move forward," Ms. Montes said, interrupting my memories.

We entered the dayroom. Babydoll sat in one of the back TV rows and put her things on a chair next to her own. Xochitl sat against the wall on the other side of the dayroom by herself. I took a seat next to Babydoll.

"Look, this is my daughter, Katrina." I placed the photo in her hand.

She gazed at the picture for a long time. "So cute. I have a little sister. She's six."

"You do? How many you have in your family?"

"Family?" Babydoll snickered before she looked away. "My mom's in the pinta, my half-sister and brother are in foster care."

"Your mamá is in prison? Why?"

"In and out ever since I can remember. Mostly using or selling drugs. She's locked up for armed robbery right now." Babydoll bit at her thumbnail. The skin around her slender fingers was pink and ragged.

"You don't have to tell me more if you don't want to."

She lifted the photograph close to her eyes, held it for a long time. "Pretty baby. So tiny." Her eyes moistened. She lifted her chin and sniffled.

"It's okay. I understand you have your heart broken, and you are sad."

A scowl wrinkled her forehead. "What?"

"Did you try to hurt yourself because of Jester?"

"Pfft, Jester's a player. All players lie."

"You miss your sister and brother then? Your mother?"

She turned away from me. I bit my lip. I'd asked too many questions. "I miss my family, especially my Katrina."

"Do you ever wonder what she's doing?" Babydoll asked.

"Every day I think of her. Every minute."

Tears came up but I blinked them back, smiling at Babydoll because I didn't want her to feel sadder. She dropped her head into her folded arms, leaned against the back of the chair in front of her.

I don't know why, but I touched her shoulder. "It's okay. I know my sister Lupe takes good care of her, but I wish she'd write to me."

"You're lucky, you have a sister who can take care of your baby," she said. "I've never been lucky."

"Don't worry." I patted her back. "Things will be okay."

"No, they won't. I'm pregnant."

"Ay, no." My words came out too loud but no one seemed to notice us. How could a baby survive an attempted suicide and drugs? "Es un milagro," I whispered while making the sign of the cross over my heart. "How many months you are?"

Babydoll moved her hand from beneath her long hair and held up four fingers. "Almost. That's what the doctor said."

"How you don't know before?"

She turned to see where the others girls sat before she answered. "Drugs mess up your period. I was using before the jura busted me. I really fucked things up for a baby."

Babydoll slumped back into her chair and sighed. A small rise in her stomach lifted and fell. She pulled her loose tee shirt down to cover up the bump.

"When do you parole?"

"Montes recommended I do the maximum time. Eighteen months."

"Who will take care of the baby?"

"Probably be messed up because of the drugs and the stupid shit I did. I don't have a family. I can't do this."

"No, it's a miracle the baby's alive."

"They're giving me extra food and gigantic prenatal vitamins to keep it alive. At the same time, they tell me to think about getting an abortion. Fucked up, huh? I gotta decide in a couple of days."

My breath sucked into my chest. "Don't do that. Have the baby."

"You just don't know how it is." She picked up her papers and clothing from the chair next to her. "I have nothing or nobody for a kid."

I stared at her as she dragged her feet across the dayroom floor and sat curled up in another chair. What could I do to convince Babydoll to keep her child? I had to help her baby live.

THIRTY-TWO

The ice maker in the corner of the dining room churned while the refrigerators hummed. Ms. Montes flipped open my folder while we sat in the empty kitchen. She held the custody letter up. "Juana Maria *Flores*?" The edge in her voice was as tight as her smile.

My fingers gripped the sides of the hard plastic chair. I swallowed to wet my dry throat. "Yes. I'm not married."

"You lied?" Ms. Montes shook her head. "Tell me the truth. Everything."

"I bought a fake green card in Mexicali so I go with Alek." I stared at the floor. "Uh, so we could raise our baby together. When the police arrested me, they took the card. No one asked me for my real name."

"And you let them believe your lie?"

She didn't understand. How could I tell the police I had a counterfeit card? They'd call immigration and take me to Tijuana without any questions. Alek's mother had told the police that Katrina was an American citizen and she wanted her brought back to LA. I told the police I had a green card but Alek had hidden it from me. They had already searched our apartment and found my card.

"After your board hearing, Mrs. Snow told me she sent a request to immigration about your green card status. You could have told her the truth then, saved her the trouble. It's a crime to be here without proper documents or with fake papers," Ms. Montes said.

Images of an immigration van showing up at the front of San Bueno made me grit my teeth. I hung my head. My knees knocked against the table. "What will they do to me, Miss?"

"The Correctional Board can give you more time."

I took a shaky breath to loosen the tightness in my chest. "I lied because I didn't want Alek's mother to have Katrina. Sometimes she'd say she wanted to go back to Russia and that Alek could find a better job there with relatives. What if she took Katrina with her? How would I get her back?"

Ms. Montes wrote something in my file. "This could become a court battle especially since Mrs. Ivanov hired an attorney. You're in prison, with fake documents, and no family in the United States. Once you parole, you're to be deported."

My jaw clenched at the word "deported." *Don't cry. Breathe.* I remembered what the law books said. "They can't just take my child away from me. The laws say I have rights as a mother. I want to tell the custody judge my side, in person."

Ms. Montes tilted her head, stared at me for a few seconds. "I'll have to ask Mrs. Snow."

"My sister takes care of my daughter very good. She's been with her Tia Lupe for months now."

"Does she have temporary legal guardianship? Even relatives have to go to court so they can have guardianship of a child."

"Nobody in my town in Mexico asks for papers. When I leave here, I'll go back to Santa Isabel to pick her up."

"Since your sister doesn't have legal guardianship, Mrs. Ivanov may have a better case. Your daughter is a US citizen and you're not."

"But, I'm her mother. She belongs with me."

She huffed and scribbled more notes. My neck burned hot making my skin tingle. I slapped my hand against my bouncing knee before the table shook.

Ms. Montes pushed my file aside. "Let's talk about something else, something I observed last night. You were talking to Paula Alvarez, Babydoll you girls call her, and I noticed both of you were on the verge of tears. I'm concerned, especially since she attempted suicide."

The scene in Babydoll's room flashed through my mind. I remembered the way her head hung crookedly on her skinny body, her lips puffy and purple. I shivered. My hands moved to my own neck.

"My first time seeing an attempted suicide." Ms. Montes ran her red fingernails through the side of her head, tucking stray hairs from her ponytail behind her ear. "Did she tell you anything last night?"

Ms. Montes's eyes searched my face like I had the answers. I didn't want to tell her what Babydoll said about being pregnant, the staff had to know already. Couldn't Ms. Montes put herself in Babydoll's place, figure out the reason why she was depressed? She was the counselor.

"I tried talking to Alvarez, but she says she's okay," I said, frowning.

It unsettled me to see the uneasiness on her face. She's supposed to know what to do. I glanced up at the windows lining the top of the brick wall wishing I could climb out.

Ms. Montes sighed. "Go back to your room."

My mind swirled with the thought of Alek's mother taking my Katrina to Russia. Every time I thought Katrina got closer to me, something happened to move her away. I had to stop Anna.

The darkened hallway looked gloomier than usual. I rested against the brick wall next to my cell, waited for Ms. Montes to unlock my door. I knew she wasn't going to help me.

In this place, there were no warm shoulders to cry on, no hands to hold, no hugs, no one to whisper things will work out, and no "I love you" to carry me through another day.

She locked me into my cell without a word. I didn't have the energy to change into my pajamas so I lay awake staring at Katrina's pictures on my wall. If I'm not in court, the Judge will think I don't care about my baby. There had to be some way to let them know I wanted her to remain with Lupe.

Xochitl would know what I could do. I grabbed my shoe, used it to tap on the wall she and I shared. I pressed my ear against the brick.

Her bed squeaked. "What's up?"

"I don't think Ms. Montes can help me with the letter from the attorney. What do you think I should do?"

"Demand to go to the court hearing. How else is the judge going to know how you feel? I'll help you file a grievance."

"They don't like it when we write complaints. They'll call me a troublemaker."

"Remember when I filed the grievance for giving us only

eight sanitary napkins or tampons a month, while they used a bunch of the pads for cleaning the kitchen grill? The committee agreed with me. Now it's up to the administration staff. They decide. You have to at least try."

"Okay, but let's ask Ms. Dillon too. Library, second period?"

"I'll be there."

I grabbed my composition book from my bed and wrote 15 April on the blank page. I added the words "Demand, Legal Guardianship, Notarize" on my list and tucked it back under my mattress. My open window let a burst of night air inside. Sometimes, just breathing in the outside calmed me. I moved to the screen.

One of the streetlights flickered out. The half-moon stood bright white against the black sheet of night. No chisme tonight, not one grillo chirped in the still cold.

I wondered if Lupe showed Katrina the stars and the moon or told her to listen to the night songs of the crickets. Did my baby feel the embrace of the evening air and smell the scent of the squash blossoms in my mother's garden? Did she wonder what happened to me or did she already cuddle against Lupe, believing she's her mother?

The steel frame around the window felt like ice when I pushed it closed. Dropping onto the mattress, I took my pillow, pressed it against my chest and imagined holding Katrina close to me, then Calexico Alek, and then my mother. I reached for my blanket, wrapped it over me, shielding my family from the frigid air. Rocking back and forth, I tried to feel the heat from their bodies seep into mine. Nothing happened. No amount of pretending brought them back to me. I lay down, streams of tears flooding over my face, the chill returning into my empty arms.

THIRTY-THREE

Xochitl picked up a grey plastic binder from the library table where she and I sat. "Ms. Dillon, come look at this. I think I found the right part for Juana's case in the facility manual."

The librarian pushed her glasses up with one hand, steadied the book with the other. She smiled, her fair skin crinkling over her rosy cheeks. "Yes, you're right."

"Read it to me, Xochitl." I moved closer to follow the words in the book:

"It is a legal right of the parent to be present when decisions are made about your child. It is the responsibility of the Sheriff's Department, in the county where you were committed, to transport the offender. Ask your attorney for assistance. You can request a free legal phone call from the unit supervisor or parole agent or contact a public defender for more details."

"Did you have your own attorney or a public defender when you went to court?" Xochitl asked.

"Public defender. I think his name is on my papers. He talked to me one time in juvenile hall and once at court. He said I had a good case to get out because even though I ran from Alek, I came back the next day. But the judge, he didn't think so."

Ms. Dillon unsnapped the rings in the binder and picked up the page. "Show this to your correctional counselor. I'll make you a copy."

Xochitl nodded. "You need to have proof. Keep it in your room, okay?"

They looked happy for me, but I was afraid to be excited for myself.

"You're the smartest girl I know, Xochitl. You're not afraid to ask questions or tell someone what you think."

"I planned to go to college, become a lawyer like my brother, but with my charge hanging over my head, I don't know what'll happen. Juana, you gotta learn to speak up. I won't always be here."

She was right. I didn't speak up to my father or LA Alek or in San Bueno even when I really wanted to say something. The words floated in my head like I was talking to myself. My father expected obedience and when there wasn't any he got angry. With LA Alek I didn't know what to expect. One wrong word could mean a slap in the face. San Bueno was like that too. With Alek, I watched out for only one person. In San Bueno, I had to watch out for many people.

On the way into the Mariposa living unit from school movement, I darted out of line near Mrs. Snow's office. With my pencil ready, I signed the list taped to her office door, ignoring the handwritten message from her: "Did you ask your counselor first?" Ms. Montes was on her days off and my problem couldn't wait. I slipped back into line as a group of girls moved into the dayroom.

"Did you sign up for an appointment?" Xochitl asked.

We sat in the TV rows hidden from the view of Gina and Bruja.

"Yes, five names ahead of me. Maybe next week she'll call me. Lend me some paper? I need to start on a letter to the judge, let him know I disagree with Alek's mother and tell him I'm asking staff to take me to the hearing."

"I'll ask if I can go to my room." Xochitl headed to the staff desk.

Babydoll popped her head over a chair in front of me. "What're you doing?"

Even though Jester wasn't in the unit, I didn't know if Babydoll wanted to warn me about Xochitl being on the leva and remind me I wasn't supposed to sit with her, or if she was really interested in what I was doing.

She left her seat and stood in front of me. "Whose stuff is that?"

"Xochitl's, but you can sit here too. I'm not a gangbanger, so I'm not going to act like one."

Her thin eyebrow arched. She coiled the ends of her long hair around her finger, holding it against her mouth, and stared out to the dayroom. "I don't care about them anymore. I'll sit where I want."

I turned to see where she looked. LaLa, Bruja, and Gina were at the other end of the room playing cards.

"But they'll beat you up. You have to be careful, remember?" I stared at Babydoll's stomach.

Her eyes darkened while her forehead creased. She twisted her hair for a few more seconds before she moved away.

"What did she want?" Xochitl asked, sitting one seat space away from me.

"She says she don't care about Jester and her friends anymore."

Xochitl sucked her teeth and handed me two sheets of paper and a stamp. "Babydoll will be back with Jester in a day or two. She's so weak."

"Maybe she needs to have someone because she doesn't have a family like you. Babydoll needs a friend."

Xochitl rolled her eyes. "Pfft."

"Don't get mad. I'm lucky I'm not alone. I have Katrina, Lupe, you, and Mariana."

"Speaking of Mariana, I haven't seen her all day."

"Maybe she comes out tomorrow."

"Don't hold your breath. Let's start on the letters. Tell me what you want the judge to know and I'll write it down."

After we finished, I handed Xochitl another piece of paper. "Tell me if my English is okay."

Dear Mrs. Anna Ivanov,

I want to keep custody of Katrina. She is safe and taken care of by my sister. I know you do not like me, but I wish you would believe me. I didn't kill Alek. He fell down those stairs running after me. He got up and yelled at me again. I loved him but I was afraid of him too sometimes. He was a hard worker when he had a job and I know he loved Katrina. I will be in court to tell the judge I can take care of my daughter and be a good mother when I parole.

With respect, Juana

"Great letter. Hey, what *really* happened that night?"

"Like I said in group, Alek chased me through our apartment, acting like a crazy man. I grabbed Katrina and ran out the door. Then I heard him fall down the apartment stairs and stopped to look back. He lifted himself part way up, with his arms. He kept saying 'Give me the money, Juana,' over and over. He wasn't dead. He yelled at me so I started running again. Ms. Montes said I should have called the ambulance, but I didn't."

"You didn't mention money in our group."

"The police must not have thought it was important because they didn't ask me any more questions. A long time before that night, when Alek came home drunk, he told me he owed a lot of money but he didn't say for what or how much."

"Who do you think he owed it to?"

"He said his friends." I shrugged my shoulders because he never introduced me to any friends.

"Someone must've come looking for him."

I thought about the time two Russian guys came to our apartment. "Two weeks before Alek died, two guys banged on our door late at night. He went outside to talk to them and they went away. The next day, after I returned from the market, our front door lock was broken. The house was a mess, and our TV was stolen. Afterwards, I started hiding our money."

"Dang, crazy. You think those guys killed him?"

I sat up, clutched the pencil in my hand. "Why would they do that?"

Xochitl scratched at her neck. "What if Alek owed them more money than a television? How do you know they didn't go back and kill him after you ran away? Do you remember what they look like?"

My insides knotted remembering the night those men came to the apartment.

"I saw them through the window. One of them was about my father's age, around forty, a short stocky man who wore an old brown leather coat. The other one, a little older and taller than Alek, had muscles and a tattoo of a dagger on his forearm. Both men had Russian accents. Alek kept rubbing his chin."

"So who did he say they were?"

"He didn't, but after he shut the door, he paced around the apartment. The next day, when our apartment was broken into, he wouldn't call the police."

Xochitl faced me. "Did they find the money you hid?"

"I don't know because the police didn't let me in the apartment. I had almost forty dollars in the diaper bag when I ran. The rest I kept secret under the bathroom sink, in the tampon box."

"How much?"

"Close to one hundred dollars. The money I had in the diaper bag, I used for a bus ticket to get to Calexico. When I arrived, I called my cousin Maribel in Mexicali. It's right there across the United States border. She asked me to go with her, to her house, but I wanted to go back, talk to Alek. I wanted to tell him I couldn't live as we were living and we could move back to Calexico. Life was better there for us."

"You should've told the judge about the robbery or stayed with your cousin and your baby."

I twisted the bottom of my tee shirt. "Every day I think of my stupid mistake. When I got to our apartment the next day, a lock was on the door with yellow tape and a sign. I telephoned

Alek's mother, but she hung up on me, so I walked to her apartment to look for him. She screamed at me that I killed him."

"Juana, I bet those men came to your place after you left and found Alek messed up at the bottom of the stairs. Maybe they killed him. Did you read the coroner's report?"

All the breath came out of my body like a balloon losing its air. "I don't want to talk about this anymore."

"Alright, but that could've happened."

Xochitl pressed one of her stamps on the letter addressed to Alek's mother while I sat in the chair, stunned at what she said. Could someone have killed Alek after I left? Why didn't I remember all those details before so I could have told the public defender and the judge? Why didn't anyone ask me if Alek had enemies or if he owed money?

"You know what?" Xochitl said. "Bring out your court papers and the police report tomorrow at breakfast. There has to be more information in there to tell us what really happened."

"I don't have a police report. How do I get one?"

"Ask Montes or Ms. Dillon. You need to know how and when the cops found Alek. It's important."

I scraped my hand over my hair. Those men could have killed Alek. "I don't know, I can't think."

"You don't have a lot of time before the custody hearing. Do you want to keep your daughter or not?"

THIRTY-FOUR

Ms. Montes handed me a ward movement pass. "Library? Why're you going there?"

I slipped the pass into my pocket and ran to the unit door, pretending I didn't hear her question. She'd tell me to wait and ask the social worker but finding out who killed Alek was more important than Ms. Montes's rules. I jogged down the roadway to the school area.

"Walk," a booming voice came from a crackling speaker in the communication tower.

I glanced up to see a CO wearing shiny sunglasses standing inside the glass-enclosed tower, a microphone in his hand. A security van appeared behind me, trailing me. I didn't care if I had the whole security team watching, I had to find out what I could do to stop Anna.

"Hi, Ms. Dillon." I handed her my pass. "I need to find out information about my case, but I don't have all the reports. Can you get them for me?"

"Juana, I'm a librarian, not a law clerk. Why don't you tell me what you're trying to do so I can direct you to the correct books or facility manual."

This meant I had to tell her about the night of Alek's death. I didn't want to but she was a caring person and I trusted that she wouldn't be disgusted by me or ask why I didn't report him before. I sat at the table and motioned for her to sit. My body began to tremble, knowing that I'd relive that night.

"Ms. Dillon, I'm here for manslaughter. The police accused me of letting my husband die. He had hit me and chased me and my baby all the way down three flights of stairs. Then he fell."

I made myself glance at her face. The lines on her forehead creased slightly while her head lowered. She was listening.

"When I turned back, I saw him get up. He yelled at me and I kept running. Now I need to know when the police found him and where."

Her eyebrows came together as she touched her chin and nodded. "Let's get this figured out. I take it you don't have a police report. Do you have the coroner's findings?

"What is that?"

Ms. Dillon pointed to her office. "Let's go in there. More privacy." She left the door open and sat behind her desk. "Juana, the coroner is a medical examiner who inspects the body. The information in his or her report indicates how a person died and the time of death. Surely those facts were brought out during the hearing."

Most of what happened in court was fuzzy in my memory. I shook my head. "If I had the report, I'd let you read it, Ms. Dillon. I didn't kill Alek, but his mother thinks I did. What if someone else killed him?"

"A judge requires proof. You'll need to get those reports and go through them to find anything to support your claim. I suggest you talk to your correctional counselor or the living unit social worker."

"I signed up to see Mrs. Snow already, but she takes so long to call us. This is important and I need to find out before the custody hearing in three weeks. Maybe I can do this myself. How long does it take to get those reports?"

"Ms. Dillon?" A girl poked her head in the door to the library. "My teacher needs a book."

"The facility manual should have that info for you, Juana. You can go on back and find it. Excuse me."

I made my way down to the bookcases, found the manual, and returned to the table at the front of the library. Flipping through the binder, I found the section on reports. It said I needed a Request for Reports form from a staff member. It could take several weeks for the report to be sent.

A hard sigh escaped my mouth. I swallowed to unloosen the tightness in my throat. *Several weeks*? There were only three weeks until the hearing. By that time the judge could give Katrina to Alek's mother, or my baby could be in the US and I'd be in Mexico. Either way, I lose Katrina.

My feet dragged across the prison grounds back to my living unit, my composition book and important papers held tight against my chest. A life without my daughter would be worse than it was now. At least I had the hope of seeing her in two or three years, but to not see her ever? If the court took Katrina . . . my heart couldn't stand another break.

After my mother's death, I felt like a bad windstorm swept

me up, sucked a hole out of the middle of my heart, and dropped me to the ground. For a long time, I was empty inside.

When I met Alek the hole in my heart was a little smaller. Later, Alek, Katrina, and my life filled me up again. Now only the photos of Katrina and walking through my memories kept me alive. If I lost my baby, I'd lose everything worth living for.

THIRTY-FIVE

I pushed a broom across the dayroom floor. Working every spare minute was the only thing that kept me from breaking down and crying. I was afraid if I began, I wouldn't stop.

"Juana, great news." Mrs. Shaffer hung up the telephone on the staff desk. "Warden says we can have a garden."

Growing vegetables didn't seem important anymore. I had to get ahold of those reports and convince staff to take me to Katrina's custody hearing, but Mrs. Snow hadn't called me into her office yet and Ms. Montes was out sick. I continued sweeping the area I'd already swept.

Xochitl rolled the mop bucket across the floor towards me. "Hey now, we finally get something normal."

"The maintenance man will shovel out a square of grass in the unit's backyard later today," Mrs. Shaffer said. "I'll need your skill to make the garden bloom. I'm counting on you."

"Don't." I'd just let them down, like everyone before.

"What's that?" Mrs. Shaffer said.

"She said you can depend on her." Xochitl bumped my feet with the mop and whispered. "What's wrong with you?"

"Can you lock me in now, Mrs. Shaffer?" I put the broom away in the hall closet.

She huffed and followed me down the hallway. "We'll talk later."

Through my room window, I gazed at the brown patch of dead grass, flattened and sparse like everything else around here. How could I make things grow when I was dead inside? I didn't care about that gardening stuff anymore. It would just be another disappointment if it didn't work out. Another failure. Another reason for the girls to tease me. Mouse who can't speak English right, who doesn't know shit, who doesn't speak up for herself, who's scared of getting hit again. Mouse who lost her baby.

The evening program came too soon. I wanted to stay in my room after dinner movement but Mrs. Shaffer told me to wait in the dayroom. She needed to talk to me. Most likely she'd scold me for not getting excited about the garden.

"Ms. Ivanov and Alvarez," Mrs. Shaffer called out from the back office.

Babydoll and I stared at each other from across the dayroom. Half of the girls turned in their seats to watch us walk into the staff office. I searched for Bruja, Jester, and Gina. Thankfully, they were on evening room restrictions.

"Have a seat, you two." She pushed the cardboard box across her desk towards me with a wide grin. "Here's the garden tools, seeds, and tomato plants from our volunteer ladies."

The tomato plants, with their thick vines, sat in green plastic pots. I touched the soft leaves, brought them close to me and inhaled. The grassy scent flooded my mind with pictures of my mother's garden, of happier times, of watching vegetables grow from seedlings to leafy plants. In the box, seed packets with colorful photos of marigolds, zucchini, chile peppers. I couldn't help but smile.

"So many seeds. Thank you, Mrs. Shaffer. Thank the volunteer ladies too."

"From your reaction earlier in the day, I didn't think you'd be excited."

"Why'd you call me in?" Babydoll slouched in her chair, arms crossed.

"To help Juana with the garden."

She sat up, pressed her fingers against her lower lip. "But I don't know nothing about plants."

"She can teach you," Mrs. Shaffer said.

The corners of Babydoll's lips perked up. "Oh, uh, okay." She wound her finger through a strand of hair.

"When I dismiss the group for the night, stay behind and I'll show you where the box goes when you're not outside. Paula, you'll work with Juana beginning on Saturday. Any problems?"

Babydoll's leg jiggled. "Nope."

"Good to hear. Make the garden come to life."

While several of the girls in the unit went to Saturday visiting, Babydoll and I worked in the backyard. We mixed bags of soft bright brown dirt into the crumbly clods. The moist scent of the new earth took me to Mamá's garden again, to a time I felt safe and cared for.

"Ugh, I'm getting so dirty," Babydoll said.

She stabbed at the chunks of dirt with the plastic scooper, scattering dust into the air, spotting her pale cheeks. Her skin still had a slight yellow coloring like she was sick and needed better food and vitamins. She needed to be healthy. For her baby's sake. I was happy I could help her.

"I'll make the rows for the plants," I said. "You can drop the seeds in afterwards."

Babydoll tossed the trowel to me, sitting cross-legged on the dry grass. She wiped her hands against the dead lawn. "Do you think I should get an abortion?"

My hand shovel stopped in midair. She asked so casually like she wanted my opinion on whether she should buy chicken or chile-flavored noodles on her next canteen order.

"So, what do you think?" She looped a strand of hair around her finger, waiting for an answer.

"I don't believe."

"It's legal over here. Isn't it legal in Mexico?"

"Si, pero soy catolica. Tu bebé es un milagro."

She blew her breath out, folding her knees against her chest. "What if it's deformed or something? I'm not Catholic and I can't take care of a messed-up baby. I can't be a mother."

I drop the trowel and moved closer. "When I got pregnant, I was scared too."

"But you were out there, not in here." Babydoll dropped her head to her knees, laced her fingers around the back of her neck. "I don't have nobody. I'll probably parole to a foster home anyway."

How and where could Babydoll raise a child? Sixteen years old, a heroin user who tried to kill herself last month. But I had to get her to talk about the baby so she'd have something to look forward to.

"Did you tell the baby's father?"

"The father? Fuck, are you kiddin' me?"

"Did you tell your mother?"

"She won't care."

"But she's your mother."

"Pfftt. I'll tell you what kind of mom she was, always letting her boyfriends live in our apartment. One creepy guy after another." She picked at the patchy grass, pulling up strands and flicking them away.

"You don't have to tell me, unless you want to," I said.

"This one guy, way older than my mom, like grandpa old, was the worst. *I'll put her to bed,*' he'd say. When he pulled the blankets over me, he'd pat my chest, kissing me on the cheek. A week later, he's sliding his hands under the covers, touching me between the legs. I ran out of my bedroom and told her, but he lied, said I didn't like him. So, I went to live with my grandma. She already had custody of my brother and sister."

What little I knew about Babydoll's life was worse than I wanted to imagine. She must be miserable about her situation. I needed to find a way to bring a little hope into her life. Something to keep her going so she wouldn't try to kill herself again.

"You liked your abuelita, Babydoll?"

"She took good care of us, but she was real strict. I started hanging out with friends, ditching school, drinking, you know? Then I met a guy at a party who got me started carrying heroin for him. We made lots of money but I got busted."

Babydoll wrapped her arms around her knees and rested her head. Her long hair fell to one side, draping her leg like a blanket.

"When I got out of the Hall, I looked him up again, but he'd hooked up with someone else. Never wrote to me when I was inside."

I patted her shoulder, small pats like I used on Katrina to soothe her. Her back tensed for a few seconds, then relaxed.

She raised her head. "Want to hear something more fucked up? I don't even know who the baby's father is. I was loaded most of the time and slept with whoever gave me drugs."

Her breathing grew shallower. Quiet and low until she lowered her head again and sighed.

Humming like when I quieted my baby, I continued patting her back. She trembled against my shoulder. "Maybe you do adoption, Babydoll."

"Who wants to adopt a drug-addicted kid?"

"But what if everything turns out okay?"

"You think it could be all right?" Her long lashes blinked against wet eyes. She stared at my face so intensely I looked away.

"Ask the nurses at the clinic. They could tell you better."

"The nurses who tell me to get an abortion? Those nurses? Please." She snickered.

With no mother or relatives to help her raise a baby, what could she do? But something told me to try again.

"I tell you a story my mamá told me one time when we took our vegetables to the mercado. The calabaza had pretty orange blossoms and I picked them for the market, but I ruined the crop because I picked them too soon. Instead of scolding me, she told me I needed to know which blossoms to pick and which ones to leave alone. We need patience and faith when growing things."

Babydoll's thin eyebrow rose, one eye squinting. Her hand

flew to her mouth to stop a laugh. "You sound like my abuelita with her stories and dichos." She leaned over, sprinkling some soil over the chile pepper seeds. "Anyway, what does that have to do with anything?"

"We need faith things will work out and good things will happen."

"Nah, it's a dog-eat-dog world and only the strong survive," Babydoll said. "My mom always said those words. The only thing outta her mouth that was the truth."

I scraped the dirt with my trowel. Babydoll's saying—only the strong survive—rang through my ears.

Sprinkling earth over the seeds, she patted the mound lightly and finished a row. She looked up at me with a big grin. "We did it," she said, sweeping her dusty hand through the air.

Our rows were a little crooked, the dirt dried out, but I had confidence our garden would grow and produce.

"Put some water in that can. We need to sprinkle some on the seeds."

"You really think vegetables and flowers can grow here in this messed-up prison yard?" Babydoll said.

"If we take care of them, yes."

"You ever see how sometimes a flower grows through cracks in the sidewalks?" Babydoll said. "Or on the side of a trashy ditch?"

"Or from a hard squash?" I giggled. "See, proves things can grow anywhere. Strong women can grow here too."

Babydoll laughed. "I never heard that dicho. You're like a seventeen-year-old grandma."

"It's not a proverb, but something Mamá told me. After Papá

lost his arm at the railroad job, Mamá cried all night. That scared me, but she said she cried because she was sad for his loss and she was angry at his bosses. Life for us would be harder. She said sometimes the strongest women are the ones who cried all night but got up in the morning to take care of their family anyway. They didn't give up."

Babydoll glanced up at the cloudy sky and sniffled. "Cool story." Then she grabbed a seed packet and held it up to me. "These look like weeds on the cover."

"Oregano. My mother planted it near the vegetables so the bugs stay away."

"My mom never showed me anything, except how to score drugs," Babydoll said. "I'm going to show my baby how to do lots of things."

"You will? Me too. I'm going to show Katrina how to work the soil, plant flowers, and grow vegetables like my mother did for me."

"Juana," Mrs. Shaffer shouted from the back door of the unit. "Mrs. Snow wants to see you. Paula, you can stay out here for a few more minutes to finish up. You have a pass for an appointment in half an hour."

"I hope she gives me the phone call to the lawyer." I held out the garden can to her. "Water the rest of the rows while I'm gone, okay?"

Babydoll grabbed my hand instead of the can. She held on to it, her grip getting tighter, studying my face. Her smile was like when a girl is attracted to someone. I thought of pulling my hand away but maybe I was wrong. I didn't want to hurt her feelings.

"I'm glad you want to keep the baby," I said.

"I don't know yet, but come back out as soon as you're done." Babydoll released my hand. Her eyes examined my face like she was searching inside of me.

A tiny flutter swept through my stomach. Kind of happy, kind of nervous.

THIRTY-SIX

M rs. Snow stood at her door and waved me inside. I sat in front of her cluttered desk while she crossed my name off the list taped to her office window. She waddled to her seat, fell heavily into her rolling chair.

"What is it that your counselor couldn't help you with, Ms. Ivanov?"

I took a breath and curled my fingers around the seat of my chair. "Ms. Montes is off sick. I need a phone call to my public defender."

"Whatever for?" Her round eyes looked more bulging than usual.

"For the custody hearing. I found the lawyer's name and phone number on my paperwork. I need to tell him Mrs. Ivanov wants custody of my daughter, Katrina, but I don't want that. Can I get permission for a legal phone call?"

"A public defender can't do anything for you. The attorney represented you in a criminal court proceeding, and custody is a family court issue."

I shrank back in my seat and then remembered what the state manual said. I memorized the words. "Mrs. Snow, the rules say I can be present when decisions are made about my daughter's custody. I need to ask a lawyer for help."

We stared at each other for several seconds, my foot tapping the floor, my hands cramped from clutching the chair seat. I had to remain seated until she did something, even if it meant she threw me out of her office.

She pushed back her chair, opened a drawer in her metal cabinet, and flipped through files. Her fingers jabbed the numbers into the phone. "Yes, on the case of Katrina Ivanov. Her mother, Juana Maria Flores aka Juana Ivanov, is incarcerated at San Bueno Correctional Facility."

After waiting for a minute, she handed me the telephone. I swallowed to loosen all the words I'd need to make the person on the other end of the line understand.

"Yes, this is Juana. I want to be in court, yes. I don't want to give Katrina to Mrs. Ivanov. I plan to take care of my baby when I parole. Right now, my sister takes care of her." My heart thumped into my ears while I waited for the lady to speak.

"I'll note your request on the paperwork for the hearing, Ms. Flores."

She didn't question or argue with me. My body relaxed. "Okay, thank you, thank you."

I handed the phone over to Mrs. Snow who told the lady she wasn't positive if the Sheriff's Department could transport me to Los Angeles, but she would call her back.

"Why you not sure I can go?"

"First, I need to check with my supervisor, Ms. Palomarez. Why don't you write a letter to the judge, instead? That should be sufficient."

She wasn't going to call the lady back. I heard it in her tone of voice and the way her eyes rushed to the pile of papers on her desk. I couldn't let those papers be more important than my baby. I thought about how Xochitl let people know what wasn't right, how she spoke up.

"A letter is not the same as being at court, Mrs. Snow. The law books say I have the right to attend the hearing."

She stopped shuffling files. "You're reading law books now?"

"Yes, I can read. The rules here at San Bueno Correctional say the Sheriff's Department has to take me to my hearing."

Her face scrunched, filling with wrinkles. We stared at each other again. The narrow office walls seemed to close in, squeezing me from all sides. My chest tightened against my ribs, but I wouldn't look away from Mrs. Snow. I wasn't going to give up.

"Please. My baby is everything to me."

"Ms. Ivanov, I'll ask but your chances of retaining custody are slim, especially after we discovered your fake green card." She opened her door. "Go back to the dayroom."

My lies caught up with me at the worst time. I sighed, lifted myself out of the chair, and left the office. How could I demand anything now?

I searched for two empty spots in the TV rows, far away from the tables and the noise of slapping cards, the whoops of the players. Jester sat at one of the tables with Gina and Bruja. All of them holding their cards close to their chest.

"Pssst, hey," came from my left side.

Babydoll poked her head above the wide back of a chair in the middle of the TV rows. She motioned for me to come over. I paused for a few seconds but moved one seat away from her.

"I thought you stayed outside, watering the seeds."

"Got an appointment. Plus I didn't want to be out there without you."

She smiled and glanced away from me. Her words startled me but made me feel good too. "Where you going?"

"The psych. They made me see him in the clinic that time. I gotta talk to him once a week now."

"You like him?"

She shrugged. "What did you see Snowball about?"

"The custody hearing for my baby. I want to be there."

Babydoll nodded, moved closer to me. "When my mom was in jail, the Sheriff's Department took her to court. I used to go to those with my abuelita."

"The social worker says she has to get permission from her supervisor for me to go. She tells me to write a letter to the judge."

Someone cleared her throat behind us. I turned ready to jump up if it was Jester or Bruja. It was Xochitl. She glared at me.

"Babydoll, you let Xochitl sit with us, then I can hear you both?"

"Can't, but sit in the row behind me with her. I'll listen from here."

Jester and Bruja were busy studying their cards. I moved to Xochitl's row.

"What's up with that?" She lifted her chin toward the back of the chair where Babydoll sat.

"She says her abuelita used to go to court for her and they brought her mom from jail."

"Adult jail. I don't know if it counts for us," Xochitl said. "Did you tell Snowball it was your right to be at court?"

"I don't think she cared. She said she'd ask her supervisor."

"Put in an emergency grievance. You can't be waiting."

"If I do a complaint the staff will get mad. That's not good for me."

Babydoll looked over the back of her chair. "My abuelita had a dicho: Decirle a una mujer todo lo que no puede hacer es decirle lo que ella puede hacer."

I laughed at the saying. Xochitl looked startled before she nodded. "So true. Tell a woman what she can't do is to tell her what she can do. Yeah, I like it."

"Me too," Babydoll said as she slid back down in her seat.

Hearing them talk of dichos made me remember my mother's courage. She stood up to my father's foreman and had her say even though the security men escorted us out of the office. A week later, a worker delivered the money to my father from the railroad company. It wasn't much, but he accepted the cash. My mother didn't say a word.

"Juana, file a complaint. It's your daughter's life," Xochitl said. "You have to fight for her."

"And you told me yourself that I needed to be strong," Babydoll said. "You got nothing to lose by asking. That's what the grievance system is for, que no?"

"Okay, I'll write a complaint to the warden this time."

They were right. I tried to follow everyone's rules, Jester's and Ms. Montes's, but nothing worked to get what I really wanted—to keep Katrina safe. I needed to do what was right for me and Katrina no matter what the staff or others thought about me. I had to be brave like my mother. I didn't have much time. The hearing was three weeks away.

THIRTY-SEVEN

"Everyone's dismissed—*except for Ivanov*," Ms. Montes said at the end of our group. Her voice, tight and high, got everyone's attention.

Gina and Bruja smirked. Mariana raised her eyebrows at me. I shrugged because I didn't know what Ms. Montes wanted.

Xochitl's hand brushed mine as she passed me on the way to the hallway. "You got this," she mouthed.

"Let's go in the office," Ms. Montes said. "Sit. I need to give you some information."

Her lips pressed themselves in a tight line. If she was going to yell at me, I'd rather stand and take it.

"You talked to Mrs. Snow before seeing me about the custody appearance."

"But you were out sick."

Her eyes glanced up to the ceiling before she looked at me. "Well, we don't have the transportation available for you and neither does the Sheriff's Department. So you can't go to the hearing."

I stepped back like I could move away from her decision.

"Okay then." She stepped to the office door, held it open.

Ms. Montes needed to hear me out. I pulled out a chair and sat. "Miss, I have to go. It's for my baby. Can you give me another emergency grievance?"

"Out of our hands. Write a letter to the judge like Mrs. Snow told you."

She strode out of the office like she was in a hurry. I followed her to the counter. CO Isadora glanced up at me from her chair.

"Isadora, can you do the hall checks?" Ms. Montes said. "Hurry up, Ivanov. Go stand by your door."

I didn't move. "The San Bueno manual and the law books say I have the right to go to the hearing. The judge will think I don't care about my own daughter if I'm not there. Why can't the Sheriff's Department take me to court?"

"Your fake green card didn't help your case."

"But I explained that already, Ms. Montes. I don't have to be an American citizen to be at court for my daughter, that's what the—"

She waved her hand, dismissed me like I didn't matter. My baby's future didn't matter to her either.

"Ivanov, I don't have all night. Go to your room."

I remained planted. "Por favor, escuchame. You're not listening. My baby means everything to me. You can't let them take her."

"Go to your room. Now." She slammed her clipboard on the staff desk.

CO Isadora rushed back up the hallway. "Ms. Ivanov?"

I turned to her, and back to Ms. Montes who moved from the desk to the other side of the counter where I stood.

"They all care when they're in jail," Ms. Montes said to the CO and snickered.

My fingers tightened in my palms. "I've always thought of my daughter. The judge needs to know that I—"

"Your cell. Now, Ivanov." Ms. Montes stared down at me, her hands on her hips.

"Nobody wants to be bothered, you only want the girls to do what you say when you say it. I'm not asking for paper or tampons. I'm begging you for my daughter's life. Alek's mother can say anything about me, tell the judge I killed him on purpose, say I'm not a good mother, but I am Ms. Montes, I am."

She stepped closer to me.

Blood rushed to my hands, my fingers pulsating. "I need to be there. I want an emergency grievance."

"You think I'm going to jump to get you a grievance? Move it." She flicked her wrist at me.

I grabbed the magazines on the counter, crumpled them in my hands, threw them to the ground. "Why won't you listen? Why don't you care?"

Her eyes became gashes against her forehead. Her chest rose and fell. She moved her hand to the mace can on her thick belt but I didn't move. I wanted to be heard.

"Why don't you understand?"

"Ivanov, I'm warning you."

The sound of her voice, those room keys she held, her clipboard, reminded me of everything she controlled. Everyone tried to have a hold over me. Alek, the police, the staff, Jester, Anna Ivanov, even my sister Lupe. I wasn't moving anywhere.

Ms. Montes jabbed at the alarm button on her belt. Everything slowed down as she unsnapped the can holder and lifted it off her belt. I knew the mace would sting my eyes. I wanted to run but I wouldn't budge.

"Ms. Ivanov, come with me," I heard CO Isadora say.

I glanced to my right, saw her standing close to me. Her face and body relaxed. She reached out and motioned with her hand. "Come on, let's talk on the way to your room."

"Ms. Isadora, please, I have to go."

"We'll talk after you're in your room, but you gotta go down now. Don't make it worse."

Her eyes were sincere, her voice low. I turned away from Ms. Montes and stomped out of the dayroom.

"Don't think you'll get away with this, Ivanov, Flores, whoever the hell you are," Ms. Montes yelled.

The front door buzzed and a CO burst into the unit.

"Hook her up," she shouted. "Take her to seg."

THIRTY-EIGHT

y wrists handcuffed, the CO lifted me by the arm up onto the running board of the van. "What'd you do to piss off Montes?"

He should have asked what she did. My jaw throbbed through clenched teeth that held back the screams I had in my throat. My eyes held tight against the images clouding my mind. Alek's mother in the courtroom, crying and saying what a horrible person I was. Her attorney telling everyone that I was in prison and not to be trusted. The judge deciding my daughter's fate. Without me.

"The quiet ones surprise you," the CO said to a female staff at the seg unit. "Montes sent her."

The lady CO stood inside a glass-enclosed area in front of two shadowy hallways. She strapped on a thick vest. The belt on her waist, heavy with keys, mace, alarm, and a long black stick, looked huge on her slender body.

"Come with me, ward Ivanov," the lady CO said.

She led me by the elbow to the shower area, waited for the other CO to unlock and pull back the metal gate covering the entrance.

The smell of iron and dampness, grief and misery hit me. The floor, clammy with moisture, made sucking sounds as I walked over to the spot to where she pointed. She unlocked one of my handcuffs, attached it and me to a large ring on the shower wall. I was a mouse trapped in a cage.

"Arm out. Shake out your hair. Now, strip down to your panties and toss clothes to the corner there."

The male CO at the desk stared right at me.

She moved in front of me. "I'm blocking you from view. He has to be here, so do it."

I wriggled off my clothes, dropped them on the floor. The CO uncuffed my other wrist. Although my back was to the staff, I moved my hands in front of my breasts.

"You can't keep your panties." She held out her blue gloved hand until I gave her my underwear. "Two-minute shower." She handed me a yellow jumpsuit and plastic slippers, pointed to the shower stall with a short curtain.

The cold water dampened the fire I had left in me. My anger turned to a heap of cold ashes that pooled in my legs. I wanted to shrink and disappear. The water shut off but the chill stayed with me even after I changed into the jumpsuit.

The lady CO handcuffed me and walked me to the top of a hallway so dark I couldn't see where it ended. Her huge keys clanked against the steel door as she turned the lock. I stepped inside with a thin blanket she handed me.

The sound of the lock bolting echoed in the hall. A shiny steel toilet, a flat mattress on a concrete block filled up the icy room where the walls and floors were the color of storm clouds.

I dragged myself on top of the mattress. The overhead ceiling light shone like a dulled spotlight since a screen covered the bulb. Every time the CO passed my door and peered in, I glared at him like he was the one in a cage. He'd watch, wait a few seconds, and leave.

A small camera sat in a little metal cage in the top corner of the wall. They were watching. How many girls went crazy in these rooms? Who saw them? Who listened? Who cared?

Trembling uncontrollably, more from my nerves than the cold, I remained wide awake. I yanked the mattress off the bed, propped it up against the corner of the cell, and wrapped myself in the blanket. With my knees to my chest, I rested my head against the cushioned wall thinking about my mother. I couldn't sink into my grief, I had to stay sane. I remembered the stories she told me about her youth. I searched for a warmer spot against the mattress and visited her in my head.

Mamá was Tarahumara, born in a stone hut. Her family left the mountains for the city because there wasn't any food. She didn't know Spanish until she was a teenager, only the Tarahumara language, but she learned. She found a job and later met my papá. Our family didn't have a lot but we had a home, a garden, and enough food to eat. Mamá was happy she was able to give us a better life.

My life wasn't as difficult as hers, but it felt more punishing because I was alone. I wouldn't be able to give Katrina a better life. Maybe it was best for her to think of Lupe as her mother or to be given to Mrs. Ivanov. They were in a position to give her a chance in life.

A crack against the wall sounded. A CO hit his flashlight against the iron bars of the window outside. Three taps and he was gone. I pretended someone knocked on the door to my parents' house, a neighbor visiting, my friend wanting to play.

A train whistled in the distance. I wanted to be on the train. Go back home. Tomorrow would be Katrina's first birthday, May 1st, a day when I should be with her, celebrating. Instead, I wouldn't see her again.

I slid onto the icy floor, so tired of my life here, tired of keeping hope. Better to forget everyone so I wouldn't hurt so much. I wrapped the blanket around my face. Maybe I could suffocate myself, stop breathing. Over and over, I pictured Babydoll hanging in her room. How ugly and harsh it all looked. She wanted to stop her pain. I wanted to stop mine.

In my mind's eye, I caught glimpses of Katrina's smile, her hands, her baby sounds. All more distant now, fading. I forced myself to picture her and Mamá. I imagined her holding Katrina in a rebozo and pointing out the squash blossoms, smiles on both their faces. They harvested vegetables, took them inside to make a caldo de pollo. Spices and aromas drifted into my nose from our kitchen. My mind filled with beautiful pictures of my childhood. I threw off the blanket. I couldn't leave Katrina alone. I couldn't give up.

"Mamá, help me."

Praying, I asked her and God for help to endure my life and the strength to go on. I wasn't a little girl anymore. I was seventeen. A mother. My baby depended on me. I pleaded for my mamá to help me find the courage to continue. If I was going to survive in San Bueno, keep my baby, and go home, I'd have to find a way to fight for what I wanted.

THIRTY-NINE

The CO walked me past the caged-in showers of the segregation unit. I glanced up at him and opened my mouth to ask a question, but nothing came out. I sighed instead, my body too worn out from crying and not sleeping.

"Mrs. Shaffer said you could return to the unit," the CO said.

He escorted me out the front door and into the windy night where the overhead streetlamps shone on the van. Yellow glowing lights surrounded the living units in front of me and the control tower. The walkways that divided up the buildings were empty. I tried to guess if it was seven o'clock, nine, or midnight.

CO Isadora sat at the Mariposa staff desk when we entered. I glanced at the wall clock. Nine thirty. Everyone was locked in their cells. She uncuffed me and sent me to the back office where Mrs. Shaffer sat at her desk.

"I don't understand why you didn't go to your room when instructed," Mrs. Shaffer said. "We could've talked about your situation later, come up with more options. You know better, Juana."

All my life, my parents told me I had to do what the authorities and my elders said, but this didn't work here in San Bueno.

"If you had a baby, you'd want to be at the custody hearing, wouldn't you, Mrs. Shaffer?"

"I guess I would, but there are other ways to go about getting what you need. Try writing out your feelings instead of yelling them out." She handed me a composition book but it was purple instead of black like at school. "Write your feelings in here."

I stared at the book, flipped through the lined pages. "Thank you," I murmured.

"Do you want to talk about what happened with Ms. Montes?"

Even though Mrs. Shaffer's tone of voice was soothing and she wore a sad smile like she understood, I didn't want to talk with anyone.

"No, not anymore, Mrs. Shaffer. I'm sorry I lost my temper."

"When Ms. Montes returns tomorrow, I want both of you to talk in front of me."

Not that it would make any difference to Ms. Montes. She wouldn't suddenly see things my way.

"You sure you don't want to talk about the problem?"

I shook my head.

Mrs. Shaffer adjusted her gold rimmed glasses. "All right, child. But you need to talk this out with someone."

"Saw your name on the detention list," Ms. Dillon said. "What happened?"

Xochitl jumped in front of me and threw her pass on the desk. "She told Ms. Montes off, told her she could take her—"

"You weren't there, Xochitl." I blew out my breath. I was tired of her speaking for me.

"Why'd you end up in seg, then?"

The thought of the incident made my stomach churn. "Because staff said I couldn't go to my baby's custody hearing. I got angry and threw some magazines."

"Oh, I'm sorry to hear that, Juana," Ms. Dillon said.

"I should have asked Miss Isadora for a grievance, but I wasn't thinking right. Mrs. Shaffer gave me a grievance form last night when I got back. I'll ask Mrs. Snow's supervisor about going to the custody hearing."

"Give it to me," Xochitl said. "I've written a lot of them."

"No. I need to do this one myself—but thanks."

"Follow me." Ms. Dillon waved us over to her desk.

"Finally, the new computer came in," Xochitl said like she just saw the best thing in her life. "Now I can catch up with what's happening on the outs. I need the info for my letters to the politicians in the Bay area."

That Xochitl, she was so passionate about her beliefs. I wanted to be more like her and less like a scared mouse. Writing my own grievances was a start.

"Took three months to get in," Ms. Dillon said. "I printed out some sections from the California Welfare and Institutions Code for you, Juana. You'll find more information to help you with your custody case. I marked the spots."

I read the pages with the Post-its stuck on the top. "This part says what Mrs. Snow told me. I can write a letter to the judge."

"Couldn't hurt while you wait for your grievance to be answered," she said.

"At least I can tell the court and Mrs. Ivanov that I'm a good mother. I only wanted Katrina to be safe, that's why I ran. I'll write a letter, but can you type for me?"

Ms. Dillon pointed to a tablet attached to the computer. "You can do it."

I never used a computer before, not even in ESL classes I took when I was in LA. Everything was on the whiteboard and on worksheets. I stared at the board that had typewriter letters.

"Didn't you take keyboarding in school?" Xochitl asked.

"My school didn't have computers for the students."

"This is where you type," Ms. Dillon said. "I'll show you what a computer can do another time."

"If you want to work anywhere nowadays, you're going to have to learn how to use computer programs and type fast," Xochitl said. "You'll get the hang of it."

Hope warmed me up inside because they believed I could learn the keyboard and the judge would read my letter.

Ms. Dillon placed my fingers over the black squares with letters. "I think I can do this better one letter at a time." I jabbed at the keyboard. Letters made words. My words flew into sentences and then a paragraph.

At the end of library time, I had a letter to the judge put together without any mistakes. Ms. Dillon struck a few keys and we watched as the printer made noise and the paper moved out to the tray.

I held up the paper with crisp and clear letters. "Thank you. I feel a lot better now that I have a plan."

"Can you write the guardianship letter and bring it back after school? We could see the school clerk who does notarizations," said Ms. Dillon.

After the library, I rushed to my English class. The teacher passed out the spelling worksheet and I finished in a few minutes. I had fifteen minutes left to write the letter.

To Whom It May Concern,

I give custody of my daughter Katrina Anna Ivanov to my sister Guadalupe Flores Garcia to take care of, for temporary because I am not able to do so. She is a responsible woman who is a good mother to my baby. When I parole, I will get a job and take care of my daughter.

Sincerely, Juana M. Ivanov (Flores)

Using my Ivanov signature made me think of Alek and our life together. As much as I loved him, leaving my family in Mexico was one of the worst decisions of my life.

Over the last few months, I wondered how my life would have been if I had told my father about my pregnancy and begged forgiveness. Giving him the truth would have hurt him, but I could have avoided so many lies and so much trouble. I'd be with Katrina right now instead of writing a letter from prison.

FORTY

The night staff slipped two sheets of paper through my door. I scrambled out of bed. A letter? My grievance?

A discipline report from Ms. Montes. "Refusing to follow instructions necessitating additional staff intervention," was written in the allegation box. The punishment typed on the bottom of the sheet said: "Disposition: Four twenty-four-hour room restrictions in the seg unit."

The other sheet, my emergency grievance: "Denied. Transportation not available for child custody appearance."

Mrs. Snow signed the complaint although I'd asked for her supervisor to read the grievance.

I crumpled both sheets and threw them against my locker. Mrs. Shaffer told me to write out my feelings instead of yelling them out. That sounded stupid, but I took the notebook from my locker to give it a try.

The small calendar of the Virgin of Guadalupe stared at me with the number ten circled in pencil. The date of the child custody hearing: May 10th, Mother's Day in México, reminded me further what I could lose on this day.

What if the letter I sent to the court didn't arrive on time?

Or the judge ignored what I wrote, or Anna said horrible things about me?

The judge would determine the rest of my life, just like the last one who put me in this place. I didn't have a lawyer fighting for me, just words on paper from an inmate in prison for her baby's father's death. Why would a judge believe I'd be a better mother than Anna?

My eyes and jaw clenched as tight as my throat. Who was I kidding? I wasn't a good mother. I did stupid things. I made things worse, not better for me and my baby.

In the shadowy light, Katrina's picture pasted on my locker stared through me. Innocent, helpless, and so far away. She deserved more than I could give.

They were going to take her away. I threw my pencil and myself on my bed. Groans grew inside my belly, threatening to come out until my chest heaved. Katrina deserved the best life. I wanted to give her one, but I failed.

Everything I held inside fell out onto the pillow. I wiped my tears with the back of my hand. *Stop crying*, I told myself. I was tired of tears that did nothing. They didn't make me feel better anymore.

I paced back and forth until I bumped into my locker. Stupid, stupid Juana. Stupid staff, stupid life. I kicked the side of the locker over and over. The blow against the hard metal made me feel heard. Each smack a sound staff would pay attention to even though they didn't listen to my words.

"Stop it." Mariana banged on the wall adjoining our rooms. "You're going to get in trouble."

"It's five fucking o'clock," a voice yelled.

"Shut the fuck up," another voice shouted.

"No, you shut up," I yelled.

"Juana, get a grip," Xochitl said from the other side of my wall. "What's wrong?"

"I want my baby, I want my baby," I screamed.

The night staff pounded on my door, but I ignored her like she and all the staff ignored my need to be in court fighting for Katrina. I hated them for not caring, for thinking it was okay to treat me and the other girls like we didn't have hearts. Worse, I hated my helplessness to do anything but cry and hit my locker.

"Ivanov, stop your yelling or I'll call the COs," the staff shouted.

"Who the fuck cares anymore," I heard myself say like another Juana took over.

Rage shook me. I flipped over my mattress, threw my notebook against the wicket. Why should I write down my words or the dates of my sentence? It was stupid, none of that mattered any more. Only one thing kept me going in this place, only one thing was important: Katrina. Now they were taking her away from me and I couldn't do anything to stop them.

"Ivanov, knock it off." The night lady's fist banged on my wicket. "Stop it or I'll call a code."

"Fuck your code."

Kicking the locker again, I threw my mattress back on the bed and crawled on top. I hadn't seen my baby in seven months. She was the only piece of my life that I had left. The innocent part, the best part. Even if the court didn't give Katrina to Anna, they would order Lupe to hand Katrina over, then she would leave to Arizona. My father would be alone, no one to care for him and worse off than when I left Santa Isabel. He'd hate me more. All of them gone from my life.

I'd failed as a daughter and now a mother. My mother didn't fail, except for dying too soon. Dying wasn't her fault, but being in here was my fault—I wanted to die.

Loud, dark, mournful sounds like the palomas near the church in Santa Isabel drifted in the air. I went to my window and pushed it open.

Piercing, heaving sobs came from the room next to me. Mariana.

"Mariana, I'm sorry for yelling. I know you have your hearing this morning. I'm sorry."

Silence.

"I didn't mean to keep you awake. I'll stop. I'm okay now."

Her crying became low and muffled. My shouts about my baby probably reminded her of her own and what happened. I made things worse for me and my friend. I lay on my bed. All I wanted to do was sleep, hope for a dream where I could escape for a little while.

"Heard you had a rough night. I'm sorry you can't attend your daughter's hearing." Mrs. Shaffer slid a breakfast tray through the food slot at the bottom of my door. She waited for a few seconds but left when I didn't answer. The night staff put me on room restriction for twenty-four hours for not stopping my noise.

I picked at the mushy oatmeal spread out in the square compartment and sniffed at the pineapple chunks, the fruit I did like but couldn't eat. I pushed the tray aside.

May 10th, a day meant for celebration, love, and honoring mothers would turn out to be another day in prison, on room restriction. Tears seeped out of my eyes. Little rivers of salty misery slid by the corners of my mouth.

Soon, the memories of my first and only Mother's Day came to me, something I could hold onto so I wouldn't go crazy with grief. Katrina was ten days old when we celebrated both the Mexican and American Mother's Day, one at the park and the other with Alek's mother at a restaurant. We laughed that day, each taking turns holding and feeding Katrina. Later, I visited the church and lit a candle for my mother and said a prayer.

It was better my own mamá was gone. She'd be ashamed of me, just like my father. I'd messed up again and let my anger get me in more trouble. The complaint was supposed to help me with Katrina's hearing, instead my counselor was mad at me and Mariana wouldn't talk to me. Mrs. Shaffer told me she was sorry and I ignored her like I didn't care. Was I turning into Jester and Gina who did bad things to get what they wanted?

The deep rumble of the floor buffer echoed in the hallway. I threw my blanket aside and stood at my wicket to see who was out cleaning in my place. Xochitl gripped the buffer handle as the pad removed the old wax from the floor. Mariana mopped up behind her.

"Mariana, what happened at your hearing?"

Xochitl shot me a glance and shook her head. Mariana stared at the floor, mopping the same place over and over.

"Three years," Xochitl mouthed and flashed three fingers at me.

Mariana received the maximum time for her crime of involuntary manslaughter. I knocked on my wicket, pointed at her until Xochitl tapped Mariana's shoulder. She moved closer to my door window.

"Mariana, I'm sorry I made a bunch of noise last night. I should have helped prepare you for your hearing."

She nodded. "It didn't go well. I froze up. Sorry you don't get to go to the custody hearing. Keep trying, okay?"

"I will." I sat back on my bed staring at the photo of Katrina. I had an idea and sprang back to the door. "Xochitl, get me the grievance clerk."

"Didn't they already deny it?"

"If they're not taking me to the hearing, they could at least let me make a phone call to the court and say something over the phone. Couldn't they?"

Xochitl stuck her face at my door wicket. "I'll be back."

"Great idea," Mariana said.

Her smile made me feel better. I took a deep breath and told myself to calm down and think. I needed to talk to someone off this living unit.

A form slid under my door.

"What are you going to say?" Xochitl asked.

"It'll be an emergency grievance. I asked to talk to Mrs. Snow's supervisor before, this time I'm asking the warden before the custody hearing is over this afternoon."

"Alright. Knock on your door when you're done. I'll give the grievance to the clerk."

I couldn't think with all the noise in and outside my head. Putting down my pencil, I opened my room window. LaLa's voice rose above the chatter flying back and forth between the rooms and across the wings of the living unit.

"Fuckin' Gina's a rata. Her fault the compa's dry."

"Fuck you. It wasn't me. It was Wozzy, you stupid bitch," Gina yelled. "He gave up the info and resigned so he wouldn't get fired. The staff is trying to give me a new charge. I'll be transferred up north to the women's prison if it sticks."

"I'll find my own connection, and it won't be with a bofo like Wozzy or any staff. They always turn rat," LaLa said.

I shut my window. This was my life now. Crushed between staff and inmates, good, not so good, and evil. Trying to figure out how to survive another day. A life where memories faded to the dull brown of the bricks around me.

But I wasn't giving up. I wrote out my emergency request, signed my name.

"Xochitl." I knocked on my wicket. "Here's my complaint form. I want to talk to the warden."

FORTY-ONE

An hour later, the loud click of my room lock sounded. I sat up in bed, brushed my hand through my hair. My stinky food tray still lay on the floor. Ms. Montes was probably going to yell at me for putting in another grievance. Instead, it was Mrs. Shaffer.

She poked her head inside my room and picked up the tray. "Appointment for you in the admin building."

"I'm sorry about the other night," I said and followed her up the hall to the staff desk. "I wasn't angry with you."

"Thank you for the apology. I hope there aren't any more incidents." She handed me a movement pass.

"Where are *you* going?" Ms. Montes came around the counter and glanced at the sign-in/out sheet.

Her hair pulled back into a high ponytail, making the tight frown on her face look worse.

I glanced at both staff.

"She has a pass," Mrs. Shaffer said.

Ms. Montes let the sheet drop. I rushed to the door, waited for it to buzz open, and jogged up the concrete pathway between the living units up to the administration building.

"Walk," the microphone crackled.

The CO in his black sunglasses stared out of the tower, looking down at me.

"Movement pass?" he said through the loudspeaker.

I held the small piece of paper up like I had a magic key and waved it in the air. "Room 110."

He buzzed the lock open. "Past the visiting room. Find the door sign, 'Supervising Parole Agent.'"

The pass was to Mrs. Snow's supervisor, not the warden, but at least I was seeing someone off the unit. *Stay calm*, I told myself and practiced what I'd say to the supervisor.

A few women and children sat in the visiting room. I'd never been in the area when the families visited. I stopped, glanced around at the half-full room scented with potato chips and sweet honey buns, with happy voices and sniffling children. A CO stood at the entrance, his eyes scanning the people seated at several tables.

"Foster family visiting pass?" he said.

Shaking my head and holding up the movement pass, I kept moving. The people in the visiting room must have been the foster families who brought the girls' kids to visit them once a month.

I glanced at each door number until I found the right room and knocked.

"Come on in," a woman's voice said.

Behind a desk full of folders and papers sat a lady with a pencil holding up her dark brown hair, her red eyeglasses halfway down her nose. "Ms. Ivanov, or Flores I should say, I'm Ms. Palomarez. Sit. Your grievance asked to see the warden about your child's custody hearing. He can't see you, but I'll act on his behalf."

I remembered the lady from my board hearing. She knew all about me, my crime, and what the board members decided. I took a deep breath, sat straight in the chair in front of her, and folded my hands in my lap.

"Yes, I wanted to be at the court to tell the judge myself that I'm against Mrs. Ivanov taking my baby."

"The Sheriff's Department couldn't take you, so Mrs. Snow was correct in advising you to write a letter. Your grievance requests to talk to someone at the hearing. Is that right?"

"Yes. I'm not sure the letter I wrote got there in time, so I want to tell the judge how I feel about my daughter and why she should stay with me." I braced myself for her to say "no," or to laugh and scold me.

"The judge can't come to the telephone, as he or she is in court, however, I could ask for a departmental representative. You could talk with them."

The representative might or might not tell the judge what I said, but I had to take the chance. "I'll talk to the person. Thank you."

Ms. Palomarez dialed a number and spoke. "Ivanov's the name the case is under. She's here in my office." She passed me the telephone.

"Yes, I did write a letter but I want the judge to know I asked to be at the hearing. My social worker said the Sheriff's Department couldn't give me transportation, that's why I'm not there. Please tell the judge that my daughter's taken care of by her aunt, my older sister who's married. I'm trying to do the best I can in here, going to school and working. As soon as I parole, I'll pick her up, find a job and provide for her. Can you give the judge that message?"

My fingers cramped against the phone receiver. I was out of breath, but I remembered to say everything I planned. The lady on the phone said she would give the judge the information and asked me to pass the phone back to the supervisor.

"This is the fax number you'll need. Thanks for your time." Ms. Palomarez hung up the phone. "You did a fine job, Ms. Ivanov. We'll receive a fax on the judgment after the hearing. I'll call you back here when it comes in."

Wearing a big smile, I floated down the hallway, passed the visiting room. I talked to the court.

The school movement lined up on the roadway outside the living unit. I passed them on my way back from the admin building. Xochitl was first in line. Babydoll should have been behind her and Mariana, but neither of them were there.

"What happened?" Xochitl asked.

"Mrs. Snow's supervisor answered my grievance. I got to talk to someone in the court. They'll tell the judge what I said."

"See, I told you."

I nodded. "Where's Babydoll? I want to tell her my news."

Xochitl's smile turned into a frown. "I don't keep track of her. But I overheard someone say she has cramps and didn't come out of her room."

That couldn't be true because she didn't have a period anymore, but none of the girls knew Babydoll was pregnant. She probably just wanted to sleep like I did during my first months of pregnancy.

"Ivanov," the staff supervising the group said. "Move along."

The door buzzer sounded off as I entered the unit. Ms. Montes jerked her head up from the staff desk. I handed her my pass and signed back in.

"So what were you doing in admin?"

"Talking to the supervisor about my custody hearing. I need a pass for school, please."

"Did you tell her you had a fake green card too? You're not a citizen, so it's a whole different ballgame." She scribbled out a movement pass and handed it to me.

I wasn't going to let my anger overtake me. While I waited for the door to open, Ms. Montes picked up the phone and dialed, all the while staring at me. "Hello, Ms. Palomarez?"

The dayroom clock showed five o'clock. I'd watched the minutes slowly tick by for the last hour. Five o'clock was the end of the day for the social workers and their supervisors and still no word from Ms. Palomarez.

"Ivanov, admin," the dayroom overhead speaker crackled. "Ivanov, admin."

I jumped from my seat, almost yelled, "Yes, the custody results."

Mrs. Shaffer wrote me a pass while I bounced on my feet. Everything in my body sped up like I was in fast motion.

Pass in hand, I speed walked across the facility, up the sidewalk, and stopped at the communications center. Ms. Palomarez stood there, flipping through the file folders in her hand.

"Let's go into the visiting area." She took my pass, waved me by the com center. "Have a seat."

The visiting room, empty of sounds and smells, didn't look like a happy place anymore. Stomach acid flooded my insides. Ms. Palomarez had no expression on her face.

"Bad news?" I gulped.

"No, you're one lucky young lady. The judge said your baby was cared for by a family member and there was no reason to remove her from your sister's care. But the custody matter isn't finished. In ninety days, the judge will review the case again."

My breath whooshed out. Katrina could stay with Lupe, she'd be safe.

"Thank you, Ms. Palomarez, thank you."

She held her hand up. "There's more. Mrs. Ivanov, your victim's mother, told the judge your daughter is an American citizen and you used a fake green card. Ms. Montes also reported that you admitted this to her during counseling."

I shrank into my seat. I wanted to lie, but I couldn't do that anymore. Things only got worse.

"Yes, I told Ms. Montes and Mrs. Snow. I bought a green card to follow Alek here because I was pregnant and we weren't married."

"You do understand that your decision made things worse for you."

I cleared the lump in my throat and took a breath. "I left home at fourteen, something my father told me not to do, but I wanted to make money. At fifteen, I fell in love with Alek. At sixteen, I made a desperate decision. But I'm seventeen now. I'm trying to do better. If Katrina stays here in the US with Mrs. Ivanov, I'll never be able to get her back, legally. When I parole, you'll take me to Tijuana and drop me off. I'm not supposed to come back."

The Garden of Second Chances

"We're following the law."

"It's a bad law to separate me from my baby. She didn't make the mistake, I did."

"Nevertheless, Mrs. Ivanov appealed the judge's decision because you're incarcerated for a felony. I need you to understand something. Custody can be removed from a parent because of a felony conviction."

The words "removed" and "felony conviction" buzzed in my ears like hungry biting flies.

Take deep breaths, I told myself. I placed my hands on the table to steady them and my trembling body. Right now, Katrina was safe. Safe.

"Ms. Ivanov?"

"I need you to understand something too, Ms. Palomarez. I loved Alek and I didn't kill him. I didn't like what he became but I was younger then and I thought he'd change. That's why I went back to Los Angeles. I'd die if the judge took Katrina away from me. A slow ugly death."

"Your fake green card is a problem. It's a crime to have one."

"Another charge? More time?"

"We're checking into the situation and will report the findings to the Corrections Board with a recommendation. Were you employed while in the United States, receive benefits, or use a fake social security number?"

"No, I stayed home, took care of my baby. Alek had insurance with his job until he got fired."

Ms. Palomarez wrote something on her tablet. "I hope you're telling me the truth."

"I am. I didn't kill Alek but to prove it to the Corrections

Board, I need to read the coroner's report and the police report. The information in those papers is important. I've already asked my social worker but she hasn't given me the forms."

She tapped her pen on the table, stuck it back into her hair. "Wait here." She called someone on the visiting room phone.

I prayed she wasn't calling the COs to take me to seg for lying about the green card. A woman came into the room and handed papers to Ms. Palomarez who slid them on the table in front of me.

"This one is to review your master file with your social worker. You'll find the police report in there. The other form is for the coroner report. Fill it out. You should receive a copy in a few weeks."

"Thank you. Can I have a copy of the judge's decision?" I asked, remembering what Xochitl taught me about keeping my own paperwork.

Ms. Palomarez gave me a slight smile. "I'll send a copy to your unit tomorrow."

The weight pressing against my chest drifted away when I exhaled. "Thank you."

Only ninety days before my daughter's next custody hearing. I had to make the most of that time to prepare a case to keep my baby.

FORTY-TWO

I clutched the papers Ms. Palomarez gave to me against my chest believing the coroner and police reports had something in them to help my case. The lines on the concrete sidewalk reminded me that I'd crossed a lot of places since I left Mexico. I figured things out on my own, and although I made mistakes, I also kept going. I had to remind myself that I wasn't as stupid as my father said.

But what if Ms. Montes took the forms away? I slid the papers halfway under my waistband and tee shirt, praying staff didn't do a pat down on me when I returned to the living unit.

Ms. Montes's deep-set eyes studied me when she locked me in my room. I tapped on the wall adjoining Xochitl's cell.

"You there?"

"Got stuck watering the garden because Babydoll's sick again. I saw you going to the admin building. What happened?"

"Ms. Palomarez gave me papers to fill out for the coroner report."

"Send them out quick, sealed, 'cause they're legal documents. You don't need stamps when it's legal stuff."

Smoothing out the papers, I wrote in the date of my offense and my address, and signed them.

A slip of paper slid into the doorframe. "Spanish translation needed," the form said.

I peeked out of my door wicket, watched Ms. Montes peer into every room for a count, and waited for her to walk by so I could give her the sealed envelopes. She stopped with a jerk at Babydoll's room and banged on the door several times.

"Mrs. Shaffer, " Ms. Montes called out. Her high-pitched voice traveled up the hallway.

The panic in her voice made me think Babydoll tried to hang herself again. I pressed my face against my wicket for a better view.

"Can't leave the desk," Mrs. Shaffer shouted.

"Call for a nurse." Ms. Montes pressed the alarm on her belt and swung open Babydoll's door. "She's bleeding."

Babydoll's groans reached down into the pit of my stomach. I squinted into my wicket again.

"Bleeding?" Voices yelled from the dayroom. "Who's bleeding?"

The front door buzzer shrieked. Two COs ran down the hallway, stopped at the open door with Ms. Montes.

"So much blood," one of the COs said.

Screams shot out of Babydoll's room and into the hall followed by moaning.

"Call a nurse, Montes," Xochitl shouted from her room.

"Be quiet, Anaya," she said.

"Ms. Montes, take the desk. I called for a stretcher," Mrs. Shaffer said.

"That's what you should have done, Montes," a girl from across Babydoll's room shouted. "She told you she was cramping bad for two days."

After a few long minutes, another CO showed up with a stretcher and took Babydoll out of her room. Her head moved side to side. Her face was drained of color. She clutched at the sides of the stretcher, arched her back, and let out another scream. Splotches of deep red soaked her white underwear and streaked her pale thighs.

"Told you she was pregnant," "Staff shoulda done something before," came the shouts through the doorframes up and down the hallway. "They had to know."

Babydoll was nearly five months pregnant, much too early for contractions. Recently, she decided not to have an abortion. She said an older cousin would help her and she could start a new life.

But now she was losing her baby. I felt a loss of hope, too, like a bright balloon that quickly lost its air, never having a chance to rise. Babydoll's dreams to start over, to be a mother and do better, were gone.

Babydoll's groans made me think about my own labor pains. Alek was so excited when my contractions started, he telephoned my cousin Maribel in Mexicali to tell her the news. His mother came to the hospital too. Everyone was happy and excited.

Pobrecita Babydoll, she had no family. No one to be with her.

Howling sounds loud enough to cut through the walls came from one of the cells. The girls in the hallway shouted, "What's happening?" "Who's crying?"

The cries came from Mariana's room. I hit my wall with my shoe, shouted for her, but only a burst of roaring sobs followed.

"Mrs. Shaffer," I called out.

CO Isadora stopped at my wicket. "She's gone to the clinic."

I pointed to Mariana's room. "She needs help."

"Ms. Johnson, what's wrong?"

The crying became muffled.

"She's okay," Ms. Montes shouted to the CO.

But she wasn't okay. I heard soft crying like a sad cat mewing.

CO Isadora unlocked Mariana's door. "Talk to me."

"I'm, I'm fine." Her words were hushed by the choking sounds of a tight throat.

"You're not okay. What happened?"

Silence. I didn't understand why she pretended she was fine. She pretended she didn't know she was pregnant, or she had labor pains at school, and her baby died. Pretending it didn't happen was what she did to make it through the day like Xochitl said. That's how she survived.

CO Isadora sighed and walked away.

I waited a few seconds before I opened my window. "Mariana? Does Babydoll's pain make you think of yours on that day?"

She sniffled. "It's just, yes, this brings back a lot of memories. Things I don't want to think about."

"No one wants to go over the ugly parts of their past. I understand. Everyone deals with their pain in different ways. Babydoll with drugs, Jester with her gang rules. Who am I to say they are wrong? Maybe they're like me, they didn't know any other way. And two years ago, you didn't either."

"Yeah." She inhaled and blew out her breath. "Do you think I'm a terrible person or stupid?"

"No, you're real smart. You're not a bad person."

"Every night I wake up from the same dream. I'm back in the school bathroom on that day. Now, I remember more and more of what happened."

"I think you should tell Ms. Montes in your individual counseling."

"She's not someone who listens," Mariana said. "I like Ms. Isadora though and Mrs. Shaffer."

"Tell them. Tell somebody."

Just then, Jester yelled out, "I love you, Babydoll."

Other voices began shouting how Babydoll had a miscarriage and it was Ms. Montes's fault. Soon, lots of voices shouted stuff about Ms. Montes.

"Tight ass."

"Bitch."

"Worse staff ever."

The lights shut off in our rooms, leaving us in dark cells. Girls knocked on their doors, yelling, "Turn on the lights," "What the fuck?"

"Knock off the noise," Ms. Montes shouted. "To your wicket for count."

Several girls banged on their lockers. "Fuck you!" "You're an asshole." "Turn the power back on."

"I said to knock it off," Ms. Montes shouted. "You want to lose the water too?"

"Why?" voices yelled. "What's your problem, Montes? You already have us in the dark."

"Then you need to shut up," she yelled.

"Give me a grievance," Xochitl said. "Mrs. Shaffer, this isn't right."

"Shaffer's not here, Anaya. So shut the hell up."

That woman made a bad situation worse. Girls kicked at their lockers, pounded against the walls, beds, and cell doors.

"I'm writing your asses up," she shouted.

Mariana began wailing again.

Ms. Montes pounded on her door. "Stop it or we'll hook you up, take you to seg."

"Fucked up," Xochitl said.

"Leave her alone, let her cry," I said. "She's not hurting anyone."

Everyone started banging on their door again. With each pound of my hand, I remembered my own labor and my baby. Over and over girls yelled out, "Let her cry."

Screams filled the hallways, over and over, until a terrible moaning filled every space with drumbeats of sorrow, anger, and pain. Echoes of agony filled the hallways like each brick in the walls that held us prisoners. It's as if we all remembered every loss we ever had. The girls who were mothers, those without mothers, those betrayed by fathers, raped, thrown out, beaten, all of us remembered. With each bang and kick against our cell door we grieved the things we lost or never had.

"Stop it," Ms. Montes said. "Last warning."

I strained to see out of my wicket. She stood at Mariana's door, pushed the alarm on her belt. In seconds, the front door buzzed open. Boot stomps ran inside.

"COs are here," Ms. Montes said. "Isadora, I'm sending Johnson to seg for failing to follow staff instructions. That'll quiet everyone down."

"Montes is cold shit," someone said.

Ms. Montes unlocked Mariana's door. She stood at the door with her head down. Shoulders slumped, her hair matted against her wet face, she stepped into the hallway and offered her wrists.

FORTY-THREE

rs. Shaffer escorted me into the back office. While we walked, I tried to read her expression. I couldn't think of any reason she needed to see me until I saw her wave over Ms. Montes.

"Did I do something wrong?"

"No. I asked your counselor to come in a few minutes early so we could talk. You two don't appear to get along."

My stomach fell. Ms. Montes wasn't easy to talk with, but I was tired of not speaking up and trying to avoid difficult subjects.

"Ms. Montes makes things worse. She doesn't listen. I don't think she cares."

Mrs. Shaffer blinked. Her mouth opened and then closed like she didn't know what to say or thought it was better to say nothing. The office door swung open.

"I'm here. What's this about?" Ms. Montes said.

"Juana, is there anything you want to say to Ms. Montes?"

"Uh, I'm sorry I got mad."

"Can you tell her why you became upset?" Mrs. Shaffer said.

"I just wanted her to listen to me. My baby's custody hearing was important."

"Do you feel she listened or offered a solution?"

Before I could answer, Ms. Montes gave a loud exhale. She didn't like the question. I glanced at her and back to Mrs. Shaffer.

"She wanted me to shut up and go to my room, but I couldn't accept that. That was like telling me to give up trying to keep my baby."

Mrs. Shaffer nodded. "If Ms. Montes had offered you an emergency grievance or helped you to write a letter to the judge, would you have used either of those options?"

This time it was me who nodded. "I didn't know about emergency grievances until another girl in here told me. If she offered to help me write a letter, I would."

"Ms. Montes. What would you like to say?"

"I think Ms. Ivanov can't take no for an answer." She stood and pushed back her chair. "And now it's time for my shift."

After she left the room, Mrs. Shaffer told me to go outside and work in the backyard.

There was little shade under the sparse leaves of the tree in the backyard, but a few tiny leaves budded on the outer branches. For weeks I'd watered and shoveled the earth around the trunk. Xochitl and I sat pulling weeds between the chile plants spotted with reddish peppers.

"It's been two days since Babydoll left for the clinic."

"Heard she went off after her miscarriage," Xochitl said. "Staff must've taken her to the looney ward."

"Don't say 'looney.' Babydoll's upset and sad. You'd be depressed too."

"Yeah. I guess the whole thing brought back memories for Mariana. I overheard Gina talking, saying Mariana made up the story of her stepdad molesting her. Saying she must be guilty because she never denies it in group."

"Maybe the way she explained really happened. He's in prison, isn't he? She must be telling the truth."

Xochitl shrugged. "You say you're innocent, but you're in prison. I'm innocent and I'm here."

"You don't believe Mariana?"

"Sometimes I do, sometimes I don't. Right now, she's acting guilty. The other girls can see it. Everyone's going to take a shot at her now. She can't hide out for three years."

Three years. I chewed on my lip and shaded my face from the heat in the backyard. I had to stop thinking about the months and years ahead of me. I had to get through this one hour, and then the next.

"Hey, I heard Mrs. Shaffer had you and Montes in her office. What happened?"

"I said I was sorry for losing my temper." I shrugged. "Ms. Montes said I can't take no for an answer, got mad and left."

"Whoa, so she made it your fault? I bet it's true then. I overheard Shaffer scolding Montes, telling her she could've handled the situation better. She came down on her ass for cutting the power and sending Mariana to seg. Heard there might be an investigation on her too because Babydoll complained about cramping the day before."

"And staff knew she was pregnant. Ms. Montes acts worse than some of the girls in here."

"Really. Like she could've given you the forms you needed

from the get-go. She's a hard head. Hey, when do you get those reports anyway?"

"Ms. Palomarez said they might take weeks. I wrote Lupe a letter telling her the judge said it's okay for Katrina to be with her and I wrote to Alek's mother, Anna, to tell her that Lupe takes good care of Katrina."

"In English, by yourself?"

I nodded. My English was much better and I was proud of myself for writing Anna without anyone's help.

"I told her again that Alek was alive when I ran and I thought he had a drinking or gambling problem. I described the two Russian men who came to the door to collect money."

Xochitl filled up the watering can from the wall faucet and brought it back to the tree. "Have you told Montes the story yet?"

"She always looks mad, so I'll wait."

"Oh yeah, listen. That staff, Mr. Jay? Heard he dumped her."

"Where you hear this?"

"From the kitchen lady. She told me when we were on the loading dock during her smoke break. Montes is bummed out."

Ms. Montes brokenhearted? She wasn't a soft woman so it surprised me she was upset. But I couldn't worry about her; I was more concerned about Mariana. Mrs. Shaffer brought her back from seg but she hadn't come out of her room.

I put my trowel down and picked up the watering can. "Watch the back door, Xochitl. I'm going to Mariana's window to talk to her."

"If you're caught, you'll be restricted from the backyard. Who'll take care of the garden?"

"Right now, she needs help." I backed up to her window,

tapped it with the water container. "Talk to me." A few seconds passed. I raised my voice. "I know you hear me, Mariana. Please say something."

"Juana, stop." Xochitl motioned to me to come back to the garden.

"Mariana." I became afraid she wasn't answering because she was trying to hurt herself like Babydoll did. "Mari-a-na, Mari-a-na." I peered between the bars but the screen blocked most of my view. I shouted into the window. I couldn't stand by and let her hurt herself. "Ma-ri-a-na!"

"Shut the fuck up," Jester yelled from her window.

"You shut up," I shouted.

Chantilla's voice blared out her window, "Hah, Jester's got no control."

"Oh, shit," "told her," a couple of girls shouted.

What had I done? Jester or one of her friends would make me pay for that mistake.

Mariana pulled open her window. "Juana, be quiet. I'll come out for choir tryouts tonight."

Our Catholic church in Santa Isabel didn't have a choir. But in San Bueno Correctional, the priest, Father Anthony, wanted one. He invited girls to sing together at Mass like the Protestant service.

Everyone wanted to be in the choir because we got out of our room twice a week, saw the other girls, and did something different. Most of the unit signed up, but Mrs. Shaffer took Jester and Bruja's names off the list because they were in the lowest phases of the program. Xochitl came even though she said she didn't believe in the church. Gina came although she was a Protestant.

Half the pews were taken up by girls from the eight housing units. Each unit wore a different color tee shirt for their compa. Mariposa girls used light blue, Gaviota used yellow, and the others were orange or green, every color except red and dark blue because staff said those were gang colors.

Every unit sat together with one empty pew between the groups. We looked like a rainbow against the dark wood rows and brown bricks of the church.

"I have a list of forty names, so we'll need a sing off." Father Anthony's fleshy face stretched out with his smile. "Unfortunately, we can only select ten girls. Only eight can participate with two alternates."

"Sing in front of everybody?" a girl from Gaviota asked. "Alone?"

"Three verses, yes."

"I'm out," the girl said.

"Anyone else?" Father Anthony said. "Raise your hand."

Half the girls raised their hand, me included, but we were happy to stay and watch.

"First is Gina Jones, Mariposa." Father Anthony slid a CD into the player.

She jumped from her seat, her ponytail bouncing until she took the microphone where she made a big deal of adjusting it and clearing her throat. "Lemme show you how this is done." Her voice came out so high pitched her words sounded like screeches.

"Our rooster back home sings better than that," I said to Xochitl.

"Oh my god." She laughed out loud, slapped her knee. "Check out CO Isadora, she's trying not to laugh."

Four COs stood against the wall and smothered their smiles with their hand.

"Shut up." Gina hissed the words as she took her seat.

"Next is Mariana Johnson," Father Anthony said.

A couple of girls booed, some sneered when her name was called.

"Knock it off or you'll go back." CO Isadora stepped in front of the group. "Have some respect."

Everyone straightened up because CO Isadora could be nice and helpful, but when she gave you an instruction you better listen.

Mariana stepped up to the side of the altar, tugging her tight shirt down around her stomach. I waved to her so she would look at me and stop twisting the paper in her hand. Her voice, soft at first, got stronger by the second line. All the murmurs in the group stopped.

By the time she finished, Xochitl and CO Isadora clapped, then I clapped and the other girls did too. Mariana rushed off the altar and slid into the pew next to me, her face flushed and perspiring.

"Damn, you sing like a professional," Xochitl said.

"Father Anthony smiled so big when you sang. The church lady too," I said. "Gina's jealous."

"Do you think I'll make it?" Mariana said.

She was the best singer out of the twenty girls who sang. Sooner than I wanted, the audition was over.

"I'll send a list of those chosen to the unit supervisors,"

Father said. "Thank you for coming and sharing your talents."

"Mariposa unit," CO Isadora said. "Line up at the chapel entrance."

"Juana, would you be my assistant for choir practice?" Father Anthony asked when I passed him. "I need someone to take care of the song sheets and hymns."

"Yes, I'll help you and the church lady. Thank you, Father."

We turned into the chapel entrance where a long table held pamphlets about baptism and catechism. CO Isadora moved in front of us and stood outside on the sidewalk talking with another staff.

"Fucken baby killer," someone behind me yelled.

A girl pushed past me. Mariana hit the ground, face down. I moved out of line to reach her, but Xochitl grabbed my hand, yanked me back.

In front of us, Gina and a few other girls turned to watch, so it couldn't be them who yelled out "baby killer." We stood on the sidewalk outside while CO Isadora escorted Mariana away from the walkway. Blood dripped from her lower lip.

"I'm okay, nothing happened," Mariana said.

Her lip quivered and her hand jerked when she lifted it to smooth back her hair.

"You were on the ground," CO Isadora said. "Evidently, something happened."

"I tripped, on the rug, or over my feet," Mariana said. "I'm fine."

The way her eyes shifted away from me told me she lied.

"Arm length apart, hands behind your back," the other CO said. "Move out."

"Why didn't you fight back?" I asked.

"I'm not a fighter, Juana," she said in a low voice. "Neither are you. You didn't hit Jester back when she pushed you into the ice bin."

"I'd do something different now. I know it's scary, but you can't hide for three years. Your life will be miserable."

"My life's already miserable."

We walked back to the unit in silence. I thought of how parts of my life had been miserable too. I stayed with Alek and look what happened. My life went from good to okay to terrible trying to avoid his anger and fists. No matter how quiet I stayed, or if I left the room, he'd find me when he wanted something. Doing nothing didn't help me. Doing something got me accused of killing him. There had to be a choice in between.

Xochitl sat with Mariana in the dayroom right in front of the staff desk. I sat sideways on a chair facing them.

"Mariana said you told her to fight back," Xochitl said.

"She has to."

"Juana, you need to be careful yourself," Mariana said. "I overheard Chantilla say Jester has to put you in line now."

My heart sped up. "What else did you hear?"

Mariana's eyes widened and moved upwards until they stopped at something above my head. Her mouth opened like she wanted to tell me something, but no sound came out. I sensed body heat, smelled greasy pomade.

"So, you think you can tell me to shut up?" Jester's voice made a sharp sound behind my chair. "I've been easy on you, paisa. Too easy."

Never stay sitting down if someone rushes you. Xochitl had given me this advice once. I turned my body to face her, since there was no room to stand. Her legs pressed against my chair. Her fingers curled into fists. Xochitl scooted her chair back.

"Ms. Gonzales, sit down," Mrs. Shaffer said.

Jester moved around to the front of my chair with slow steps like a lion stalking its prey. She turned back like she decided to say something. My eyes followed her until her leg brushed my knees. The nerves on my neck and shoulders tingled as I stared into her penetrating eyes. She held my gaze the entire time.

"Gonzales, I said sit down." Mrs. Shaffer's voice boomed.

Jester murmured something under her breath and left.

"Day-um," Xochitl whispered. "I thought we were going to have to throw down."

"I couldn't stand, there wasn't any room," Mariana said.

She could have scooted her chair back like Xochitl, but I didn't say anything. I glanced around the dayroom to see who else was watching. LaLa and Bruja lifted their chins at Jester. Chantilla and her friends snickered, pointing to Jester's table. Jester mad-dogged them until they smirked and sank back into the chairs.

My whole body shook, ignoring my will to stay still. "I should go to my room."

Mariana gathered up her papers

"Hell no, don't anyone move. We're gonna stay here," Xochitl said. "Act strong, like nothing happened."

My hands trembled. I put them on my lap, pressed them together. Mariana cracked her knuckles. Xochitl stared straight ahead, her body a sitting statue. I wasn't as strong as she was, but

I had to act like it, especially now. Guarding the space around me, I leaned back into my chair, my jaw clenched.

Mrs. Shaffer strolled over from the staff desk into the day-room and stood near Jester's card table. LaLa cleared her throat and sat up. After a few seconds, Mrs. Shaffer moved over to the TV row where Chantilla and her friends sat. The whole day-room quieted. We knew very little escaped the eagle eyes of Mrs. Shaffer and today that was a good thing.

"Alpha hall, time to go down," she said.

"When we come back out to clean, let's talk," Xochitl said while we stood at our doors waiting to be locked inside. "You're going to need protection."

FORTY-FOUR

ochitl wiped down the chairs in the TV rows while I pushed a broom across the dayroom floor. She glanced at the staff desk a few feet away and called me over. "Only us two out."

"Yeah, more work for us."

"Quick, put this in your pocket." She pressed something wrapped in toilet paper into my palm. "Don't look, just do it."

The object, hard and stiff, felt like a regular-sized pencil not the three-inch ones staff gave us.

"What is it?"

"Protection. I think Jester's gonna jump you."

My stomach sank into my legs, stiffening them like cement. Jester meant to make an example of me, shut me up for good.

"Get a move on ladies, I have showers to run," Ms. Montes said.

"Juana, you need to be ready," Xochitl said. "Keep it with you."

Tape bound one end of the object making it thick. I pushed the smooth thin handle into my pocket. About an inch stuck out of the top so I kept my hand at my side, covering the end.

Ms. Montes locked me in my cell. In the weak glow of my

nightlight, I moved to the toilet seat, near my window, and took the "protection" out of my pocket.

The missing utensil.

The ridges along its sides had bumpy spots where Xochitl had rubbed the hard plastic against bricks. I unraveled the masking tape. The end was sharpened to a point and the other wider end had a broken razor blade melted into the plastic. Masking tape had held the bottom of the razor in place.

Rolling the fork handle in the palm of my hand, I curled my fingers around the middle. The bottom tip was spikey enough to leave a dent in my thumb. The top of the shank could cut. The thought of stabbing the razor into someone's flesh made my stomach turn, but Jester could attack me anywhere, anytime.

Could I push the filed edge into someone's flesh? Could I stab Jester even when I couldn't bear to wring the necks of our chickens back home? I never hit anyone with my fists, never slapped anyone, not even Alek.

Jester stabbed two girls for walking in her neighborhood park. Stuck each of them in the stomach, twice. She believed gang rules had to be followed. The Mariposa unit was her territory and I didn't follow her rules. Instead, I made her look stupid in front of her friends, and in front of Chantilla.

The gang leaders in the other living units must have heard about what I said to her in the backyard. Jester warned me, told me she let me slide before.

I rewrapped the base of the razor with tape and fingered the shank's length, rolled it in the palm of my hand. Xochitl was right, I needed protection. I needed to be ready.

FORTY-FIVE

Xochitl thumped her shoe on the wall between our cells. "In-coming."

The kite slid beneath my doorframe. I grabbed at the paper and read her message. *Keep it on you all the time, especially during showers.*

Shower movement could be the most dangerous time if someone wanted to attack a person. Girls slipped between the metal stalls or crawled underneath the partitions whenever staff got distracted.

I pressed my palm against the hip pocket of my thin robe and touched the handle of the fork. Could I use this? Would I have to? I wasn't a violent person like Ms. Montes and the rest of the staff thought because of my crime, but prison changed me.

On the outside, there are places to run, disappear, or go back to. In here, your cell was the only safety you had, and even then, someone could creep into your room. If one of the lazy staff unlocked a bunch of cells and returned to the desk before they called us out, a girl could slip out of her room into someone else's to either fight or to make out with them. It happened every week only staff didn't catch the girls.

My shower area was on the A side of the hallway. Jester's

area was on the B side, but the entrance to the two places was only a few feet apart. It wasn't hard for someone to slip into the opposite shower side.

On the flip side of Xochitl's kite I wrote, *Gracias, but what about you?* and threw it back. My fishing line didn't make it under her doorframe but Xochitl had a wire hook she made. She swept the kite into her room and tossed it back within seconds. *Toothbrush.*

Xochitl must have made herself another shank, either a razor blade melted into a toothbrush head or the handle sharpened to the point. Either way, she was prepared too.

"Alpha hall, showers," Ms. Montes shouted.

The showers held six girls. We had five minutes to shower once staff turned on the water. I hung my robe on the edge of the steel divider, leaving the shank inside the pocket, my towel draped on top. I kept my back against the wall and my eyes on the short shower curtain.

Over the sound of running water, shouts ran through the shower area.

"Lopez. Get back in there until the entire group in B hall is ready," Ms. Montes said.

"Fuck you," LaLa shouted.

The water in the Alpha hall shower shut off, sending complaints into the damp air. I wrapped a towel around my wet hair, pulled on my robe, and stepped out of the stall. The steam clouded over the large plexiglass window and blocked my view of the staff desk. All of us rubbed the haze off so we could see better.

Across the hall, in the B wing, LaLa turned around and returned to stand at her door. When Ms. Montes was ready, she called them up. Jester was in the group. Once they were in the shower area, LaLa stepped out again. She paced outside the entrance, in front of the hall showers on both sides.

"Damn it, Lopez," Ms. Montes shouted. She stepped around from the staff desk to the front of the counter. "You fried up meth head, go stand by your door."

Mrs. Shaffer stood, waved her arm. "Ms. Montes, come back to the desk."

Her mouth opened to say something but she backed away. LaLa stepped quickly in her direction. Ms. Montes scurried behind the counter.

"Lauren, turn around," Mrs. Shaffer said in her loud no-nonsense voice.

I tightened my fingers around the shank in my pocket. This could be a distraction. Jester could have sent LaLa to fight me. She could run to my shower area in two seconds.

"Shut the shower room doors," Mrs. Shaffer shouted at us.

I reached over and shut the door but it wasn't locked. LaLa could yank it open. Better for me to stand at the window so I could see her movements.

LaLa cocked her head, laughed, stepped closer to the staff desk. Back and forth she moved, giggling and pointing at Ms. Montes until she turned to the Alpha hall shower window. She faced us. Her pupils large, almost covering up her green eyes. "Monkeys in a zoo, ha-ha-ha."

"Go back down the hall, Ms. Lopez," Mrs. Shaffer said. "Now."

"Oh-kay." She drifted back towards her room, knocking on every cell door in B hall.

"Ladies, out of the showers. Everyone down. Alpha hall, you first," Mrs. Shaffer said. "Ms. Montes, I'm going to go lock Ms. Lopez in." My group shuffled down the Alpha hall, grumbling from the shortened shower time. Water from my wet hair and towel dripped onto my shoulders as I moved past Mariana's and Xochitl's cells to mine in the middle.

When was all this yelling going to stop? Arguments, cussing, and threats took place every day. I was so tired. Worn out. Leaning against my door, I clutched my robe tight against my body and closed my eyes.

"Juana!" Xochitl yelled out her door. "Trucha!"

My eyes blinked open. Thudding footsteps. Jester. She shoved into my shoulder. I fell sideways, sprawled on my hands and knees. Her fists slammed the back of my head. My nose bounced against the floor.

"Code 3, Code 3!" Ms. Montes's voice sounded in the distance. "Everyone down, down on your knees."

The pain stunned me, but I pushed myself over, scooted backward on my butt until I hit the back door of the hallway. Jester stepped closer. Her broad chest heaved while her hands curled into fists. I groped my pocket, grabbing for the shank.

"Fucking wetback. I let you survive in here and you disrespected me?"

Warm blood flooded over my tongue. Cold air hit my exposed chest. My fingers gripped the handle of the fork. I pulled it out. Jester stepped back, a crooked grin on her face.

"Get up, Juana. Get up," Xochitl's voice rang through her wicket.

I wriggled myself back against the wall.

"Get up," shouted voices from all directions.

Jester stood a few feet in front of me, blocking the hallway and Ms. Montes's view. My shower slides slipped on the floor as I struggled to stand.

"What you gonna do?" Jester snickered.

Her body loomed in front of mine. She stepped closer.

Standing, I wrapped my fist tight around the shank handle.

"You don't have the balls to use that, chúntara."

I bent my head down, ran full force at her stomach. She stepped to the side, grabbed my wrist, and yanked the handle back. The sharp tip sliced into her forearm. With her other hand, she bent my wrist back, forcing my fingers to loosen their grip on the handle, and pulled down on the shank. The razor cut across my palm. It dropped to the floor.

"Kick it here, kick it," Xochitl shouted.

Jester bent to grab the shank, but I punted it, sent it sliding down the hall. At the same time, my foot hit her in the face. She slapped her hand over her nose. Blood oozed between her fingers.

Someone grabbed my arm and forced it behind my back. Jester crouched against the wall, pressing her hand against her mouth.

"Hands behind your back, Gonzales," Ms. Montes said.

Jester snorted, shook her head. Sgt. Cuellar took ahold of my other arm and handcuffed me. I kept my hand curled so he wouldn't see the cut.

"Take them to the clinic first," Mrs. Shaffer said.

"Let's go, Ivanov," Sgt. Cuellar said.

The thump of heartbeats pounded in my throat and ears as

Sergeant Cuellar half-dragged me up the hallway. I scanned the floor for the shank but didn't see it anywhere. Straightening up, I walked out of the unit without wobbling, experiencing the burn across my palm, and tasted warm blood in my mouth.

FORTY-SIX

The nurse in the brightly lit clinic checked the cut over my eyebrow and applied an ointment that stung. She dabbed my lip with a puffy cotton ball and pulled my lower lip down.

"You don't need stitches but sign up to see the dentist."

I ran my tongue over loose bottom teeth which made my gums and jaw hurt. I kept my fist balled up in my lap, wiping blood onto my towel. The phone in another room rang.

"Wait here. Sergeant Cuellar wants to talk with you," the nurse said.

As soon as she stepped out of the room, I grabbed gauze from the counter, wrapped my palm and wound the gauze around my wrist. I tossed the stained towel into the trash bin and hopped back on the chair.

"Ms. Ivanov." Sgt. Cuellar entered the room. "So what happened?"

"I was attacked." I slid my wrapped hand under my thigh.

He scanned my face, down my arm, and stopped. "What happened there?"

If I showed him my palm, he'd realize a shank cut me and the unit would be on lockdown again. I wanted to be truthful but I couldn't get myself in more trouble.

"My hand? The nurse thinks I sprained it when I fell. When Jester jumped on me."

"Hmm," he said.

Ms. Montes locked me into my room. "We'll talk about this later, Ivanov. The COs will be here to take you to seg."

I wanted to yell, "She started it," but my mouth and jaw hurt too much.

Xochitl tapped on the wall. "I got it, don't worry. While you guys were gone, the COs searched a few rooms, found some drugs in LaLa's cell. She was high, that's why she acted all crazy with Montes. They didn't find anything in your room. Glad they didn't search mine."

I pressed the ice pack against my jaw, remembering LaLa's wild eyes, her huge pupils. Alek had the same strange look when he chased me around the apartment, screaming for the money.

"Heard it was meth," Xochitl said. "The COs put her in seg. Probably incommunicado."

"I'm on my way there too."

"What the hell? She attacked you."

Xochitl's voice drifted around me as the hard edges of the ice pack and the throbbing in my jaw softened while I waited for the COs to come for me.

The COs in the seg unit never checked my palms, either. They were busy dealing with Jester and LaLa who were arguing and trying to twist out of their handcuffs.

For two days I sat in the bare cell and slept most of the time, waking up when the ache in my jaw and neck got too bad. The aspirin the COs gave me did little for my pain, and nothing for the loneliness growing inside of me. During those hours, part of me drifted into memories while the other part struggled to stay in the real world.

Time slowed in the cell, nothing but brick and steel. During the day, I stood by the small window, covered by a screen and bars, and watched the shadows on the rooftop of the unit across the way.

I scratched at the bricks just to touch something, tracing the outline of the window to feel the smooth cold. During my two-minute shower, I stood in one place, breathing in the dampness, catching my breath.

On the third day, a CO brought me out of my cell, hand-cuffed my wrists in front of me, and led me to the empty day-room. He sat me at the round steel table.

"Crisis intervention."

The big word meant I had to talk about the fight before staff decided if I could get out of isolation. I didn't want to talk to Jester. What was there to say anyway?

Ms. Montes strode into the unit, sitting across the table from me. "I'm going to uncuff her. Stand by. Let me see your arms, Ivanov."

Palms down, I stretched my arms away from my body.

"Palms up."

I flipped over my sweaty hands and spread out my fingers. They ached.

"You have a cut across your palm. How'd you get that?"

Staring blankly at her face, I shrugged.

"Gonzales has a similar cut on her forearm. Don't think we

don't know a shank was involved." Ms. Montes stared into my eyes.

I looked through her, not flinching.

The CO brought Jester into the dayroom, sat her opposite my seat, and stood behind her.

"Gonzales, what started this problem?" Ms. Montes asked.

Didn't they see Jester hit me first or only me hitting her?

"We don't have any problems." Jester tilted her chin up at me. "Do we?"

Ms. Montes scowled. "You were out of bounds from your shower area, Gonzales, so you must have been looking for a fight."

Jester smirked. I remained silent.

"Where did this long scratch on your forearm come from?" She peered down at Jester's arm.

"Must've been when you pulled my arms to handcuff me. You got long dagger nails."

"And Ivanov's cut on her palm? I didn't cuff her."

"Shit, I don't know. Ask her."

"Cut the bullshit or you can stay here for the rest of your sentence. You must've had a shank."

I tried not to look surprised but I gulped. What if she told staff I had the shank?

Jester tilted her head, shifted her eyes from me to Ms. Montes. "I don't know what you're talking about. All I knows is she disrespected me."

"You called me wetback. You disrespected me."

"Pfft. It's over, Montes." Jester shrugged.

I nodded.

"Well, Gonzales, since you left your shower area and were

out of bounds, Mrs. Shaffer says you initiated the fight. I'm leaving you here in seg for a week while we figure out what to do with you. You've had one too many incidents."

Jester blew out her breath, leaned back. "Whatever."

Ms. Montes escorted me back to the Mariposa unit. "Anything you want to tell me?"

She had to know that I was at a disadvantage with Jester. I shook my head and kept walking, pretending the road ahead led out the gate.

We sat in the dayroom, pretending to watch a TV program so we could talk without Bruja or Gina bothering us.

"Hey, slugger, now the other girls won't pick on you since you stood up to Jester," Xochitl said.

Chantilla stood by the row where we sat. She stopped and raised her chin—the gangbanger sign of respect. Xochitl was right. I showed the other girls I wouldn't let someone hit me. If that someone was Jester, an enemy of Chantilla, that was even better. But being okay with Chantilla didn't protect me from Jester or Bruja. They'd find a way to mess with me again.

"What did you do with the thing?" I asked.

"Hidden in my ceiling vent."

"Good. I don't want you getting into trouble. You should have told me before that you had the missing spork. I worried every day."

Xochitl turned around in her chair. "Can't say sorry because I needed to do what I needed to do."

I slouched into my seat, waited for our dayroom time to be

over. I wanted to be inside the four walls of my room, by myself. I had a lot to think about.

"What's bugging you?" Xochitl asked.

She was the only one who ever listened to me about Alek so I decided I could ask her questions. "Do people who take meth act like LaLa did? Her eyeballs bounced funny."

"Yeah, pretty much. Why?"

"Alek must have used those drugs too. His eyes were like LaLa's when he grabbed me and put me against the wall. Maybe that's where all our money went, to buy drugs. Those men didn't come looking for him because of gambling debts like he said. It had to be money for drugs."

"If he was high on meth, that'd explain why he fell down the stairs and still got up. You really need that report. Three weeks have gone by."

The coroner's report was something I could show Ms. Montes and Mrs. Snow, a document to get them to believe me if the report said Alek had drugs in his body when he died.

Mariana and I sat at a dining room table with the other food servers.

"Applications are open for kitchen crew," Ms. Montes said.

There were no kitchen openings. Mariana and I glanced at each other.

"Due to Ivanov's fight the other day, she's fired."

Giggling erupted from Gina, who sat across from me.

I apologized and spent days in seg but that wasn't enough of a punishment for Ms. Montes. I didn't make much money, just pennies, but they added up to buy stamps and noodles at canteen.

Mariana nudged my shoulder. "If you're fired, I'm not working," she whispered.

She didn't say that because Ms. Montes was wrong. She didn't feel safe in the kitchen without a friend.

We filed out of the dining room and into the empty TV rows. In two minutes half the dayroom filled with girls.

"Are you coming to choir practice tonight?" Mariana asked.

"No, I don't want Father to see my big lip. I'll be there for confession."

"But you told Father you'd help with the choir." She scratched behind her ear, chewed on her thumb nail.

"Xochitl's taking my place. Next time I'll go with you, I promise."

Babydoll waved me over to her seat. She had just returned from the clinic where she had to stay a few days after her miscarriage.

"Don't go over there," Xochitl said.

"I'd rather be in my room but we have to be in the dayroom until you guys come back from choir."

Mariana and Xochitl took their passes and left the unit. Babydoll waved at me again. I scanned the dayroom to see where Bruja sat. She shuffled cards at the table with a couple of other girls. Two staff sat at the desk, watching. I made my way to the front TV rows, to a corner chair where Babydoll sat.

"Aww, look at your swollen lip," she said. "I better teach you how to fight, huh Mouse?"

"Call me by my name, Juana. Okay? And don't worry about

me. How are you feeling?" I looked down at her stomach, no longer swollen.

"No biggie. Better this way. Don't talk about it. It's over," she said. "Anyways, tell me what happened with Jester."

"She came after me, we fought." I folded my hands in my lap, glanced up to the TV screen. "I'm fine."

Babydoll bumped my shoulder. "You're lying. You're worried about going home on time now. Getting back to your daughter."

My nose prickled with surging tears. I nodded.

Her hand dropped on top of mine. She held it there, sliding her smooth fingers over the top of my hand. So gentle. She bent close to my face. I turned away, but her lips brushed against my cheek.

"Sorry, your lips probably hurt, huh?"

I slipped my hand from under her fingers. "Uh, Babydoll, um—"

"Jester and her friends don't know you like I do. Or how sweet you are."

Her eyebrows drew together, softening the usual hardness in her eyes. My face warmed but I couldn't break away from the gold flecks sparkling in her eyes, her upswept eyelashes.

"Did you miss my kites while I was gone?" She slipped a note into my hand.

I opened the paper: "*I like being with you, you're so sweet. Missed you.*" I focused on the large print. They were like those other kites the girl in the movement line passed to me the month before. "Those other kites were yours?"

"You didn't know? No wonder you didn't write me back. I thought you were afraid to because of Jester."

I swallowed. She couldn't like me. I was Jester's target already. I pulled my hand into my lap but she leaned into me, her dark bangs covering up half of her face. Her hand covered mine again.

"Stay here with me. Okay?"

Her voice faint, warm like her touch on my hand, surprised me. I couldn't speak. I glanced down the row of chairs, hoping nobody saw us. I wanted to tell her she couldn't kiss me again, but she made me feel like I was alive and someone noticed me, someone cared. But I couldn't be close like that to Babydoll. Jester said she loved her and Bruja waited for her to show interest.

"I need to finish ironing." I stood, moved to the ironing board.

Sadness covered her downturned eyes. Not wanting to cause her more grief, I smiled and waved at her. Her lips pressed together before they curved slightly.

Xochitl and Mariana plodded into the dayroom from choir practice. Xochitl wore a frown while Mariana had her head down. I took my clothes and sat near them.

"Chantilla's wannabe girlfriend in Gaviota hit Mariana while she got in line from choir practice," Xochitl said. "Tell her she has to fight back, even if she gets beat up."

"It was more a push than a hit." She clasped her hands in her lap, her thumbs rotating around each other. "It could've been an accident."

"Twice? She's jealous because Chantilla pays attention to you," Xochitl said. "It's gonna keep happening unless you fight back."

"Listen, Mariana. I didn't want to fight either, but I had to do something when Jester came after me."

"We're just friends." She picked at a thread on her jeans. "I'm not a fighter. There has to be another way to do my time in here. I need to think about my options."

"When Jester pushed me into the ice bin, I didn't do anything and she jumped me. You have to defend yourself."

"What's the worst that can happen?" Xochitl said. "You get beat up like me and Juana, but you go down fighting."

Mariana raised her head, nodded. I knew then she would not be the same anymore, just like me and Xochitl. We had become people we didn't want to be but had to be.

FORTY-SEVEN

I glanced around the large room in the San Bueno administration building. The place looked like the library in the school area except there were no books, just rows and rows of light brown files on the shelves along three walls.

We sat at one of the two tables in the room. Mrs. Snow opened a folder with my name typed onto a stickie label and flipped through several reports.

"Here's the police report." She stuck a pink Post-it on the side of the paper and moved the file in front of me.

My public defender never showed me anything like this before. I placed my purple notebook on the table and wrote down the time the police came to the apartment. I made notes on everything they said about finding Alek.

Mrs. Snow tapped her pen against the desk. "Are you done yet?"

I glanced up, saw her staring at her gold wristwatch as she sat across from me. She didn't like having to show me my main folder, but the form Ms. Palomarez gave me said I had the right to review my file.

"No, still reading. There's so many little boxes and numbers here. And this part has white tape over it."

"Penal code numbers. The covered section lists the names of witnesses, which you aren't privy to." She huffed. "What exactly are you looking for?"

"What time the police were called and how they found Alek."

Mrs. Snow scanned the report and tapped her finger on a section. "Here."

From the time a neighbor called the police it had been over two hours after I ran from Alek. The report said he had no pulse, he wasn't breathing, and blood stained the concrete near his mouth.

Flipping to the next page, I found a drawing, squares, arrows, and the name of our street. Mrs. Snow explained that the apartment buildings were the squares, next to them a squiggling line for the stairs. Behind the stair line was a stick figure, arms in front of the circle for the face, the line of legs crooked. Alek.

Nausea rocked my body. I gulped and pushed the file away. Mrs. Snow slammed it shut, put it back on the shelf with hundreds of others.

"Here's your pass. Run along now."

The twisted stick figure floated around in my mind and followed me as I rushed down the administration hallway and onto the sidewalk to the living unit.

Something in the drawing was wrong. Our apartment was in one corner of the square while Alek's body was behind the staircase of another section. When I bolted, he followed me and fell to the bottom of the stairs—in front of them, not behind or one staircase away. He pushed his chest up with his arms to get off the concrete. What was he doing behind the neighbor's staircase two hours later?

The coroner's report hadn't come in the mail yet and it was almost the end of May. I needed that report so I could read what the examiner said happened to Alek. Something to tell me what happened after I ran. To make sense of the drawing.

I handed Mrs. Shaffer my pass from the admin building. She took it and waved me over to the dayroom side of the staff counter. Everyone was locked in their rooms for lunchtime, so the place was quiet. In the back office, Ms. Montes talked on the phone.

"Did you find what you were looking for in your file?" Mrs. Shaffer asked.

"Yes, thank you. Any mail for me?"

"Sorry, no."

Maybe she wanted me to tell her why I was in the admin building. I hadn't told her or Ms. Montes why I needed to read my case file because I didn't want anyone to tell me to stop looking for answers. Ms. Montes went by whatever the court papers said so anything I found out didn't matter to her unless the information was in a report. If I told her about the police report drawings, then she'd believe me.

"How's your daughter?" Mrs. Shaffer asked.

"Last week I received the Spanish Translation form but I haven't gotten the letter yet. I don't know how they are, but I hope they're okay."

Lupe hadn't written to me in months. In that time, I sent three letters to her, one to her husband in Arizona, one to my brother, and one to Maribel. Only Maribel wrote back. She didn't have any news about Lupe's plans and she said no one answered the telephone at my papá's house.

What if Lupe already left Mexico with Katrina? Or she left Katrina with my papá? Either way wasn't a good situation. The not knowing was taking bits and pieces of my heart. Every day I slipped down into misery, lost in my memories when I went to bed. The only difference was I didn't cry anymore.

"Have you written to your sister?" Mrs. Shaffer asked.

I shook my head. "I don't have a job anymore, so no more stamps to write every week."

"Well, you have a new job. I've assigned a new work position. Gardener." She winked at me.

"Me? You're hiring me, Mrs. Shaffer? And paying me too?"

"You're doing a fine job out there. I am assigning you a helper, part-time, on a trial basis."

"Xochitl or Mariana are good workers."

"I'm placing Paula Alvarez with you. She worked with you once and you both seemed to do fine. Teach her how to care for the plants and harvest them when the time comes."

I tried to form the words to say I was grateful but having Babydoll help me wasn't a good idea. Still, getting paid would provide me a way to buy canteen and more stamps to write to Lupe and Maribel.

Mrs. Shaffer cleared her throat. "You're surprised, I see. You don't want the job?"

"Um, yes. I'll do the best job I can to train her. Thank you, Mrs. Shaffer."

FORTY-EIGHT

Mrs. Shaffer assigned me and Babydoll to take care of the garden for an hour every other day. Whenever she was in the unit, she made sure we got out to the backyard, but when Ms. Montes was there, I had to remind her and she'd grunt or roll her eyes at me. I didn't care how she acted when I asked as long as she let me and Babydoll outside.

We'd take our supplies out to the end of the vegetable patch and start working. Sometimes we weeded the area or picked off bugs. I had to do that part because Babydoll always made a face and refused to pick up a snail.

The damp, crumbly dirt between my fingers made me feel like I was still in the real world. I breathed easier. Different smells drifted in the air when I watered or turned over the dirt or inspected a leaf. The earth smelled a little different than it did in Santa Isabel, but the plants grew bigger and bushier every week.

We talked like my mother would with her comadre but we never talked about Babydoll's miscarriage. Instead, we described our hometowns or the kind of house we each wanted or guessed what kind of animal a cloud resembled.

Babydoll's dream house was two stories high, sky blue with white trim and a wrought iron gate surrounding the front yard. My dream house was two stories too, with balconies so I could see the yard outside. I wanted a big magnolia tree in the front yard and lots of geraniums. In the back, I wanted a vegetable garden, sunflowers, and a big fountain like at the mercado plaza.

"Or we could have our own house, together. We'll have three rooms," Babydoll said while she traced rooms on the ground with her finger. "One for us, one for Katrina, and one so you can sew clothes."

"Yes, a whole room to sew dresses for Katrina. For you too."

"In our bedroom, we'll have a queen bed with—"

"We have one bed?"

"Uh-huh, and a big-screen TV." She stretched her arms out wide. "We'll have a cat too. One of those orange stripey ones."

When she described the furniture and colors of the house, I thought Babydoll having dreams was a good thing. I didn't want to take them away so I went along with her fantasy. I wondered if this was the type of home she always wanted but never got?

"Do you ever wish your life had been ordinary like going to high school or dances?" I asked.

She lowered her head, her hand fingering the dirt. "Sometimes, but I get sad when I think about it, so I don't."

I knew what she meant. Whenever we spoke about regular things on the outside, the memories were contagious, infecting our minds with things we used to have or used to do like go to the store and buy candy or a soda.

"Time to pick the tomatoes, the güeros, and oregano." I dragged the cardboard box over to the row of chiles.

The Garden of Second Chances

"*Güeros?*"

"The name of the yellow chiles."

"Oh, okay." Babydoll yanked a chile off the plant, bending the slender stalk.

"Wait." I crouched in front of her. "Hold your hand on the stalk, like this, and tug. Slow."

She covered my hand with hers, pressing her chest into my shoulders. "Like this?" she whispered in my ear.

My breath caught. Tiny goosebumps ran down my back. I pulled my hand away. Something like excitement filled me but confusion crowded into my mind. My body wanted to lean into her but my brain said, *It's Babydoll, we're friends.*

She laughed. "You're so pretty when you blush."

"I'll pick tomatoes, you, uh. . . ." I couldn't make my mouth work. "The chiles."

We harvested the plants in silence. I glanced over to where Babydoll knelt, plucking pale yellow chiles carefully from the bush. She held up each güero and inspected it before she dropped it into the box. I'd never seen her look so happy.

"When we get out, I'll help you take care of your baby while you go to business school, or work," she said.

When I got out, I wanted to return to Mexico for Katrina. There I would start a new life with my daughter, alone.

I had to tell Babydoll what I wanted to do, but if I didn't agree with her, I was afraid she'd try to hurt herself again. I'd have to find a way to let her know my plans. Soon.

FORTY-NINE

The social worker's office was crowded with three of us. Ms. Montes sat next to me and across from Mrs. Snow for my sixty-day evaluation. They shuffled papers and files. I rubbed my palms against my thighs and waited to give them the new information about my case.

"Tell us anything else you remember from the night of your committing offense," Ms. Montes said.

This was my chance. "Mrs. Snow took me to read the police report. It said they got to the apartment two hours after I ran from Alek and found him with no pulse behind the staircase. He wasn't at the bottom, where he fell."

"He could have crawled to the location," Mrs. Snow said.

The image made me wince, but I went on. "That night, I ran through the apartment parking lot to the bus stop and waited a couple of minutes. Alek wasn't behind me. He must've gone back up to the apartment. I think someone killed him after I ran away."

Ms. Montes sighed. "There's no evidence of that, Ivanov."

"You should have called 911 emergency," Mrs. Snow said. "At least provided care for him in his last minutes of life."

"I wasn't thinking he was hurt." I rubbed my forehead massaging my growing headache. "I didn't want to be hit again or have my baby injured. That's why I ran."

"Still, you need evidence, proof of what you claim happened," Ms. Montes said.

"Proof? I've waited weeks for the coroner's report. Would you call the office to see if they got my letter?"

"It's only been three weeks, wait at least one more," Mrs. Snow said. "Now back to your evaluation. We took points off your progress because of the fight and your discipline reports."

"But I didn't start the fight. I defended myself."

"Funny, how you always hurt someone when you defend yourself," Ms. Montes said.

"I've never hurt anyone in my life."

"The crime, your fight? You need to find other ways to solve your problems. You didn't earn any time off this month," Ms. Montes said.

I wanted to scream at her foolish statement. She should open her eyes and see how hard it was not to fight inside this place, with people cursing, hitting, and threatening you all the time. I paused, steadied my breath like Xochitl told me, and thought about what to say.

"If I didn't run, Alek would hurt me or the baby real bad. Jester came into my hall and hit me when I wasn't looking. I don't know what you want me to do. Tell me."

Neither of them said anything. Ms. Montes shut my folder.

Mrs. Snow leaned forward against her desk. "One more thing, Juana. Ms. Montes said you and Paula Alvarez seem to be very close. I don't think it's appropriate."

"Why? She's a nice person and Mrs. Shaffer assigned her to work with me."

Ms. Montes stood and opened the office door.

She wanted me to leave, but I needed to know why she'd say not to be friends with Babydoll. "Why is it wrong?"

"You lose yourself in relationships with other people. Paula has a lot of problems, ones she needs to work out," Mrs. Snow said. "You have a child and you have to plan your future with her in mind. Relationships will distract you."

"Think about it." Ms. Montes waved me out of the office.

The comments didn't make sense. I liked Babydoll and she needed me. She always asked me what I thought about things and told me I was a good mother. When she asked about what happened with Alek, she didn't call me stupid for staying with him. I didn't want to stop talking to her and I didn't want staff to be right.

Babydoll plopped into a TV row chair next to me. The wide seats had a tall back so the staff and the other girls couldn't see when shorter girls, like Babydoll and me, sat in them.

"Got you something." She pulled a pink hairbrush from under her tee shirt.

"My brush." I glanced up at her smiling face. "Thank you."

"That bitch has all kinds of stuff already. Turn around, I'll do your hair." Babydoll parted the back of my long hair into sections and brushed. "In group, you told us you ran away from your husband because he hit you. Didn't he hit you when you guys were going out?"

"No. He became a different person after I had the baby."

"Guys always change. You can't depend on them. Girls, either."

"He got worse after he lost his job. After those two men came to our apartment, he was nervous all the time."

I told her how Alek messed up our apartment looking for money and when he overturned Katrina's bassinet and hit me.

"Messed up." She shook her head. "I bet he burned those guys for drugs or money, and they came looking for him."

"That's what Xochitl said. I asked to read the police report and coroner's report so I could have proof, but Ms. Montes still doesn't believe me."

Babydoll snapped her fingers, her eyes wide. "What if those guys saw him after he fell down the stairs, took the chance, and killed him?"

I bit my lip, imaging the men dragging Alek. "The police found him behind the staircase of the apartments next to ours, not in front where he fell."

"See what I'm saying? He could've gone back to your apartment, then they came and threw him over the side of the stairs."

My shoulders tensed. We lived on the third floor. What if what she said was true?

She leaned into my shoulder. "You're shaking."

"What if they did that?" The image that flashed before my eyes sickened me. I curled into a ball in the chair. "Poor Alek."

"I'm sorry, but it's a dog-eat-dog world." Babydoll shook her head and put her arm around my shoulders, held me tight.

It felt comforting but inside I was confused about what really happened with Alek and what was happening between me and

Babydoll. I remembered when her lips brushed my cheek and how I liked the feeling, the tingling of excitement.

This was how I felt with Alek long ago during the time before we left Mexicali when everything was good. When we laughed and hugged each other and got lost in time. I glanced at the desk.

One of the counselors watched the girls in the dayroom while the other did a hallway count. I stood, but Babydoll grabbed my hand, pulled me back.

"Stay." She moved my hair away from the side of my face, brushed her lips on my cheek, and sent shivers down my back.

I lurched away from her body. "Babydoll, don't. I um—"

"You don't like it?" Her thin eyebrows rose into small tents on her forehead.

"I um, I like you. I like when we spend time together, but, uh—"

"But what? What is it?" Her voice, irritated and hard, rose.

How could I tell her I cared for her so much but I knew she wanted more from me? She wanted love, but I didn't have the kind of love she wanted. Still, I was afraid to lose her friendship. I had to explain myself.

"You are my very good friend. Like a little sister. We can hold hands, and hug when staff isn't looking, but we can't kiss. When I leave, they're deporting me to Mexico. I can't come back here, to the US. I can't live here. I need to be with my baby. You understand? I love you as a friend, Babydoll."

Her long lashes moistened with tears. She blinked them back. Oh my God, what did I do? Her tee shirt lifted and dipped with her deep breaths. I reached for her hand but she frowned and pulled away. Then she walked away from me and didn't look back. My heart sank.

All night, Babydoll wouldn't answer me or take my kite. I knew she was upset and I prayed she didn't hurt herself.

During breakfast movement, I sat at my table with Xochitl and Mariana. Babydoll moved into the kitchen with her group of four girls. She shuffled by me. I noticed her eyebrows were painted black and arched, pink blush on her cheeks with lip gloss on her mouth. I waved, but she turned her head away.

"Damn, where's she going?" Xochitl said. "That malflora's on the hunt."

"That's an ugly word. So she likes girls, so what?"

"Damn, whatever." Xochitl raised her palms. "Doesn't matter to me but I heard Bruja broke up with LaLa and started sending kites to Babydoll. That could create problems for you."

"Why do you tell me that?" I picked at the oatmeal on my tray. "I don't care. We're just friends."

But I did care. Bruja would hurt Babydoll just like Jester had. Telling her how I really felt was the hardest thing I did in here but not telling her would've been worse. I'd be pretending just to go along with her dream and forget that I had my own. I needed to return to my baby, be part of the family again. Nothing could get in the way of that hope.

"I heard Bruja tattooed 'Babydoll' on her leg," Mariana said. "Jester got mad when she heard, even though Sadgirl is still her girlfriend."

"Who told you?" Xochitl asked.

"Chantilla. I was doing her hair."

A couple of Chantilla's friends in the unit played cards and were friendly with Mariana now that she was the hair stylist for the unit.

"So, you're in with the Crips now?" Xochitl asked.

"I'm not *in* the gang. I can still be friends with you guys, so don't worry."

"Aren't you afraid of her girlfriend? The one who hit you."

Mariana swiped the air with her hand. "Everything's cool. Chantilla said she talked to her. The girl won't even go to choir anymore."

"Scrape," Ms. Montes called out.

The row next to ours stood up to take their trays to the garbage bins. Babydoll passed in front of our table. My glance caught hers for a second before she cut her eyes at me.

"I don't think she's your friend anymore," Xochitl said.

Chantilla strolled into the dayroom and called Mariana over. She jumped from her seat, next to me, and left with a "later." I watched them talk and laugh like they were the best of friends. The way I thought we had been. I studied my vocabulary list until someone bumped the foot of my chair.

"Don't ask me to help you no more." Babydoll stood in front of me, her mouth twisted like she wanted to spit. "Tell staff to find someone else for your stupid garden."

"I didn't mean to hurt your feelings. I like you so—"

She walked away leaving me with a sinking feeling and wondering if I'd made a mistake. I moved over to where Mariana stood behind Chantilla's chair, braiding her hair, sharing a honey bun.

"You help me in the backyard later?"

"Geez, I don't think so. I have choir later."

Xochitl entered the dayroom from an appointment.

"Come sit next to me," I said.

"You sure?"

"I'm tired of everyone's rules. Sit here."

"Looks like Mariana made her decision. She's gonna hang with a group for protection. Stupid."

"Don't blame her. It's real hard to be alone."

"Don't I know it," Xochitl said. "You look like you're hard-timing. Snap out of it. Shake it off before the feeling drags you down and gets you depressed."

As if my sadness could disappear in an instant. I turned away from her so she wouldn't see the anger rising to my cheeks. "Easy for you, you'll be leaving soon."

An ugly sense of darkness had been with me for days. Over and over I dreamt of Katrina and Lupe wandering in the desert, the mountains. They moved in and out of my fitful dreams. Hoping to lose the heaviness in my mind and body, I prayed the rosary like Father Anthony suggested. When I prayed, I stared out at the moon, hoping to remember my mother's consejos or a sign to help me go on, tell me what to do, but there was nothing.

"Juana, are you listening to me?" Xochitl shook my arm.

"What if Lupe crossed the border? Maybe that's why I haven't received a letter from her."

"Nah, your cousin Maribel would tell you."

"I heard stories of the places where they put immigrants.

Places with metal bunk beds like ours, in big dorms with toilets out in the open, worse than here. Children and babies, young women and viejitas, everyone together."

Xochitl sighed. "Yeah. The detention centers are all over the US now. Fucked up. Exactly why I was protesting. People don't get due process rights."

"If Lupe comes to the United States, she could be stopped by the Migra. They'll take Katrina away when they find out she doesn't belong to her."

"No they won't," Xochitl said. "Will they?"

"They can. Happened to a girl in Centre Juvenile Hall."

"Sucks. One of the worst things about being locked up is not knowing what's happening on the outside," Xochitl said.

A long sigh escaped from my lips, along with some of my hope. The feeling I had was worse than not knowing what was happening on the outside. I didn't know what was happening to me on the inside either.

"I'm going to my room." The bright lights, the TV laughter, the smell of the floor wax and detergent coming from the laundry room were too much to handle. I sank into my chair and covered my eyes with my arms.

"Stay out here and talk," Xochitl said.

"What if Lupe tries to cross and is arrested? What if she's in one of those detention centers now? Will Katrina be with her? Will the Migra ask her if the baby is hers and to prove it?"

My stomach rolled. I grasped my knees to my chest and huddled myself in the chair, trying to keep steady. The questions bouncing in my head now weighed on my chest, crushing the breath out of me.

"Juana," Xochitl shook my arm. "You look like you're gonna throw up."

I shook my head. "I can't take this anymore."

FIFTY

All evening my worries piled on top of each other and drowned me in misery. Xochitl's advice to "snap out of it" was wrong but right too. It wasn't easy to change in an instant.

The food slot door opened with a groan and clanked shut. I turned in my bed to see something plop on my cell floor. The squeaky steps of tennis shoes faded in the hallway as I struggled with whether to climb out of bed or not. Letters delivered bad news. The thick envelope lay near the door. I had to take a step forward. I wrestled out of my bed covers.

The return address said, Los Angeles Department of the Coroner. Finally, five weeks later, the information. I hesitated. What if there were descriptions of how Alek looked when the police found him? Or pictures of his body? What if the coroner didn't prove he had taken drugs? What if the information inside this envelope showed Ms. Montes and the staff that he suffered and died because I didn't call the emergency line?

I couldn't take that right now, not in the dark of my room, by myself. I slid the envelope under my mattress, near my feet, afraid it might give me nightmares if the pages were under my pillow. The information would have to wait until I met with Ms. Dillon and Xochitl in the morning.

I glanced around the library as soon as I entered. I didn't want anyone to know my business. Ms. Dillon and Xochitl sat at the table.

"I got this last night from the coroner, but I don't want to see any pictures. Would you open it?"

Ms. Dillon's forehead creased as she slid a pencil through the top of the envelope. She flipped through the pages. "They don't include photographs, Juana. Do you want me to read the report aloud?"

Xochitl wriggled in her chair next to me. "Yeah."

"No, you finish reading it first, Miss." I slid out a chair and waited.

She grabbed a pen and scribbled on a piece of paper. "What time did the incident happen?"

"Around nine at night."

"This report says the time of death is estimated to be 11:00 p.m."

"Does the report say where Alek was found? The exact place."

"Behind the staircase of apartment building D."

Like in the drawing in the police report. I shook my head. "No, something's wrong. We lived in the C building. He fell coming down the last set of stairs and pushed himself up from the ground. He kept yelling at me."

"Perhaps he crawled to the other staircase?"

Why would Alek do such a thing? If anything, he'd return to our apartment and wait for me to return. I left everything there.

"Does it say if anything got broken?" I asked.

"The injuries are listed." Ms. Dillon peered at me over her eyeglasses. "Do you want to hear them?

I braced myself. The police didn't tell me what happened to Alek, but his mother yelled at me plenty of times, telling me his nose was broken. This was the official report, so I nodded. I needed to find out.

Xochitl moved closer to me. "She needs to know if he had drugs in his system too."

Ms. Dillon scanned the empty library before she began. "I'll read directly from the report: 'The external injuries seem to be more than one would receive by falling down one flight of stairs. Subject had contusions, nasal fracture, and a cervical dislocation.'"

Xochitl nudged my shoulder. "That means he had bruises, a broken nose, and a broken neck."

I pressed my hands against my ears. That couldn't be true. After Alek fell, he pushed himself up, his nose wasn't bleeding.

"This report does say your husband had methamphetamine in his body." She stopped, pointed to the coroner's words under the part which said, Conclusion. "Read this, Juana."

"The injuries are inconsistent with a fall from apartment stair steps." Inconsistent?

"Could be that the coroner means the evidence isn't reliable," Ms. Dillon said. "I think you should talk to your counselor and social worker."

"Either way, she has a case for an appeal," Xochitl said. "Juana, you can say not all of the information was given at the time of trial."

"This could help my case. Alek was alive when I left and now, I have proof." My voice came out high-pitched and excited, which made my body tingle. I grabbed Ms. Dillon's hand. "You think I have a chance?"

"I'm not an attorney, but you might have a valid case here."

"Means a good case." Xochitl grabbed onto my other hand.

"You think the appeal comes back before my next hearing?"

"You'd need to do research," Ms. Dillon said. "I'll make a copy of this for your records, but please, take this to your staff. They need to know."

With the last two sheets of my birthday stationary, I decided to write two letters.

Dear Hermana,

I pray this letter finds you in Santa Isabel and you are feeling well. You must be six months pregnant by now. I'm sure you're very busy, but I need to hear from you.

How is Katrina? My papá? So much has happened since I last wrote. I've found out how to get more information on how Alek died and I can use that to tell the authorities. It's called an appeal. If I win, they'll let me out sooner than two or three years.

If you stay in Santa Isabel until after your baby is born, I can be home, take care of Katrina, and help you. I've had nightmares thinking of you both crossing the desert. Please don't leave. I'm praying a novena for good news from you. Please write.

Siempre, Juana

I wrote to Alek's mother, Anna, too. I began by saying I appreciated her concern for Katrina, but she was safe with my sister. Again, I told her I was sorry for Alek's accident and hoped she believed me, but in case she didn't I told her I read the coroner's report. I copied the section "External Injuries, Internal injuries, and Coroner's Findings" for her to read.

The injuries were awful things to write. She probably didn't know Alek took drugs, but she needed to hear the truth so she would understand he wasn't in his right mind.

I described the two men who came to our apartment the week before Alek died when our television was stolen. I think the men came back to the apartment after the accident and killed Alek, then put him behind the staircase or threw him off the third floor, like Babydoll said. Although Alek hit me and threw Katrina in anger, I told Anna I didn't want Alek to die but I couldn't live with him anymore. I urged her to look for the two men I described.

My memory traveled to the night when Alek fell. His raspy voice calling for me while I ran. His words, his anger, came with me when I sat down on the bus with Katrina in my arms and my whole life in my diaper bag, leaving Los Angeles.

A chilly breeze blew through my window as I used my last stamp on Anna's letter. I slipped both envelopes through my doorframe for the night staff to pick up.

How many more girls in here hadn't read their police reports? Or were without an attorney to spend time with them? Or who didn't understand the court process? How many of them had longer sentences because not all the facts were given to the court?

Feeling more awake than ever, I gazed out of my window. The streetlights around the yard glowed like dying candles in the evening fog. Although I couldn't see the vegetable garden, I tried to breathe in the aroma of the tomatoes and oregano. Some scent to tell me the plants were growing, or there was a change in the air, something to keep me hoping for better things to come.

FIFTY-ONE

During the night, better things did not come. Instead I had nightmares of Alek chasing me and falling down the stairs over and over. I'd run past the crowded parking lot, crash into cars, and fall. Then I was running in the desert, under a dark moon, over dirt and jagged rock, coyotes howling in the distance. A city bus raced past me and I yelled, "Stop, stop, I need to get on." But it sped away. Alek caught me, threw me to the ground, and broke my fingers. Katrina disappeared from my arms like a ghost. I kicked Alek away, but he hit me in the face, blood spurting from my nose, dripping into my mouth, where I gagged on the metallic taste.

I woke, wet with sweat, gasping for breath. Sitting up, I uncurled stiff fingers from the tight balls of my fists. The swollen cut in my palm ran from the end of my pointing finger to the bottom. My hand throbbed.

"Ms. Ivanov, didn't you hear me knocking?" Mrs. Shaffer poked her head in my room and held an envelope in her hand. "I need you to sub in the kitchen. Here's a letter for you. Be ready in five minutes."

I nodded and reached for the letter. From my cousin Maribel and stamped May 2nd. I slipped the paper out.

My dear Juana Maria,

There is no easy way to tell you. Lupe crossed into Arizona two weeks ago to join her husband. Yesterday I received a phone call from him telling me the Border Patrol picked her up. He said there are several detention centers in Arizona but he didn't know where she was placed. She could be in a center or a county jail.

"Nooo. . . ." I moaned, sunk to my bed, the letter clutched in my hands. I forced myself to breathe and kept reading.

If they question Lupe about Katrina and she says she isn't her own child, the Migra will take her to protective services because she is a US citizen. I'm so sorry Juana. I called every agency I know of for help, but I can't get any answers except one of them said sometimes it takes months for the Migra to deport people.

There had to be a mistake, this couldn't be true. Maybe it's not Lupe the Migra picked up, but another Guadalupe Flores Garcia. Who was this protection services? Protection from who?

I'll continue looking, even if I have to go to all those places. I have my green card and maybe they'll give me Katrina if you write me a guardianship letter. I called your papá but he didn't have Katrina's birth certificate.

Please write to your papá and tell him what's happening

with you. He should know. Send me a letter when you receive this information. If you can call me that would be better. We are praying this turns out well.

Your prima, Maribel

Stupid, stupid Lupe. Why did she take a chance and cross the border? Tears fell on the crumpled paper as I read it again; maybe I read it wrong. *I'm so sorry Juana. I called every agency I know of for help, but I can't get any answers.*

My throat dry, my vision blurred, I fell to the floor. Katrina's gone. My chest tightened like a coil wire in a ballpoint pen, curled up, ready to spring loose. Groans climbed up my chest, forced their way into my throat and out of my mouth.

"Ivanov? Juana, Juana," Mrs. Shaffer called my name, banged on my door.

Tears slid down the side of my nose, into my mouth. "Leave me alone. Just let me cry."

The overhead light clicked on. A flood of light made me wince when the door opened. The suddenness snapped me back into reality.

"Breathe, Juana," Mrs. Shaffer said. "Tell me what happened."

The sound of her voice surprised me. I stood, wiped my face, and handed her the crumpled letter.

"My baby, the Migra has her and my sister Lupe. I don't know where Katrina's birth certificate is or . . . I don't know what to do."

She took the letter from my hand, smoothed it against the wall, and read it. When she handed it back to me she sighed.

"When Ms. Montes comes in, we'll talk with Mrs. Snow. In the meantime, write out a letter of guardianship for your cousin."

She shut the door. I sat on my bed, stunned she read Maribel's letter and offered to help. Smoothing back my hair, I washed my face. The guardianship letter I wrote for Lupe last month must not have gotten to her before she left. Another one might work or not, but I had to do something—I couldn't continue to sit in my room and cry.

I followed Ms. Montes to the staff office, clutching the coroner's report in my hand. CO Isadora sat at one of two desks in the staff office, reading file folders.

"I'm studying for my interview to be a counselor," she said. "Okay if I'm in here while you two talk?"

"Sure." Ms. Montes's eyes darted to me. "Have a seat."

"Ms. Ivanov?" CO Isadora said.

I jerked my head around. She was asking me? I nodded.

"So, Mrs. Shaffer told me what happened with your sister," Ms. Montes said. "She's allowing you a telephone call."

"Yes, my cousin Maribel is going to try and find Lupe and my baby. They're in a detention center in Arizona."

"You can call after school movement."

"Thank you, Ms. Montes. Can we talk about the coroner's report too? I just got it in the mail, I want you to read what it says."

"We have a few minutes before school movement." She glanced at her wristwatch.

She took the papers, sat back in the chair, and read the report. "I asked you several times about your crime. Why didn't
you mention Alek's drug use before or the men who came to
your apartment?"

"I didn't think of the men before or realize Alek took drugs.
I didn't know what the coroner's report said, either. I wrote and
told his mother about the information because she wants custody of Katrina. But with that information, I want to make an
appeal of my case." I ran out of breath talking so fast.

Ms. Montes swiveled her chair back and forth, watching me
so intently I wanted to look away, but I remembered what Xochitl told me. I stared back at her, straight into her eyes.

"I'm telling you the truth."

"Ivanov, you can't appeal your court case anymore. You can
only appeal within sixty days of the judge's order."

My mouth dropped open, sucking in all the air around me.
Words stuck in my throat. I pressed my lips shut with the palm
of my hand, feeling the scar. I wanted to run out of the room, out
of the unit, across the field, back into my former life when I had
parents to take care of me. When I wasn't alone.

Don't scream. Breathe. My hands trembled. My stomach
jumped like I had been hit.

"Take a breath, Juana," CO Isadora said.

I nodded and inhaled. "The Correctional Board needs to
have this information. I have the right to appeal."

The CO scribbled something in her notebook.

"You can use this info for your annual evaluation, next year."
Ms. Montes stood and moved to the office door. "I'll talk to Mrs.
Snow about this tomorrow."

"I have to wait nine months to tell the Board what happened? It'll be too late."

"Isadora, would you take her to her room?" Ms. Montes said.

The sound of her voice, the way she dismissed me made my neck muscles stiffen and legs twitch. My chest heaved. I fought the urge to spring up from my chair, slap my hand on the desk, do something to make her listen.

"Walk with me," CO Isadora said in a low voice, tilted her head towards the door.

Don't lose it and get sent to seg again, I told myself. I drew in a long breath and turned to the CO.

"Let's go to your door and talk," CO Isadora said as we walked across the dayroom. "Do you ever wonder why your mother-in-law asked for custody of your daughter?"

"Because she don't like me."

"Maybe it has more to do with missing her son."

I hadn't thought about that. Of course, she missed him. I thought about him a lot too. "Ms. Isadora, I'm all twisted up inside. I keep thinking of my sister and baby in a detention center, in a cell like in here. I'm scared for them."

She nodded. "I understand. This is a bad situation, but you do have your cousin on the outside to help, and Ms. Montes granted you a phone call today." We stopped at my cell. "Tell me about your baby's grandmother."

"Anna? Well, she visited with us a lot. Almost every day. When she picked up Katrina, she called her angelochek, my little angel. All the time saying Katrina was big for her age like when Alek was a baby. She would be so very happy, hugging and kissing Katrina."

"Sounds like she cared for your baby."

"Yes. I wrote to her yesterday and told her about the coroner's report and all his injuries. And about the Russian men who came to the house."

CO Isadora's lips squinched together.

"Did I do something wrong?"

"Juana, do you think you should have mentioned his injuries in a letter?"

"I can't phone her. She'll hang up on me."

"Alek's mother lost her son and her only grandchild. How do you think she feels reading that information?"

"Ms. Isadora," Mrs. Shaffer said. "Need you at the desk."

"Alek's mother isn't your enemy. She's grieving too," CO Isadora said and locked my cell door.

Sitting on my mattress, I thought about what she said. Anna suffered too. She must miss Alek and Katrina terribly.

I pulled my rosary out of my locker along with the photo of Katrina and held them to my chest while rubbing the brown beads between my thumb and finger.

While I said the ninth rosary, the last one for a novena, I thanked God for the phone call to Maribel. Hearing her voice and her plan to visit detention centers would give me more determination.

I prayed for Maribel to find Lupe, for my guardianship letter to keep Katrina from protective services. I prayed for forgiveness for not calling an ambulance for Alek and to be forgiven by his mother for not thinking about how she'd feel when she read a letter about her son's death. Lastly, I prayed for a way out of San Bueno Correctional.

After I finished, my mind filled with Ms. Isadora's words and the look of concern in her eyes when she talked about Alek's mother. Telling a mother about her son's horrible injuries was a mistake. Now she would have nightmares like those I had after reading the report.

My eyes prickled with tears. Prison made me a different person. I wanted to do the right things, be the way I was before, but the rules changed the way I acted, who I talked to, even who I was.

Maybe I changed because I was losing hope. I'd become like the other girls, the ones with coldness in their eyes who I thought didn't care about anything or anyone. And then I realized we had a lot in common. The coldness they showed wasn't because they didn't care anymore. They did, deep down inside. But their hopes were covered up with heavy blankets of hurt, pain and hopelessness. So many tears smothered any warmth in their eyes and eventually turned them into stones.

FIFTY-TWO

Xochitl waved a large three-ring binder in front of my face while I sat at the desk in the library. "Found it. The Policy and Procedures Manual. Give me a sticky note."

I shut the manual I had in front of me. "Let me read it."

She set the book down, tapped her finger over the words. "Start here."

I read aloud, "The appeal panel may grant the appeal, deny the appeal, modify prior Board action, order a rehearing, or refer the case to the Full Board En Banc."

"What does this mean for me?"

"That the board members can change what the first Correctional Board ordered when they gave you a three-year sentence. After you give them the new evidence they could give you less time, like a year." Xochitl clapped her hands and bounced on her toes. "Even let you go."

My heartbeat raced; my fingers shook the pencil I had in my hand. "Give me less time or let me go?"

There was a chance to have someone hear me now and not in nine months? Everything stirred inside me.

"That's what it sounds like to me."

I copied the sentence from the manual. "I have to do my appeal right now. My English has to say everything I need it to say."

If this was a way out of here, I had to take it. I wasn't going to wait a minute longer. I'd ask Mrs. Snow for appeal forms as soon as I returned from school.

In math class, I couldn't sit still. I told the teacher my monthly started and held my stomach to show him it really hurt. He dismissed me. I rushed back to the unit so I could get the appeal papers before Mrs. Snow left for the weekend. The appeal could change everything.

The front door of the Mariposa unit buzzed before I got to the door. Jester. I paused. She was handcuffed, but that didn't mean much. Ever since our fight in the hallway, she'd been in segregation. The CO walked behind her, carrying a cardboard box marked with GONZALES in big black letters.

A few feet away from me she stopped, spit on the sidewalk. "Fuckers are transferring me to the pinta."

Xochitl told me Jester was charged with assault because she kicked a CO when they took her for her shower. Her next stop was the adult women's prison up north. We weren't friends, and I didn't understand the way she acted, but I didn't hate her or fear her anymore.

"Be good, Dolores. Keep drawing." I ran into the unit. Her roaring laugh followed me until the door shut.

"Why're you back so early?" Ms. Montes sat at the staff desk with Mrs. Shaffer.

Hope ran through my body like electricity. Out of breath, my forehead moistened with sweat.

"My period. Can you give me appeal papers, for the new information on my case?"

Ms. Montes leaned her chin in the palm of her hand. "We've been through your information, it's too late to appeal and Mrs. Snow left. She'll be back in a week."

Her words slapped me back into reality. Hope didn't live in San Bueno Correctional. My face dropped into folds, my lip shook on its own, tears tingled in the back of my eyes. *Don't cry,* I told myself.

"If the Board tells me no, they tell me no, but I need to try."

"Go ahead and look for the forms in the office, Ms. Montes," Mrs. Shaffer said. "I can spare you for a few minutes."

"Well, come on." Ms. Montes huffed and heaved herself out of the rolling chair.

I ignored the words coming up my throat. *Never mind, you're right, I'm wasting my time.*

"Thank you, Mrs. Shaffer, Ms. Montes," I said instead and followed her into the office.

Her long fingers walked across the tops of the folders in the file cabinet until she pulled out a paper. She pushed in the drawer and sat across from me. With the appeal form still in her hand, she leaned forward, holding it up in the air. "Not so fast."

"Ms. Montes, why do you hate me so much?"

"What're you talking about? This isn't personal."

"You blow out your breath like I'm bothering you or like you don't want to help me."

"I want you to reflect on what you did, really stop and examine your actions."

"You don't like me because of what you believe I did."

"No, I want you to think about how your offense hurt others and take responsibility for your actions. Like the other day. How did you feel when you read the coroner's report about Alek?"

"Terrible. I can't sleep."

"Can you imagine how his mom felt?" she said. "So why did you tell her about the details of the report?"

The silence between us was so still I could hear myself breathe. I squirmed but Ms. Montes didn't take her eyes off mine.

"I know now that I should not have written her the letter, Miss."

"Why?"

My head dropped towards my chest while my hands twisted the bottom of my tee shirt. I thought of the conversation I had with CO Isadora and told her what we talked about.

Ms. Montes crossed her arms. "That's exactly what I mean."

I wanted to tell her that she never talked to me like CO Isadora. She yelled or didn't look at me, and acted like she didn't care. But I couldn't tell her all of that and risk her getting angry. She held the form I needed in her hand.

"Juana, whether your appeal is granted or denied, the fact remains she lost a son. You can't undo those things, but you can try to understand how she might feel."

Of course, I realize how she feels. I rubbed the sore muscle tightening across my neck. I lost Alek and my daughter too. Then I understood—that was the point.

"We both lost Alek and Katrina." A thickness filled the inside of my throat. I crossed my arms to keep my shoulders from shaking. "I understand that now."

Ms. Montes ripped tissues out of the box and brought them

over to my side of the desk. She waved them beneath my chin until I took one. "Here's the form. Bring the appeal back to me to look over or you can mail it yourself."

I returned to my room full of memories. Now I didn't want to file the appeal papers. The rosary lay on my bed. I picked it up and rolled the beads between my fingers.

My father used to tell me I did things too fast, without consideration, like when I told him I was moving to Mexicali to get a job to help the family. "Stay," he told me. "You are too young to be working so far away."

"Papá, I can send you money for your medicines."

"I don't need your help. You're the youngest. Finish school; you find a job later."

"First I'll work in Mexicali, then the United States and make lots of money."

"Don't go there, the Estados Unidos is not safe for a girl your age. I forbid you."

"Listen to Papá," Lupe had said. "Wait two more years, Juana. Please."

"I'm going." Those were my last words to them.

My sister had begged me not to go, even as I packed and told her I'd stay with Maribel in Mexicali.

With Alek, I wanted things my way. He didn't want to marry me, but I got a fake green card to leave for LA with him. Maybe, I deserved to stay here longer. So many bad decisions.

I repeated the Our Father out loud as I fingered the large bead. "Forgive us our trespasses . . ."

Forgiveness. I wanted my papa and family to forgive me for the worry I put them through. I asked for a way to help Anna instead of hurting her anymore. And then I pleaded with God to give me a second chance and to help me get out of here so I could return to Katrina. I couldn't change what already happened, but I could try to make the best out of what was happening now.

Words might not take away the nightmares Anna had after she read my first letter, but I needed to tell her I made a mistake and I was sorry. I took a sheet of paper from my locker and began writing.

FIFTY-THREE

I hadn't looked forward to this day. Xochitl and I waited in the empty dayroom for her release call to come over the intercom. Her brother got her out of San Bueno Correctional by winning her appeal in court.

She wore street clothes that he sent to her in a package. Real denim jeans and bright tennis shoes. Xochitl's face was different today. Sunnier and happy. I hadn't seen her smile so much ever.

"When your appeal returns, I wanna know what happens," she said, handing me a slip of paper. "Call collect."

"You go to a church and pray a rosary for me, okay?"

Xochitl side-eyed me but grinned. "I'm not Catholic, remember?" She leaned in close to my ear. "I'm leaving my stamps and some other stuff you'll need. Mrs. Shaffer has them. Listen, take everything out of the tampon box, okay?"

She'd always been generous. "Xochitl, my days will be lonelier without you."

"Damn, I'll miss you." She wiped her eyes with the back of her hand. "Remember what I said. Empty out the tampon box."

"Anaya, Xochitl" a voice from the overhead speaker blared. "Anaya. Mariposa."

The sound of the static made me jump. Mrs. Shaffer buzzed open the front door. "Time to go. Good luck, Ms. Anaya."

Xochitl gripped a wad of paperwork in her hand and reached for me with the other, giving me a quick hug. "Be brave," she whispered and raced out of the front door.

I ran to the dayroom window to see her jog up the concrete path, her long braid bouncing against her back. I waved until she disappeared.

Mrs. Shaffer went through the bag of stuff Xochitl left for me. "We usually don't let a girl leave things for someone else, but Ms. Montes and I made an exception in your case."

Once in my room, I turned over the bag. Stamps, stationery decorated with cats and dogs, noodles, shampoo, and lotion spilled onto the bed. More stuff than I'd ever had since I arrived.

Xochitl left twelve tampons, for which I was thankful. But why did she made a big deal about emptying the box? Flipping the box upside down, I peered inside and found one of the state sanitary napkins stuck at the bottom of the carton and pulled it loose.

The center of the thick pad was hard, it wouldn't bend. A slit ran alongside the side of the napkin. I stuck my finger in and wiggled out the object hidden inside. The shank. It looked like a dagger with a shiny handle of silver duct tape. A note stuck to the bottom of the napkin floated to the floor.

Without me for backup, and Jester gone, Bruja or another idiot might try to jump you. Stay trucha, hermana.

Xochitl's warning was true. Bruja watched me wherever I went, not in a mad-dog way, but in a "I'm looking at you, don't move out of line," kind of way. She might try to prove to Gina and LaLa that she was in charge now.

The shank, light in my hand, had more scrape marks along the edge where the tines and razor used to be. Pressing the sharp point against my bed cover, I wiggled it and a tiny hole appeared. It wouldn't take much to hurt someone. I hid the shank in my vent, where my stinger used to be.

Two weeks passed since I mailed my appeal and the letter to Anna about the coroner's report. Since I had a lot of stamps now, I stayed in my room after showers and wrote letters to Xochitl. I never telephoned Xochitl, only Maribel. I had to find out if she found Lupe and Katrina. There wasn't much to do in the garden anymore, but sometimes Mariana went outside with me.

Xochitl didn't write back. That happened a lot in here. You could be "tights," which meant good friends, and the next day you'd be enemies. Or someone said you're like a sister, and then didn't write and forgot about you. I tried not to think too much about her out there.

The light in my room blinked on and off. Two small envelopes slid through the door. I hurried to open the first one I grabbed.

June 5

Dear Juana Maria,

It was great to hear your voice the other day. I just received your letters of guardianship, but I haven't found where Lupe is being held and I haven't heard from her husband. I called your father to tell him about Lupe and found out your oldest brother lost his job and he, his wife, and children returned to your house in Santa Isabel. My father feels bad for hanging up on you before. He wants you to know you have a home with us whenever you get out.

Siempre, Maribel

I reread the letter three times. Her words brought the promise of a family back to me even though there was no news about Lupe or Katrina. I folded it back into its envelope and placed it into my notebook.

The next letter had a Los Angeles address I didn't recognize, with no name.

To Juana Flores,

How dare you send me ugly reminders of my son's injuries, only to tell me someone else is responsible for his death. I will never forget how he looked. I was the one who the police called to identify his body. You left him lying on the ground, to die. The court found you GUILTY. This is all I need to know.

I cannot walk from my bedroom to my kitchen without thinking of him. He's everywhere, sometimes as a little boy, looking up at me, sometimes as a teenager sitting at the table. His death tore my heart apart. My soul has disappeared. That is how much I miss my Alek.

You might be in jail, but you have his daughter, my

granddaughter, my mother's namesake, to comfort you.
When you leave there, you will take her away too. I will
never be able to see the piece of him which remains. You
took away two lives from me that night. I will not give up
the battle for my granddaughter.

Mrs. Anna Ivanov

The letter remained in my hands for a long time. Anna knew the hurt the mind and body go through when you remember those gone from you. She understood the feeling I had when imagining Katrina's smile or when thinking of her outstretched hand made me remember her softness, her baby powder smell. He was her baby once.

I reread the letter but Anna's words blurred on the paper. The faint glow from the overhead nightlight in my room provided enough illumination to find a sheet of stationery. I wrote in the dark. There was not much to say except I was sorry and ask for forgiveness.

My locker door creaked in complaint when I opened it and reached inside for Katrina's photograph. Her picture was small enough to fit inside the envelope and I hoped large enough to give Anna some happiness.

FIFTY-FOUR

I sat in a soft back chair against the brick wall, in sight of the staff at the desk. Ms. Montes said I had to spend time in the dayroom if I wasn't in the backyard. So, every day I chose the same spot and made sure my back was to the wall. I needed to see everyone in front of me.

Girls played cards, ironed, did each other's hair, argued, or gossiped. Mariana was the only person who talked to me, but she spent most of her time with Chantilla and her friends.

Gray foggy mornings and evenings blurred into the sameness of the weeks before. Sometimes, I didn't know the day of the week unless I looked at the calendar in my locker.

Mrs. Shaffer called the weather "June gloom." Ms. Montes called it coastal weather, but I couldn't smell the ocean, only the fertilizer they used in the surrounding fields.

Like the concrete walls in the school and the chain-link fences surrounding me, I became the color gray. I disappeared into the background.

"How come you don't kick it wit' us, Mouse?"

I glanced up. Babydoll stood a couple of feet away from my chair. The day after Xochitl left, she began talking to me, but not like before. Now she spoke using her chola voice.

"Come on. Ain't you down with the brown?"

"Bruja doesn't like me."

"She don't know whose side you're on," Babydoll said. "Neither do I."

"I'm on my side. I need to get out of here as fast as I can, back to Katrina, back to Mexico."

"Better with us than against us, que no?"

The wrong answer would lead to more pressure on me, from them and from staff. I had years left. Too many days and months of watching my back, being alone, holding onto the shank in my room.

"I'm not against you."

She bobbed her head, "Awright, esa."

"Ivanov." Ms. Montes waved me over from her seat at the staff desk, watched Babydoll return to the card table. "Go outside, the garden needs some weeding and watering."

She followed me to the supply closet and unlocked the door.

"But I did that yesterday," I said. "I thought you wanted me to spend time in the dayroom."

"You need some thinking time." She handed me the box of gardening supplies and followed me to the door that opened to the yard. "Are you strong enough to do what's right?"

Ms. Montes didn't wait for an answer and shut the door behind me.

Was I strong enough? What did she mean? I grabbed the trowel from the box and turned over the dirt around the tree trunk before I poured more water on its root line. The grass around it had become greener with the constant watering. The moist soil sucked up the liquid slowly. Sunshine peeked between the drifting clouds. I closed my eyes and inhaled the scent of the grass around me.

A hum filled the air reminding me of my mother's voice in the kitchen, in the garden, at my bedside. The smell of earth crowded into my nose, inviting me to take a deep breath. I leaned back on my arms, my face toward the sunlight struggling to shine through the gray. Calm washed through my body. Xochitl, Mariana, and Babydoll helped me change this piece of dry lawn into a garden that grew vegetables, flowers, and herbs. We gave this dying patch a chance to be something else, something more. I glanced at the last vegetables growing. The tomatoes.

Even though they were stuck in cages they grew larger. The plants climbed and twirled their thick vines inside and outside of the wood frame, their long green leaves poking through. Tiny yellow star-shaped flowers bloomed on the stems. I lifted a narrow leaf and flicked off an aphid.

Sticking my hands in the moist dirt, I wiggled my fingers. The slight breeze took me back to my family's home.

Santa Isabel was a million memories ago that brought me too close to what I couldn't have and left me feeling farther away, but I needed to remember those times. So simple, so happy. I didn't fear anything. I trusted everyone. The people who loved me didn't hurt me.

"Stay on the roadway," a booming voice from the communications tower crackled.

A girl scurried across the asphalt to the cement pathway. Diesel fumes filled the air. I sat up, watched a security van screech around the road.

My peace left. Life hurt. Simple didn't always remain. I'd

been a happy child, a pretend wife, a mother, and now I didn't know what I was. I remembered when Xochitl talked about her identity. She knew who she was and what she wanted.

Who was I now? A prisoner, a mother, a Mexican in America. A victim of domestic violence like LaLa said in group? I wasn't a teenager anymore. I was a young woman who had gone through a lot. I was all those things.

Ms. Montes's question sat in my heart. Was I strong enough to do what was right?

There were only a few ways to do my time in here. With Bruja and the gang, alone in my room under protective custody, or alone outside my room, living my own life, no matter how difficult that would be. I didn't want to walk around afraid. I didn't want to be called a victim of anything.

I thought about how I wanted my life to be in the future. I had a responsibility not only to myself, but to my daughter. What I decided, I decided for my child. What I did, I did to her or for her. I had to survive.

FIFTY-FIVE

We waited on the asphalt road outside our living unit. Chattering sounds, snickers, and high-pitched laughter surrounded me as we moved forward to the school quad. The new staff escorting the movement either didn't know or care that we were supposed to be on quiet.

LaLa and Babydoll stood in front of me, their long hair up in ponytails wrapped around until they looked like fat donuts. They crept out of line, straining their necks to the side, looking ahead at the living units before us.

"Hold up," the staff lady shouted.

We stopped in the middle of the road.

"Be ready, Mouse," Babydoll said and whispered something to LaLa.

"Put your hair up, esa." LaLa lifted her chin at me.

A security van roared past us. The staff lady's radio crackled, "Code 3, quad, Code 3, quad."

I shook my head. I wasn't going to be a part of whatever they were up to.

Mr. Jay from Gaviota and Ms. Montes ran out their unit doors, down the roadway, past us to the school quad.

"Move to the curb. Everyone sit down, sit down!" the lady said, waving her arm.

None of us sat. Instead, we stretched our necks back and forth to see what was happening around the bend of the road. Everyone pushed into everyone else's shoulders.

"Sit down, I said. Don't move," the staff lady yelled.

LaLa nudged Babydoll. "Puro Sur," she shouted and took off running to the school area.

Babydoll grabbed my arm. "Come on, Mouse. Let's go."

My shoulders tensed. I glanced around me, spotted Mariana, her eyebrows merged. She shook her head. "Don't," she mouthed.

I pulled my arm away from Babydoll. "No. I'm not fighting with anyone."

"But you're part of us. You got to."

"You can stay. You don't have to go."

She cocked her head to the side, leaned into my face. "You're fucked now." She took off running to the quad.

My insides trembled along with my hands. Sweat covered my forehead. *Stay*, I repeated to myself. Girls paced back and forth. Another van raced by us.

"Get down, get down!" The staff lady yanked the black mace container off her belt and aimed it at us. Fear crossed her face. Her finger hovered on the nozzle of the can. "I said to sit down."

"Damn." Chantilla waved her hands at her friends to sit. "We don't want any of that shit."

Nervous laughter rose through the line. I backed up to the curb and sat next to Mariana.

"Chantilla said a gangbanger from the north disrespected Jester before she left," she whispered. "The sureñas had to retaliate."

"Babydoll said I'm fucked."

Mariana touched my hand. "Oh Juana, they're going to come after you now."

I took a deep breath to slow the racing of my heart. "They'll do what they think they gotta do." I stood and dusted myself off.

My body was wound up so tight I might crack if I didn't move. I stepped up and down the curb. The asphalt and fences surrounded me like a cage. I thought of the shank still in my room, but if I used it, I'd risk hurting someone, receive more time, or the other person could stab me.

"Are you joining them? Don't do it," Mariana said.

"I can't do two and a half more years in this place. I can't."

"Sit down. Please, Juana."

"Take them back to their unit," an ear-piercing voice came through the speakers at the tower.

I glanced towards the school quad where the others had run to. I wanted to run in the opposite direction, run until I got to the fence. No one would come after me. They'd be too busy with the fights on the quad. Girls had done it before, climbed to the top until they got cut up on the razor wire. But I'd take off my sweatshirt, fling it across the top, throw myself over.

"Juana." Mariana's hand gripped my forearm. "Don't go to the quad."

"Sit down," the staff lady shouted at me. "Now, inmate."

Every moment of my life crowded my thoughts. Alek's accident, juvenile hall, the van ride to San Bueno, the grief inside these walls. The cursing, the fights, the shank I used. My lungs hurt.

What I decide for myself, I decide for my child, came to me clearly, like a gust of strong wind. I turned away from the quad. "I know what I want out of my life and it's not here."

"Inmate, come back here. Stop."

Mrs. Shaffer came into view, standing at the open door of the unit.

"Juana?" Mrs. Shaffer said.

I jogged past her, the staff desk, down the hallway until I got to my cell and slid against the door.

Mrs. Shaffer stood at the top of the hallway. "You returned before the group?"

"They were fighting in the quad, I had to get away."

"Hmm, I see your point, but you'll receive a disciplinary report for failing to follow staff's instructions."

The remaining girls came in from the school movement. They stared at me while they waited at their doors.

Once inside our rooms, the air buzzed with news. One of the girls said it wasn't a fight, it was a riot. Another girl said staff called it a "group disturbance" between the northern Chicana gangbangers and the southern ones. Four girls stabbed. Two staff injured.

"Quiet or I'll turn off the power in your rooms," Ms. Montes's voice rang out. "The unit is on lockdown."

Thumps and kicks on the cell doors responded to Ms. Montes's threats. I knew she'd grow angrier and turn off the water. We'd be in the dark with our toilets disabled except for the one flush.

Lockdown meant room searches. This time staff would tear apart the rooms, flip mattresses into the hallway, check everywhere with their mirrors and flashlights.

The shank inside my vent, hung by a thread and paperclip wrapped around the handle. Fishing it out, I jammed the tip of the shank under my locker and bounced on the handle with my feet until it snapped. Only the top cracked off, but it was small enough to flush down the toilet. The handle I threw down into my wall vent. Even if staff flashed a light in there and saw the thing, it was no longer a shank.

"Face to wicket for count," Mrs. Shaffer hollered down the hallways.

Toilets flushed. Pills, pruno, and other contraband disappeared into the sewer. I grabbed one of the smaller drawings I had of Katrina and put it inside my bra, safe from the COs who'd search my room.

Voices raced through the hallway. From my wicket, I saw one of the new girls sitting on the floor handcuffed, her face red and sweaty. A CO threw her letters and drawings into the hall.

"You mother-fucken bastard," she yelled.

"Gang related," he said. "Shut up or I'll move you to seg with your homegirls."

"Fuck you, punk," she screamed. "Wait till I get outta these cuffs."

"Hook her up, take her outta here," the CO yelled up the hallway.

The girl hadn't been assigned to school yet but in the dayroom, she sat with Babydoll. The number XIII was tattooed over her eyebrow. She wanted the COs to take her to seg so she could show the sureñas she was with them.

For the next two hours, the same thing happened over and over again. The doors opened, some shouting, and the doors shut. I stared out of my window until someone unlocked my cell.

"I shouldn't do this after your marathon run, but I need your help to make dinner trays," Mrs. Shaffer said.

I carefully rolled the food cart down the hallway behind Mrs. Shaffer. At my room, I peeked into the wicket. My notebook, blanket, and papers covered the floor. The mattress, stripped of sheets, leaned against the wall. Jester's large drawing of Katrina hung by its corner, torn down to the middle right near her nose.

A memory made me cringe. The mess reminded me of my apartment bedroom when Alek destroyed it. My room was a cell but it was my temporary home.

"Butthole." The words slipped out as I kicked my door, startling Mrs. Shaffer.

"What did you say?" she said from the end of the hallway.

"I'm sorry. Whoever searched my room tore my baby's picture." My chin rested on my chest. The anger had gone out of me but left my mind heavy.

She strode towards me, peered into my wicket. "Scotch tape will help. Let's finish up here first." Her eyes softened while her lips came up in a slight smile.

Her kindness kept me moving. "You want me to clean the kitchen after this?"

"Sure. Let Ms. Montes know."

I rolled the empty cart up towards the staff desk. "I'm going to the kitchen to clean."

"Wait up," Ms. Montes said.

She held something up in her hand. A discipline report, I was sure. My shoulders sagged as I sighed. She handed Mrs. Shaffer an envelope.

"Ms. Ivanov, you need to see this," she said.

"Another discipline report?"

"A letter for you." She held it up.

The envelope wasn't stamped "Spanish Translation Needed."

"Is it from Mrs. Ivanov?"

Mrs. Shaffer stretched her hand across the staff counter. A black stamp said, "Legal Mail" across the top. The address said Sacramento, California.

My fingers twitched while I tore open the envelope and unfolded the letter.

June 25

Ms. Juana Maria Ivanov,

After a review of your case and the coroner's report, your request for a Full Board En Banc hearing is granted. The sentence given to you by the Corrections Board will be reexamined within thirty days and a written decision will follow.

Sincerely, Ms. Maxwell, Chairperson

The letter fluttered between my fingers before I tightened my grip. My eyes flooded with warm tears. The walls around me whirled, the floor spun. I closed my eyes and swallowed.

"I have a chance now, Mrs. Shaffer, Ms. Montes."

They took the letter and read it.

"I think you do," Mrs. Shaffer said.

Tingles ran under my skin and out of my fingertips. With

Mona Alvarado Frazier

each breath, I pictured my home in Santa Isabel, Lupe, my mother in the garden, and Katrina's warmth against my chest.

I pressed the letter to my chest. The heaviness from my shoulders fell, my breathing became deeper, surer. They granted my hearing. I'd know my fate in thirty days, not next year.

336

FIFTY-SIX

"My mother's seeing a therapist," Mariana said while we sat together in the TV rows. "She says it's not my fault what happened. You know, with my stepdad."

Hearing about him forcing himself on her made me nervous, but I let her talk because she did that for me when I told her about Alek.

"Do you remember more now?"

Mariana shook her head. "I'm afraid to know. Do you think I should ask for a therapist?"

I nodded because I knew the kind of fear she talked about, fear mixed with shame and humiliation and wondering why you could love and hate a person who hurt you.

"What happened to you is too much for anyone to deal with by themselves."

The beginnings of a smile warmed her face. "Thanks. I do want to talk in private with someone. Did you find out anything about your baby and sister yet?"

"Every week I phone my cousin Maribel. She tells me what agency she's called or visited. She still hasn't found out which immigration detention center Lupe is at, no one will give her information."

I clutched at my burning chest. If I could just turn off my brain from thinking of Lupe and Katrina every minute.

"Try not to worry." Mariana patted my hand. "I'm sure Maribel's doing everything she can."

"Lupe is close to her delivery day. What if she's taken to the hospital, where will Katrina stay? What if the Migra's waiting at the hospital and deports Lupe without Katrina? There's no way for me to find out what's happening. I hate not knowing."

"Maribel will find them. You're lucky to have someone on the outside helping you."

I nodded. "I hold on to the hope so I can get through the next hour and the next day."

"Ms. Ivanov?" Mrs. Snow said.

She stood at the staff desk glancing from left to right in the dayroom. I popped out of my seat from the TV rows.

"My office, please."

"Could be good news." Mariana grasped my hand.

Mrs. Snow waved me to the chair in front of her desk. "We received our copy of the decision on your appeal. Please sit down."

My body wiggled in my seat, my fingers twisting in my lap. I concentrated on the small tower of files on her desk while I inhaled the heavy fragrance of her perfume. Mrs. Snow slipped a letter out of an envelope, unfolded it, and adjusted her eyeglasses. When she set aside the letter, I held my breath.

"As you know, the Full Board decided to grant you a hearing. The board members can choose to either readjust your parole consideration date or keep it the same. Do you understand?"

"Yes. Will I go here to the hearing or you're taking me someplace else?"

"Here at San Bueno with four board members. I'll place you on the calendar for next week. Ms. Montes will write a short report to go with your last review."

"Can I make a phone call, Mrs. Snow? I need to tell my cousin."

She nodded. "Let her know if the Board releases you, our transportation officer will take you to the bus station in Tijuana, Mexico. You'll need to make arrangements from there."

FIFTY-SEVEN

The night before my hearing I couldn't sleep, spending hours at my open window, watching the nearly full moon move like a snail across an asphalt sky. Laying on my bed, memories crisscrossed my mind. My past and my future collided, giving me a headache.

When the sun rose, so did I. I skipped breakfast and waited for three hours. Mrs. Shaffer unlocked my door, handed me a movement pass to the administration building.

"A letter came in for you." She handed me an envelope and buzzed open the door.

The address said Oakland, California. I slipped the letter out. It was from Xochitl's brother. He said she wasn't allowed to write anyone at San Bueno because she was "technically on parole," but she wanted him to tell me she thought about me. He reminded me to telephone any evening. *Be strong, be brave, be well amiga*, was the last line written in Xochitl's handwriting.

Our friendship did mean something to Xochitl and she figured out a way to let me know. She hadn't forgotten about me. The letter gave me more confidence as the CO buzzed me through to the admin building.

Staff crowded the hallway escorting girls into and out of the visiting room, others pushed carts of mail and file folders.

My mouth went dry. A mixture of nervousness and excitement filled my body. I thrust my pass at CO Isadora who sat at the small staff desk outside the hearing room.

"Take a seat, you're next," she said. "Relax."

I sat in the chair, my knees bouncing.

The door to the board room opened. "Ms. Ivanov," Mrs. Snow called out.

Ms. Maxwell sat in the center of the long conference table, her head down reading a file. The breath I'd held came out in a whoosh when I realized Mr. Axel wasn't there. The hearing officer I had before, Mr. James, sat to Ms. Maxwell's left in front of the flag of California. Two new men sat on her right with the flag of the United States behind their chairs.

One nameplate said, Mr. Tanaka. Everything about him looked polished, from his black suit, white shirt, and short gleaming hair. The other man, with a white mustache, sat behind a nameplate that said, Mr. Valdez.

"Good morning," Mr. James said, his brown suit rumpled like his smile.

My knee jiggled beneath the table. I pushed it down with my hand while I whispered, "Good morning."

The translator, Ms. Cobos, nodded to me before she sat next to Mrs. Snow.

"Ms. Ivanov, do you need a translator?" Mr. Valdez leaned closer like I was hard of hearing.

Startled, I moved back into my chair. "No, I speak a lot more English now." My voice came out strong.

He sat upright. "If you need to have something interpreted let us know."

"Thank you, Sir. I will."

Ms. Maxwell read my appeal letter out loud and flipped through the papers in my file. "Ms. Ivanov, there is conflicting information from these reports. Please understand we can't retry your case, only a judge has the authority, but we can decide whether the information here mitigates your offense. If so, the sentence you received at your initial board hearing may be modified. All of us must be convinced."

I looked to the translator. "What does 'mitigates' mean?" She explained. "Yes, I understand now."

"Tell the Board why you filed an appeal," Ms. Maxwell said.

"The police found Alek almost two hours after I left. The coroner's report said he didn't think Alek could die from falling from the staircase and he looked like he got other injuries— worse ones. I believe someone came by and hurt him, like the two Russian men who came to our apartment a couple of days after our apartment was broken into."

"The information about the two men isn't in the police report," she said.

"The police didn't ask me if anyone wanted to hurt Alek. When our television was stolen Alek didn't call the police, but I remember the date."

"Ms. Ivanov, why did you use a fake green card to come to the US?" Mr. Tanaka asked.

Burning with embarrassment, I told them the truth. "I was in love with my boyfriend, Alek. When I found out I was pregnant I wanted to get married. He didn't want to. When he told me he was leaving for Los Angeles, I panicked, ashamed to go back home to my father. He had told me not to leave. I bought a fake card and had Alek's last name as my own, pretending we were married."

Mr. Tanaka scribbled something on his yellow legal pad and then looked up at me. "Go on."

"My father only wanted the best for me. But I did what I wanted to do without stopping to consider what my actions did to other people who loved me or to myself."

"Your counselor's report says your husband hit you on two prior occasions and broke your nose once. Why didn't you leave him before this offense?" Mr. Valdez asked.

The question still bothered me, but I'd talked about the violence with Xochitl, Mariana, Babydoll, and the others in group counseling and no one made fun of me or called me stupid for staying with him. Taking a deep breath, I looked into his eyes.

"I thought if other people knew Alek hit me, they'd think it was my fault. That I wasn't a good enough wife or mother. I was embarrassed to go home, with a baby, because I had already disappointed my father."

Tears welled up, but I blinked them back and cleared my throat.

"Ms. Ivanov?" Mr. James said. "Go on."

"I thought I deserved the beatings as punishment for disobeying my father, for disappointing everyone. But no one deserves to be hurt like that. Now I understand what domestic violence is and what I could have done."

"What could you have done differently?" Mr. Tanaka asked.

"I should have taken Katrina, my daughter, and returned to

Mexico after Alek hit me the first time and there would not have been a second or third time. I was afraid if I called the police, they would deport me and Alek would keep our baby like he said, but I could have called the phone number I used to see at the bus stop, the one for abuse, and talk to someone. I was afraid to do that because I thought Alek would find out. But my baby's safety and my own should have come first."

"Ms. Ivanov," Mr. Tanaka said, "your statements say your husband fell to the bottom of the stairs. At the least, you are criminally negligent because any reasonable person would call for help for someone who fell down a staircase."

"Alek started to get up, he yelled at me. My first thought was to run away. I ran for my life and didn't stop or think. If I knew he was injured, I would have called 911 from a payphone or knocked on a neighbor's door but I was scared. A few seconds to make one call and everything would be different. Katrina would still have her father, Mrs. Ivanov her son. Alek might be alive."

Mr. Tanaka nodded. The room remained quiet except for the squeaking of the chairs and the pens on paper.

"Juana, tell us what you learned from your incarceration to help you in your future?" Ms. Maxwell asked.

I sighed while my mind dug through the memories of the past ten months of my sentence in Centre Juvenile Hall and San Bueno Correctional.

"After my mother died it seemed my whole life was full of problems, but the hardest times were here in San Bueno, the times without my baby. Life got very difficult, even more than when I was with Alek.

"I followed some people's rules that were wrong, wrong for

me and my life. I let embarrassment and fear keep me from speaking up for myself or asking for help just like I did with Alek. The most important person in my life is my daughter and when I make a decision, I need to think of how my actions will affect both of us.

"In school, I learned more English and math. Ms. Dillon, the librarian, helped me learn how to type on a computer and do research. I'm smarter than I thought. When I parole, I'll find a job to support my daughter."

My hands ached from clasping them so tight in my lap. Sweat pooled behind my neck.

All of the board members leaned back into their tall chairs. Mr. Valdez flipped through papers, Ms. Maxwell fingered her pen, and the others watched me. I felt frozen in time, everything quiet, just the sound of the big clock on the wall.

"One more thing, Ms. Ivanov," Mr. James said. "Your counselor reported that you cultivated a garden in the backyard of your living unit. Why did you come up with the idea?"

"At first, I wanted to be away from the other girls to stay out of trouble, but then I saw how learning about planting and growing things gave other girls who helped me a better mood. I watched them begin to dream, to have hope too. Most of all, the garden proved plants could grow in the rocky, dry soil near a dying tree that no one seemed to care about until we nurtured the ground. Now we have a garden of tomatoes, chiles, and the tree gives lots of shade."

Mr. James nodded. "I see."

Ms. Maxwell cleared her throat. "Gentleman, after reading the progress report from Ms. Ivanov's counselor, Mrs. Snow's case report, and the testimony we just heard, how do you vote?"

Mr. Tanaka turned towards Ms. Maxwell and asked questions about my time in juvenile hall. Mr. Valdez asked how many months I had left on my sentence. I leaned closer to the table, as they discussed my life.

Closing my eyes, I rubbed the scar on my palm from the cut of the shank. I remembered Xochitl's voice encouraging me to speak up, Mariana's gentleness, and Maribel's faith we would find Lupe and Katrina. My fingers uncurled from their tight grip while I breathed.

I raised my hand up. "Excuse me. Can I say one more thing?
They nodded.

"What Mr. Tanaka said, about negligence, that is true. I'm sorry I didn't make a phone call to the police once I got to a bus station, but I really thought Alek was okay. He may have hurt me but I didn't hate him. People might not understand that, but it's the truth. I'm trying to make better decisions, not only for me but for my daughter."

Ms. Maxwell glanced at the other board members and closed my file. "How do you vote?"

"Mitigating circumstances," Mr. Tanaka said.

Mr. Valdez nodded. "The coroner's report should have been brought to our attention at the first hearing."

"Yes," Mr. James said. "Everything we've read and heard points to lessening the time Ms. Ivanov originally received."

"We decided there are mitigating circumstances in your case. You've completed enough time here and are released from custody," Ms. Maxwell said.

"Released?" I turned to the translator, just to be sure.

She said the word in Spanish. I jumped out of my chair. "Thank you, thank you, you'll never see me again here, thank you."

FIFTY-EIGHT

The van bumped along the dirt road outside of the chain-link fence of the prison. The same officer who brought me to San Bueno, the one I called Iguana Eyes, picked me up to take me to Tijuana a week after my hearing. He drove past the INMATE PROCESSING sign and onto the freeway. I rode in silence, breathing in the strong scent of eucalyptus from the trees lining the outside roadway.

Free of handcuffs, I spread out my arms, dug my fingers into the cracked plastic of the seat. I held on to the realness of the moment. No more steel against my skin or hands behind my back. No rules telling me who I can talk to, laugh with, or hold hands with. More importantly, I'd stop guarding every bit of space around me. I was going home. I couldn't wait to cuddle Katrina.

A tangle of thoughts knotted together while the van passed the foothills, moving between cars so fast, like a movie—but this wasn't pretend or a dream. I was traveling to my future, leaving San Bueno Correctional Facility far behind. Like the unknown roads, I didn't know what lay ahead of me. I'd be dropped off in Tijuana, a city I'd never been to before. My whole life in San Bueno sat in a small cardboard box.

I whispered prayers for those I left behind, even for Jester and Ms. Montes. I'd remember the garden where flowers and vegetables grew in the gravely dirt of a prison backyard where no one expected anything to grow, but plants bloomed nonetheless. The memories of my mother's garden in Santa Isabel had sustained me.

San Bueno was the place where my dreams dissolved and began, where I learned about life from everyone around me and where love grew in my heart for Mariana, Xochitl, and Babydoll.

How strange to remember the little things that made me happy in a place that caused me pain. The girls braiding each other's hair, the dancing in the dayroom, the volunteer ladies, and Father Anthony's choir. The kindnesses of Ms. Dillon, Mrs. Shaffer and CO Isadora kept me going. Those memories would never leave me just like the scar across my palm.

I spoke to Maribel two nights before. Beside herself with happiness at the news of my parole, she squealed with the joy I hadn't let myself feel. All I could manage was, "Sí, gracias a Dios."

My insides tingled like they were electrified when I hung up the phone and skipped to my room. Mrs. Shaffer laughed and shook her head as I stood at my door, bouncing on my toes.

Maribel would meet me at the Tijuana bus station and take me back to Mexicali where we'd go together to a new agency she had visited. They said they could help find Lupe and Katrina.

My sister and baby must be frightened in a detention center, in a place filled with strangers. When we found Katrina, I would write a letter to Alek's mother and tell her the baby was safe.

Anna probably didn't want to see me, but I'd tell her she could visit if she wanted to come to Mexicali. If she didn't, I could understand. In her eyes, I was the one who took her son's life away. She moved from Russia to the United States for a new life, too, many years ago. We were more similar than I had ever thought before.

What would I tell Katrina about Alek when she grew up? She'd want to know who her father was and how he died. Those were questions I wasn't looking forward to, questions I'd have to answer honestly not only to her but to my father. If he ever spoke to me again.

The van jerked to a stop.

"Sorry, Ivanov," Iguana Eyes said, glancing up at me through the rearview mirror.

I realized I didn't know his name. When he first took me to San Bueno, I was too scared to ask. "It's Flores, not Ivanov anymore. What's your name?"

"Hernandez, Officer Hernandez," he said, stepping on the gas. "So, you made it in there."

"Yes, barely."

"It'll be another couple of hours," he said.

I was exhausted from the nervousness over my hearing, the worry about my fate, and what awaited me beyond the bars. Nothing prepared me for my time at San Bueno, but everything in my life, every hard thing, helped me survive.

The hot sun beamed through my window. The freeway sign said OCEANSIDE, CHULA VISTA. I closed my eyes. The hum of the tires, the rocking motion of the van relaxed me enough to work out the tightness in my shoulders and release the knot in my stomach.

A thumping sound woke me from my sleep.

Officer Hernandez hit the steering wheel. "Damn, there's always a line."

The border crossing from San Ysidro to Mexico loomed ahead. Huge letters on the faded brown building read "United States Border Inspection Station." Several cars waited ahead of the van.

A Border Patrol agent motioned to the van to go to the line closest to the station. Officer Hernandez rolled his window down and flashed his badge at the agent.

"Give me a second," the agent said.

Officer Hernandez drummed his fingers on the steering wheel while we waited. "Bus station isn't far now."

I looked over to the rows of cars waiting to leave Mexico. Palatero carts with pictures of dancing ice cream bars traveled between them. The aromas of roasted corn and sugary cinnamon from the churros filled the air. Young girls carried bunches of red roses crowded into white buckets. They stood in the narrow roads, next to men jangling colorful wood puppets and waving silver bracelets. Even inside the van, I heard the singsong voices of the vendors.

The agent returned, waved Officer Hernandez through. He stepped on the gas, speeding through the streets, past multicolored buildings. Bright pink, yellow, and orange storefronts exploded like fireworks in front of my eyes. I hadn't seen so much color in a long time.

Taxis raced by, leaving the odor of diesel fuel. Fluffy white clouds drifted over the blueness of a sky so big it reached beyond my view. Excited, I sat up, pressed my nose against the window. I was going home.

Officer Hernandez drove past swaying palm trees and bright

billboards, twisting and turning through streets until we drove over the bridge of Rio Tijuana.

We stopped in front of Terminal Turista where people rushed in and out of the station, like busy ants, dragging suitcases and carrying boxes.

"Wait for me to open the door." Officer Hernandez jumped out of the van.

A young woman in jeans and a baseball cap stood with her hand by the side of her face, her eyes searching the crowd. My heart sped up.

"Hand me your property. Watch your step," Officer Hernandez said.

"Juana, Juana." I heard a voice coming closer.

I stepped onto the sidewalk and peered around the officer. The van door slid close with a thump.

He handed me my cardboard box. "Looks like someone's here for you. Good luck, Ms. Flores."

"Juana, it's me." Maribel rushed forward.

She grasped my arms and pulled me in for a hug. The warmth of her body seeped into my bones, bringing me back to life.

"My tio and tia?" I said, looking behind her.

"At work. My mother stayed in Mexicali to wait with Lupe. She called us yesterday morning."

"Lupe? They're all right? Katrina?"

"They're okay. Immigration left them in Mexicali yesterday." Maribel grabbed my hand. "My car is behind the station."

At that moment, my body folded. I knelt on the ground, made the sign of the cross on my chest. They were alive and at Maribel's.

She lifted me by the arm. "Let's go home."

We arrived at Maribel's house late in the evening. My body ached from the hours of sitting in the transportation van and her car, but I was excited to be back in Mexicali.

Maribel unlocked her front door while I waited on the porch sniffing at the aroma of red chile sauce and spices. We stepped onto the tiled hallway. I glanced around. I hadn't been there for two years. Would my aunt and uncle treat me okay or would they snub me?

My tia, in her floral apron, rushed towards me, pulling me to the living room where Lupe stood. My heart stopped. Lupe stepped towards me, waddling with the weight of her pregnancy. Her face crumpled with tears.

Sobbing, she embraced me. "Lo siento, hermana, lo siento."

I patted her back, kissed her cheek. "We all make mistakes. Me especially. Where's Katrina?"

She took my hand and led me to a bedroom. My tia and Maribel followed. Lupe opened the door. Katrina sat upright in the middle of a rainbow crocheted blanket with pillows around her little body. At fourteen months old, she'd grown and had more distinct features and much longer hair. She glanced from Lupe to me and back, wrinkling her face like she was about to cry.

"Let me hold her." I reached for Katrina, but she inched back into the headboard.

"Give her a little time," Lupe said and scooped her up in her arms.

I swallowed my tears, nodding. "Yes, tomorrow."

FIFTY-NINE

We boarded the blue and white bus to Santa Isabel and took the seats behind the young driver.

"Remember to mail the letters soon," I told Maribel from the window.

"I will. I know it's very important."

Her waving hand grew more distant as our bus raced away from the Mexicali bus station.

"Here, put this pillow against your back, your feet up on my box," I told Lupe.

"We'll travel until tomorrow afternoon." Lupe's shoulders drooped. "I don't have any money."

"Tia gave us tacos and fruta for the trip," I said, pointing at the duffle bag at my feet.

Katrina put her arms around Lupe's neck, snuggling closer to her and watching me with her wide golden-brown eyes.

"Did you see a doctor in the detention center?" I asked.

"Yes, she saved me from staying longer when she told the person in charge that I was due any minute. They didn't want me having my baby in the United States, so they released us. I'm due in two weeks."

"Gracias a Dios. Was it a terrible place?"

Lupe leaned against the window and sighed. "Let's not talk about it now."

She was right, there was plenty of time to talk about what happened to me and to her another time.

"Did you write someone at the prison?" Lupe asked.

"My friend, Xochitl, and Alek's mother, Anna. I want them to know I'm released and Katrina's safe. I hope Anna can see her granddaughter again someday."

Lupe nodded, closed her eyes. Katrina watched me from Lupe's lap.

Soon, she warmed up to me and let me touch her fingers. She laughed when I showed her how to do the rhyme "Pon, Pon, Pon," tapping my forefinger into the palm of my left hand. Although she didn't talk, she didn't hesitate to play.

"Let me take her so you can sleep." I lifted Katrina onto my lap.

I wanted to smother my baby in kisses, hug her close, and whisper so many things in her ear but I didn't want to frighten her either. Katrina poked her forefinger on the palm of my hand, on my scar, and murmured "Pon, pon." I took her hand, whispered the rhyme to her, and played the game over and over until the rocking of the bus lulled her to sleep on my shoulder.

The whole time she slept, I memorized every detail of her presence. The slight curl of her dark hair on her shoulders, the flush of pink on top of her ears, her tiny mouth. I listened to the sound of her breath beneath my neck, felt her tiny hand clutch my tee shirt.

Lupe had called Papá from Mexicali. He knew we were on a

bus back to Santa Isabel. When I asked her what he said, she hesitated. "He missed Katrina. Talk to him when we get home."

What if Papá welcomed Katrina but told me to live elsewhere? The thought of another separation from my baby or my family sunk my stomach.

There was so much unknown on the other side of the prison walls. I needed to apologize to Papá for running away, causing him and Lupe pain and worry.

As the bus wound its way towards Santa Isabel, the heat and dust increased by the mile. The hills became greener. We drove into the town's narrow streets past vegetable and fruit stands, water stores, and small cafes. We passed the bell tower and steel cross on the church. I said a prayer for Papá to forgive me.

"Santa Isabel," the bus driver announced.

The bus rolled to a stop at the plaza. I nudged Lupe. She yawned, smiling at me as Katrina slept on my lap.

Gathering Lupe's bag, I heaved a sleeping Katrina higher on my shoulder. "I'm ready."

END

ACKNOWLEDGMENTS

To my family, for understanding what a closed door to my room means and for not calling me before eleven in the morning.

I am grateful for the serendipity of being introduced to the incredible Women Who Write (WoWW) group. Their loving encouragement, critiques, and friendship mean the world to me.

My WoWW tribe: Amada Irma Perez, Danielle Pineda Brown, Eddie Leonard, Florencia Ramirez, Lori Braun Anaya, Mikko Cook, Sherri Ward, and Toni Guy. Thank you for your words of wisdom and for making memories with me and sharing laughter at conferences, writing retreats, and every other Wednesday at the dinner table for the past fifteen years.

Michele Serros, author. Thank you for encouraging a budding writer and homegirl to keep writing. Your friendship, stories, and laughter live long in my heart. May you rest in peace.

The Writer-to-Writer Mentorship program, sponsored by the Association of Writers and Writing Programs (AWP), is now in its eighth year. It gifted me with mentor author Fred Arroyo. He invested his expertise, patience, and encouragement in the first drafts of this novel.

To A Room of Her Own (AROHO) Foundation and Michel Wing, who awarded the Courage Scholarship. This gift enabled me to attend their writing retreat at the inspiring Ghost Ranch in Abiquiu, New Mexico. The camaraderie of the AROHO sisterhood has lasted several years.

Special thanks to the many honest, dedicated, hard-working employees working with youthful offenders. And to those voluteers and non-profit organizations who work with youth at risk in their communities. You make a difference.

To She Writes Press and SparkPress for furthering the voices of BIPOC writers through their Equality in Publishing contest initiated in 2018. Thank you to all the staff involved in making THE GARDEN OF SECOND CHANCES a reality! Thank you for the education in publishing and the support.

And lastly, to the readers of this novel. Thank you for purchasing this book. If you enjoyed the story, one of the best ways to support an author is to write a quick review on Goodreads, Amazon, or the site where you purchased the book. You can find my website at www.alvaradofrazier.com.

About the Author

After decades of working with incarcerated youth and raising three creative kids as a single parent, Mona Alvarado Frazier is now fulfilling her passions of writing and traveling. When not doing either of those she's reading, volunteering, watching K-dramas, and tending the family's two cats and her succulent gardens. Mona's short stories are published in the University of Nevada, Reno anthology *Basta! Latinas Against Gender Violence* and *Palabritas*, a Harvard literary journal. She is a member of SCBWI and Macondo Writers and a cofounder of LatinxPitch, a Twitter event. She is a 2021 Mentee of Las Musas Latinx children's literature collective.

Dear Reader,

Thank you for taking the time to read this novel and embark on the journey with Juana. If you enjoyed the book, I'd greatly appreciate a review on your preferred platforms, such as Amazon, Goodreads, or Barnes and Noble. Your feedback is valuable to me and helps others discover my work.

I am always eager to hear from my readers, and you can reach me through my social media accounts on Twitter @AlvaradoFrazier or Instagram: m.alvaradofrazier. Follow me for updates on my next book or other exciting news.

Also, check out my website, www.alvaradofrazier.com, where you can sign up for my monthly newsletter. This will keep you informed about giveaways, stories, and book news that I think you'll enjoy.

Be well,
Mona

SELECTED TITLES FROM SHE WRITES PRESS

She Writes Press is an independent publishing company founded to serve women writers everywhere. Visit us at www.shewritespress.com.

Purple Lotus by Veena Rao. $16.95, 978-1-63152-761-6. Tara, an immigrant woman in the American South, is trapped in a loveless, abusive arranged marriage, until she discovers self-love—a powerful force that gives her the courage to find herself and to confront a cruel, victim-blaming, patriarchal culture.

Profound and Perfect Things by Maribel Garcia. $16.95, 978-1-63152-541-4. When Isa, a closeted lesbian with conservative Mexican parents, has a one-night stand that results in an unwanted pregnancy, her sister, Cristina adopts the baby—but twelve years later, Isa, who regrets giving up her child, threatens to spill the secret of her daughter's true parentage.

The Mill of Lost Dreams by Lori Rohda. $16.95, 978-1-63152-719-7. Three immigrant families and one eleven-year-old orphan risk everything to find a better life in the textile mills of Fall River, Massachusetts—and learn what happens to those whose dreams of a better life are irreversibly and unexpectedly lost.

Lost in Oaxaca by Jessica Winters Mireles. $16.95, 978-1-63152-880-4. Thirty-seven-year-old piano teacher Camille Childs is a lost soul who is seeking recognition through her star student—so when her student unexpectedly leaves California to return to her village in Oaxaca, Mexico, Camille follows her. There, Camille meets Alejandro, a Zapotec man who helps her navigate the unfamiliar culture of Oaxaca and teaches her to view the world in a different light.

Guesthouse for Ganesha by Judith Teitelman. $16.95, 978-1-63152-521-6. In 1923, seventeen-year-old Esther Grünspan arrives in Köln with a hardened heart as her sole luggage. Thus she begins a twenty-two-year journey, woven against the backdrops of the European Holocaust and the Hindu Kali Yuga (the "Age of Darkness" when human civilization degenerates spiritually), in search of a place of sanctuary.